PRAISE FOR
ANNA QUINDLEN'S

ONE TRUE THING

"ANNA QUINDLEN HAS BEEN A WOMAN WHOM
OTHER WOMEN CHANNEL THROUGH."
—*The New Yorker*

"SHE WRITES PASSIONATELY. . . . She gets to its heart,
painstakingly uncovering all the intensity, suspicion and
primitive love that bond mothers and daughters.
It's worth the price of the book."
—*The Boston Globe*

"HEART-WRENCHING."
—New York *Daily News*

Please turn the page for more extraordinary acclaim

ONE TRUE THING

ANNA QUINDLEN

Delta
Trade Paperbacks

A Delta Book
Published by
Dell Publishing
a division of
Bantam Doubleday Dell Publishing Group, Inc.
1540 Broadway
New York, New York 10036

ISBN: 0-385-31920-7

Reprinted by arrangement with Random House, Inc.

Manufactured in the United States of America
Published simultaneously in Canada

June 1997

10   9   8   7

For Prudence M. Quindlen

PROLOGUE

J ail is not as bad as you might imagine. When I say jail, I don't
mean prison. Prison is the kind of place you see in old movies or
public television documentaries, those enormous gray places with
guard towers at each corner and curly strips of razor wire going
round and round like a loop-the-loop atop the high fence. Prison
is where they hit the bars with metal spoons, plan insurrection in
the yard, and take the smallest boy—the one in on a first offense—
into the shower room, while the guards pretend not to look and
leave him to find his own way out, blood trickling palely, crimson
mixed with milky white, down the backs of his hairless thighs, the
shadows at the backs of his eyes changed forever.

Or at least that's what I've always imagined prison was like.

Jail was not like that a bit, or at least not the jail in Montgomery County. It was two small rooms, both together no bigger than
my old attic bedroom in my parents' house, and they did have
bars, but they closed by hand, not with the clang of the electric,
the remote controlled, the impregnable. An Andy Griffith jail. A
Jimmy Stewart jail. Less Dostoyevsky than summer stock, a jail for

the stranger in town who brings revelation in the leather pack he carries slung over one shoulder and has a thrilling tenor voice.

There was a shelflike cot arrangement, and a toilet, and a floor with speckled linoleum, so much like the linoleum in Langhorne Memorial Hospital that I wondered if the same contractor had installed both. When the door was locked the policeman who had brought me down the long hall after I was photographed and fingerprinted left, his eyes more than a little sympathetic. We had once been in the same beginner's French class at the high school, he to eke out another C in his senior year, me to begin the diligent study that would culminate in the Institut Français prize at graduation. After the sound of his footsteps died away the place was very quiet.

From up front, where the police dispatcher sat, there was the sound of someone typing inexpertly, the occasional animal honk from the police two-way radios. From above there was a hum, a vague, indeterminate sound that seemed to come from electricity running through the wires just beneath the acoustical tile ceiling. Above me were those plain fluorescent tube lights.

Sometimes now, at work in the hospital, I will look up at a certain angle and I see that ceiling again, those lights, and the sense of being in that small space once more is overwhelming, but not really unpleasant.

Sitting on the cot, my hands clasped lightly between my knees, I felt relief. The lockup, I repeated in my head. The slammer. The joint. All attempts to scare myself, all those cheap slang terms I had heard come from the nasty fishlike lips of Edward G. Robinson as I watched *The Late Show* in the den, the house dark, the screen gray-blue as a shark, my father and mother asleep upstairs. The can, I thought to myself. The Big House. But overlaying them all was a different thought: I am alone. I am alone. I am alone.

I lay on my side on the cot and put my hands together beneath my cheek. I closed my eyes, expecting to hear a voice in my ear, a cry for help: for a cup of tea, a glass of water, a sandwich, more morphine. But no one spoke; no one needed me any longer. I felt peaceful as I could not remember feeling for a long time. And free, too. Free in jail.

For the first time in days, I could even stop seeing my father, with his smooth black hair and his profile a little dulled by age and fatigue; I could stop seeing him spooning the rice pudding into my mother's slack mouth, like a raven tending to the runt in the nest, all wild, weird tufts of head fuzz and vacant, glittery eyes. Spoon. Swallow. Spoon. Swallow. The narrow line of his lips. The slack apostrophe of her tongue. The blaze of love and despair that lit her face for just a moment, then disappeared.

I can still see that scene today, play it over and over again to reduce it to its small component parts, particularly the look in her eyes, and in his. But, back then, during my night in jail, for a few hours it disappeared. All I was aware of was the hum.

It reminded me of the sound you could hear if you walked down the street on a summer day in Langhorne, particularly where I lived, where the big houses were. There was always the hum. If you were attentive, stood still and really listened, you could figure out that it was the hum of hundreds of air conditioners. They were pushing cold clean beautiful air into cold clean beautiful rooms, rooms like ours, where the moldings teased the eye upward from the polished surface of the dining-room table or the cushions, with their knife creases left by the side of someone's hand, on the big brown velvet couch across from the fireplace and the Steinway.

That was how I thought about it, although that was not how it had been for the last few months of my mother's life. That was how it looked before the couch from the den had been crowded into the living room to make room for the hospital bed. Before the furniture had all been moved back against the walls to make room for the wheelchair. Before the velvet nap of the couch had been disfigured by vomit and drool.

Inside the lids of my eyes I could see a kind of dull reddish light, and it reminded me of the light on those streets at the end of the day, particularly in autumn. In the magic hour the cars, so distinct, so identifiable, would come down our street, to turn into driveways or continue to some of the small streets and culs-de-sac farther on. Dr. Belknap the pediatrician, whose patient I had been all my life. Mr. Fryer, who worked in the city as a financial consultant and was obsessed with golf. Mr. Dingle, the high school principal, who could only afford to live on our street because his wife had inherited the house from her parents.

And then, late at night, after the streetlights buzzed on, with their own hum, a few others came. Always last was Mr. Best, the district attorney. My brother Brian used to deliver his *Tribune* every morning, just after sunrise, and Bri said that every time he pedaled his bike up the driveway to the sloping sward of pachysandra that set the Best house off from the street, Mr. Best would be standing there. Impatient at dawn, he would be tapping his narrow foot in leather slippers, wearing a corduroy robe in the winter and a seersucker robe in summer. He never gave Brian a tip at Christmas, always a baseball cap that said MAY THE BEST MAN WIN, which was what Mr. Best gave out in election years.

An election year was coming up when I was in jail.

The police officer came by my cell. I knew his name was Skip, although his name tag said he was really Edwin Something-or-Other Jr. I had seen him last at the town Christmas-tree lighting ceremony in December, when my mother's tree was the nicest tree, with its gaudy decorations and big red bows. He had been on the high school basketball team and had sat out every game. His broad back had been a bookend on the bench, a short kid named Bill on the other side, both of them waiting for the team to come back from the floor so they could feel again the nervous jostle that made them part of the action for a few minutes. My brother Jeff probably knew him. He was one of the boys who lived outside of town, in one of the Cape Cod houses that punctuated the corkscrew country roads.

The county had a lot of them, out where the corn grew in summer taller than any farmer, and tomatoes and zucchini were sold from little lean-tos with a plywood shelf out front. Sometimes, in August, the zucchini would be as big as baseball bats, and, because no one wanted them, the kids would use them to beat the trees in the softer light of the surrounding forests. The only zucchini worth having, my mother always said, were the tiny ones with the blossoms still attached.

Montgomery County had acres and acres of farm and forest, and then a wide avenue of junk, auto-body shops and Pizza Huts and discount electronics places and mini-malls with bad Chinese takeout and unisex hair salons. And at the end, when you'd come through it all, you arrived at Langhorne. It was the perfect college town, front porches and fanlight windows, oak trees along the curbs as big around as barrels, azaleas in the spring and hydrangeas in the summer and curbside piles of leaves in the fall. Langhorne had a shoe store full of loafers and a jewelry store with trays full of signet rings; it had a bookstore run by an elderly couple named the Duanes, Isabel and Dean Duane, who had retired from a busier life in the city and who seldom consulted *Books in Print* because they already knew everything that was in it. They were rather like the people in Langhorne, the Duanes—they knew everything about what was going on in their little world.

The jail was not in Langhorne proper. That was how the people who lived there always referred to it, "Langhorne proper," so that you would know who lived on one of the oak-lined streets and who lived in the slapdash houses and trailers outside of town. The jail was over by the gas stations, the storage facilities, the Acme and the Safeway.

The policeman, Skip, who had played in one quarter of one game his senior year, came in to check on me that night because he was concerned that I might be terrified, lonely, weeping. He was concerned that I might be unhinged by the fact that I had been in jail for nearly four hours and my father had not arrived to post bail, to say "Dark day, darling?" in that way that made my few friends go wild about him, his blue eyes, his arch and charming manner, his aphorisms. When the police had first put me here they had waited for him to come bursting in the door, with his long stride, swearing in Englishisms: "What in bloody hell is going on here, may I ask?" My father was the chairman of the Langhorne College English department and he was famous for his Englishisms; they went down exceptionally well when he would speak at the Langhorne Women's Club or the Episcopal Book Club on *David Copperfield* ("Minor Dickens, Ellen, strictly minor—*Bleak House* is too rich for their systems") or *Pride and Prejudice*. My father had called me Little Nell when I was younger.

My mother sometimes called me Ellie.

But my father did not come to bail me out, and so the young policeman came to watch over the scared woman he expected to find in the cell. He was apparently amazed to find me asleep beneath the fluorescent lights, my knees drawn up to my chest, my hands joined beneath my cheek as though I was praying. Or at least that's what he told the *Tribune*.

I saw the story after my brother Jeff and Mrs. Forburg agreed that it was best for me to know what was being said about me. "Shocked," the story said Skip was. "Disbelief," they said he felt. He said that in school I had always been a cold person, superior and sure of myself, and he was right. He said that I was smart, and that was right, too.

But he was smarter than I was about some things, and he knew that a girl in jail, a girl just barely old enough to refer to herself as a woman when she wanted to make sure that you knew she was not to be trifled with, should be rank with fear and adrenaline, up all night contemplating the horror of her position. Especially a girl charged with killing her own mother.

Instead he found me sleeping, a faint smile on my face.

You can see that smile in the pictures they took the next morning, after I appeared in court, charged with willfully causing the death of Katherine B. Gulden. The courtroom artist didn't capture it when she drew me, with my court-appointed lawyer at my side, his pale-blue suit giving off a smell of sizing as he sweated in the small, close room.

(I remember thinking that anyone represented by a man in a pale-blue suit was doomed for sure. And his dress shirt was short-sleeved. "Going up the river," I thought to myself. "In for the long haul.")

But in the late afternoon, when the strip mall across from the municipal building was in shadow and my bail had been arranged—$10,000 cash and a pledge of a four-bedroom Cape with a finished basement—when I finally left the Montgomery County jail, the smile I had had while asleep was still on my face, just a little half-moon curve above my pointed chin and below my pointed nose.

On page one of the *Tribune* I smiled my Mona Lisa smile, my dark hair braided back from my forehead, my widow's peak an arrogant *V,* my big white sweater and a peacoat flapping over dirty jeans, a smudge faintly visible on one cheek. And I knew that even the few people who still loved me would look and think that here was Ellen's fatal hubris again, smiling at the worst moment of her life.

Some of them did say that, as the days went by, and I never answered them. How could I say that whenever I went out in public and someone leapt into my path, a Nikon staring at me like a tribal mask on an enemy's face, all I could hear was a voice in my ear, an alto voice over and over, saying, "Smile for the camera, Ellie. You look so pretty when you smile."

And my mother spoke, alive again inside my brain, edging out Becky Sharp and Pip and Miss Havisham and all the other made-up people I had learned so long ago from my father to prize over real ones. She spoke and I listened to her, because I was afraid if I didn't her voice would gradually fade away, an evanescent wraith of a thing that would narrow to a pinpoint of light and then go out, lost forever, like Tinker Bell if no one clapped for her. I listened to her, because I loved her. She'd asked so little of me, over the course of our lives, and I wanted to do this one small remembered thing, to smile for the camera.

At the end I always did what she asked, even though I hated it. I was tired to death of the sour smell of her body and the straw of her hair in the brush and the bedpan and the basin and the pills that kept her from crying out, from twisting and turning like the trout do on the banks of the Montgomery River when you've lifted them on the end of the sharp hook and their gills flare in mortal agitation.

I tried to do it all without screaming, without shouting, "I am dying with you." But she knew it; she felt it. It was one of many reasons why she would lie on the living-room couch and weep without making a sound, the tears giving her gray-yellow skin, tight across her bones, the sheen of the polished cotton she used for slipcovers or the old lampshades she painted with flowers for my bedroom. I tried to make her comfortable, to do what she wanted. All but that one last time.

No matter what the police and the district attorney said, no matter what the papers wrote, no matter what people believed then and still believe, these years later, the truth is that I did not kill my mother. I only wished I had.

PART ONE

I remember that the last completely normal day we ever had in our lives, my brothers and I, was an ordinary day much like this one, a muggy August-into-September weekday, the sky low and gray over Langhorne, clouds as flat as an old comforter hanging between the two slight ridges that edged the town. We'd gone to the Tastee Freeze for soft ice cream that day, driving in Jeff's battered open jeep with our arms out the windows. My brothers were handsome boys who have turned into handsome men. Brian has our father's black hair and blue eyes, Jeffrey our mother's coloring, auburn hair and eyes like amber and a long face with freckles.

Both of them were tanned that day, at the end of their summer jobs as camp counselor and landscaper. I was pale from a summer spent in a New York office on weekdays and house-guesting at Fire Island weekends, spending more time at cocktail parties than on the beach, where melanoma and Retin-A were frequent talking points among my acquaintances.

Afterward I wondered why I hadn't loved that day more, why I hadn't savored every bit of it like soft ice cream on my tongue, why I hadn't known how good it was to live so normally, so everyday. But you only know that, I suppose, after it's not normal and everyday any longer. And nothing ever was, after that day. It was a Thursday, and I was still my old self, smug, self-involved, successful, and what in my circles passed for happy.

"Ellen's got the life," said Jeff, who'd been asking about the magazine where I worked. "She gets paid to be a wiseass for a living. You go to parties, you talk to people, you make fun of them in print. It's like getting paid to breathe. Or play tennis."

"You could get paid to play tennis," I said. "It's called being a tennis pro."

"Oh, right," said Jeff, "with our father?" He sucked the ice cream from the bottom of his cone. "Excuse me, Pop? Mr. Life of the Mind? I've decided to move to Hilton Head and become a tennis pro. But I'll be reading Flaubert in my spare time."

"Is it possible for one of you to make a life decision without wondering what Papa will find wrong with it?" I said.

My brothers hooted and jeered. "Oh, great," said Jeff. "Ellen Gulden renounces paternal approval! And only twenty-four years too late."

"Mom is happy with anything I do," said Brian.

"Oh, well, Mom," said Jeff.

"Jeffrey man," someone called across the parking lot. "Brian!" My brothers lifted their hands in desultory salutes. "What's up?" Jeff called back.

"I'm history here," I said.

"You were history here when you were here," said Jeff. "No offense, El. You're a hungry puppy, always were a hungry puppy, and the world don't like you hungry puppies. People are afraid you're going to bite them."

"Why are you talking like a cracker radio commentator?" I said.

"See, Bri, Ellen never relaxes. New York is her kind of place. An entire city of people who never relax, who were antsy in their own hometowns. So long, hungry puppy. Go where the dogs eat the dogs."

The light was dull yellow because of the low clouds, like a solitary bulb in a dark room. The asphalt was soft in the driveway under our feet, the smell of charcoal drifting over Langhorne the way perfume hung over a cocktail party in the city. Our father came in late in the evening, but we were used to that: he stood in the den for a time, leaning against the doorjamb, and then he trudged upstairs, oddly silent.

Not odd for the boys, with whom he had the strained, slightly mechanical transactions that many fathers have with their sons. But odd for me. I had always felt I knew my father's mind, if not his heart. Whenever I came home, from college and then later, on visits from the city, he would call me into his study, with its dark furniture and dim sepia light, would lean forward in his desk chair and say, simply, "Tell."

And I would spin my stories for him, of the famous writer I had heard read in a lecture hall, of the arguments about syntax I had had with editors, of the downstairs neighbor who played Scarlatti exquisitely but monotonously on the small antique harpsichord I had once glimpsed through the door of his apartment.

I often felt like someone being debriefed by a government apparatchik, or like Scheherazade entertaining the sultan. And often I made stories up, wonderful stories, so that my father would lean back in his chair and his face would relax into the utter concentration he had when he lectured to his students. Sometimes at the end he would say "Interesting." And I would be happy.

Our mother was in the hospital that day, and as it always did, the house seemed like a stage set without her. It was her house, really. Whenever anyone is called a homemaker now—and they rarely are—I think of my mother. She made a home painstakingly and well. She made balanced meals, took cooking classes, cleaned the rooms of our home with a scarf tying back her bright hair, just like in the movies. When she wallpapered a room, she would always cover the picture frames in the same paper, and place them on the bureau or the bedside table, with family photographs inside.

The two largest pictures in the living room were of my mother and father. In one they are standing together on our front porch. My mother is holding my father's arm with both her own, an incandescent smile lighting her face, as though life knows no greater happiness than this—this place, this day, this man. Her body is turned slightly sideways, toward him, but he is facing four-square to the camera, his arms crossed over his chest, his face serious, his eyes mocking.

Back when we were still lovers, Jonathan had picked up that picture from the piano and said that in it my father looked like the kind of man who would rip out your heart, grill it, and eat it for dinner, then have your wife for dessert. Allowing for the difficult relationship between Jonathan and my father, the relationship of two men engaged in a struggle for the soul of the same woman, it was a pretty fair description.

I wonder if my father still has that picture there, on the piano, or whether it's put away now, my mother smiling dustily, happily, into the dark of a drawer.

Next to it was another picture of my mother hanging on to my father's arm. Wearing a cap and gown, I am hanging on to his other one. In that picture, my father is squinting slightly in the sunlight, and smiling. Jonathan took that picture. I have it on my dresser today, the most tangible remaining evidence of the Gulden family triangle.

My mother would be saddened by my apartment now, by the grimy white cotton couch and the inexpertly placed standing lamps. My apartment is the home of someone who is not a home-maker, someone who listens to the messages on the answering machine and then runs out again.

But she would not criticize me, as other mothers might. Instead she would buy me things, a cheap but pretty print she would mat herself, a throw of some kind. And as she arranged the throw or hung the picture she would say, smiling, "We're so different, aren't we, Ellie?" But she would never realize, as she said it, as she'd said it so many times before, that if you are different from a person everyone agrees is wonderful, it means you are somehow wrong.

My mother loved the hardware store, Phelps's Hardware, and the salesmen there loved her. My father would always tease her: "Once again, she has paid the Phelps's mortgage for the month and alone of all her sex has cornered the market on tung oil and steel wool!" My father always teased her. I was the one he talked to.

It was a charmed day in the charmed life we lived, my brothers and I, that day we went to the Tastee Freeze. I see that so clearly now. We lolled on the grass in the backyard afterward, cooked and ate some hamburgers, watched television. And then the next morning our father came downstairs, his khakis wrinkled, his blue shirt rolled back from his wrists, and told us all to sit down. He leaned back against the kitchen counter as I sat opposite him, sipping a glass of orange juice. My two brothers sat in the ladderback chairs at either end of the kitchen table. My mother had caned the seats. I don't include those details by way of description, but in tribute. Things like this were my mother's whole life. Of this I was vaguely contemptuous at the time.

When I was a little girl, she would sometimes sing me to sleep, although I always preferred my father, because he made up nonsense songs: "Lullaby, and good night, fettuccine Alfredo. Lullaby and good night, rigatoni Bolognese." But my mother sang a boring little tune that was nothing but the words "safe and sound" over and over again. It put me right to sleep. My father always jazzed me up; my mother always calmed me down. They did the same to one another. Sometimes I think they just practiced on me.

I remember. It's what I do for a living now, how I earn my keep, make my mark, through memories. I remember well. I can remember the orange juice on the table, and Brian, his torso jackknifed between his knees, throwing a ball into a mitt over and over. The glass was half full; the table was oak, a big round moon of a top on a sturdy pedestal with predatory claws at its base. My mother had rescued it from a junk shop, stripped and refinished it, waxed it with butcher wax until the muscles in her arms stood out like pale polished wood themselves.

"Cancer," my father said as we sat ringed around it. There had been certain vague signs, certain symptoms. She had felt sick for a long time. "Your mother procrastinated," he said, as though she was somehow to blame. "First she thought she had the flu. Then she imagined she was expecting. She didn't want to make a fuss. You know how she is."

The three of us looked down, all three embarrassed by the thought of our forty-six-year-old mother imagining she was pregnant. I was twenty-four. Jeff was twenty. Bri was eighteen. You looked at the numbers and you could tell we were planned children. We knew how she was.

My brothers were leaving for college that weekend. Their stereos were packed up, their suitcases standing open in the center of their rooms. And I had come back from the city for four days for a visit. I hadn't even unpacked, just pulled clothes out of a duffel bag on the chest at the foot of my bed, not putting anything away, leaving the drawers of my dresser empty and clean, lined with flowered paper. Four days seemed enough for the occasion. More, and I would miss a book party and lunch with the editor of an important magazine. A week in the hospital, she had told us. A hysterectomy, she had said. It had seemed unremarkable to me in a woman of forty-six long finished with childbearing, although every day that I grow older I realize there is never anything unremarkable about losing any part of what makes you female—a breast, a womb, a child, a man.

Funny, how the imagined pregnancy jarred us at first more than the cancer, which we could scarcely comprehend. And how I suddenly realized why my mother had seemed so joyous the month before, in town to take me to lunch on my birthday, her pale translucent redhead's skin flushed with pink. A forty-six-year-old woman aching to ask her sophisticated city-daughter where you could buy attractive maternity clothes. It makes me hurt now, just to think of what was going on in her head, before she finally discovered what was going on in her body.

"Chemotherapy," my father said. There were verbs in his sentences but I did not hear them. "Liver. Ovaries. Oncologist." I picked up my glass and walked out of the room.

"I'm still speaking, Ellen," my father called after me.

"I can't listen anymore," I said, and I went out and sat on the front porch, on a wicker rocker with a cushion that, of course, had been made by my mother.

The things they sold at antique stores in my New York neighborhood were like things my mother had bought years ago—square old chests made of russet-colored cherry wood, patchwork quilts, wicker settees painted white. We lived on the nicest block in Langhorne but in the smallest house, a white clapboard farmhouse left over from the days when the surrounding hills were farms and the college was the estate of Samuel Langhorne, who had made his money in machine parts on the cusp of the industrial revolution.

Our house looked like a pony that has somehow nosed its way in among the horses, a painted miniature to their murals. But it was as beautiful as any inside because of my mother's hard work. She had married a man who would never be rich, but she said she had not minded, because she knew he had a vocation instead. Lapsed Catholic that she was—or perhaps not so lapsed, in her heart—she had said it exactly that way, as though my father had become a priest, or at least taken vows, when his seven sacraments were only "Introduction to Victorian Poetry," "The Romantics and the Seasons of Love," and other such offerings in the college catalogue.

Even on its nicest block, where most of the residents were too rich to work at the college, Langhorne had the odd feel of a town that is about something other than itself. Washington is like that, and Orlando, Florida, which has Disney World. And Boston. When I went to college in Boston—or Cambridge, as all Harvard students learn to say—I was convinced it was because I wanted a larger pond, a more cosmopolitan setting, blessed release from the bell jar of Langhorne, where everyone knew my name and my class rank, which was number one. And of course I wanted to sleep with Jonathan whenever I could and he was at Harvard, so I went there, too. I was always afraid that if I wasn't in bed with Jonathan, keeping his cold feet warm, it was a cinch someone else would be.

But the truth is that Cambridge and Langhorne are in many ways very much alike, and not just because so many of my father's spiritual colleagues are in Cambridge, roaming the streets with the *Times* tucked under their arms, in cuffed chinos with the knees bagged out. All college towns are essentially the same. There is something strange about the roots of people settled in a place where everyone else passes through.

I sat on the porch and looked across at the Buckley house as I had done so many times before—Tudor, stucco, rhododendrons and a perennial garden fading fast, losing its pinks and whites and blues, nursery colors. They had gotten balloon shades in the living room since the last time I was home.

There were no shades on the windows in my apartment in New York. When my mother had visited the month before, it had been not only to have lunch but also to figure out which items of furniture, stored in the cellar, would fit nicely in my two small rooms. "You have no window coverings!" she had said. "The whole world is watching you undress!"

"Oh, Mama, big deal," I said. "Everyone in this neighborhood is gay." I was damned if I'd tell her that the first time I pulled off my shirt in my bedroom I'd looked across at the amber lamps lighting other people's lives and clutched the cotton to my chest. Or that since then I'd dressed and undressed in my windowless bathroom, like a virgin on her honeymoon.

But I was damned, too, if I'd put up balloon shades, or lace curtains, or those narrow venetian blinds. One of the things I loved about having my own place was the spill of white light across the scratched wooden floors each morning, the wave of mellow light that snuck slowly across the futon on my bedroom floor in late afternoon and early evening, the moon rising outside my window.

The light and sun and stars belonged to me in that place where anyone, looking in the window, would find a stranger, an unknown. Not Ellen Gulden. Not little Ellen, who, when she was eight, was dressed for Halloween as a princess in blue net and star-shaped sequins. Not Ellen Gulden, who met Jonathan Beltzer in A.P. English and became inseparable from him when she was seventeen. Not Ellen, who graduated from Harvard with a magna— "*Non sum summa est?*" said my father, who did not speak Latin and had only been a magna himself, but I got the message anyhow—and then went to work for some big magazine in New York as an editorial assistant and sometime reporter.

As I sat on the porch of my mother's house I was in a place where almost everybody knew, not only my name, but all those things. A shadow crossed my lap, and I knew it was my father.

"My train is at six-ten," I said, my voice trembling.

"Ellen," said my father, "your mother needs you. She is coming home Tuesday and she won't be well for long. The disease is apparently advanced. Soon she may not be able to bathe herself. In a month or two she will not be able to cook or clean."

"We can hire a nurse. That's what the Beldens did when Mrs. Belden's mother was sick." But even as I said it I knew how preposterous it sounded. In the Gulden household, the ethos was do it yourself, for everything from Christmas gifts to floor sanding.

"Your mother didn't hire a nurse when you had your tonsils out. She didn't hire a nurse when you had chicken pox or when you broke your arm. She wouldn't want strangers in her home. She won't even have a cleaning woman."

"Papa, I have an apartment. I have a job. I have a life."

The shadow lifted. The screen door slammed. A delivery truck slid by with a rumble as it changed gears and so I did not hear my father's muffled footsteps when he returned, when he came across the porch in his deck shoes. My linen jacket sailed into my lap, and my straw hat, and then my purse came down hard on the wooden decking, my wallet bouncing loose. My duffel bag landed at my feet.

"You"—he said, throwing a book atop the pile—"have"—and then my running shoes—"a Harvard education"—then my loafers—"but"—and the glass of orange juice rolled unbroken atop the mess, soaking the shoes—"you have no heart."

My father says this all the time, usually about writers. Pound's problem, he says, is not that he was an anti-Semite but that he had no heart. Fitzgerald's work is fatuous and second-rate because he had no heart. And now I was part of this motley crew, the geniuses and the almost-rans, all those smart people who were irredeemably flawed because they lacked something many people said George Gulden had never had at all. Something I'd spent my whole life trying to win from him.

My possessions lay strewn around me, the bright detritus of another life, and I stared at them and at the glow of the juice glass, its curving surface shining iridescent silver in the late-afternoon sun.

There were ghosts everywhere on the pavement and beneath the trees. Kate Gulden pulled Brian in the red wagon up the hill as Jeff and I dragged the quilt and the picnic basket behind. Kate Gulden tacked a sign that said CONGRATULATIONS across the porch posts, so that I covered my face when the principal brought me back from the state capitol after I won the essay contest. She planted bulbs around the porch lattices, painted the shutters Williamsburg blue, heaved groceries out of the back of the car, lived a domestic life double time.

I pictured my mother marooned in the living room, some cheery woman in a white uniform making her tuna sandwiches and folding her underthings, the house silent and a little dusty. But there was no story to go with that picture. When I'd written a false paragraph in a story my friend Jules would say, "This one just doesn't parse."

Kate Gulden and a hired nurse did not parse.

All my life I had known one thing for sure about myself, and that was that my life would never be her life. I had moved as far and as fast as I could; now I was back at my beginning. All my life my father had convinced me, almost by osmosis, rarely with praise, that I was gifted, special, that there were things other people could not do that I could do effortlessly. But I had never imagined this was one of them.

I packed up the pile of my jumbled belongings and carried it inside, the empty orange-juice glass balanced atop it all. But when I got to the door the glass rolled sideways and fell, shattering into innumerable shards, bright in the sun.

I think that the people I know now believe I went home to take care of my mother because I loved her. And sometimes I believe that was in my heart without my knowing it. But the truth is that I felt I had no choice. I felt I had to be what my father wanted me to be, even if it was something so unlike the other Ellen he'd cultivated and tutored for all those years, even if it meant that I had to go from his brightest student to his demi-wife. I had to prove that, unlike Pound and Fitzgerald, I had a heart.

I carried my things back upstairs to my bedroom. When I came downstairs, my father was in the den, talking on the phone. I waited in the doorway until he was finished. Then he turned to look at me, his silhouette black against the light coming in through the window. He looked as big as he had when I was a little girl, when I would watch him rise and rise and rise from the side of my bed at night until from below, his head, with its carefully brushed black hair, would blot out the light and make it nighttime as surely as if he had his finger on the switch to the moon and sun.

He had always been able to read me; if I had good news I had never been able to hide it past the moment when he saw my face, and if I had bad news his own face would settle, even before I spoke, into vertical planes of disappointed expectation.

"I'll be back Tuesday morning," I said, and he nodded.

"To stay," he said, a declarative sentence.

"I don't know about that," I said. "There are other options. Maybe you could take a sabbatical. It's been four years since you took one for the book."

He pressed his lips together, and the lines grew long down either side of his face. "It seems to me another woman is what's wanted here," he said. I've never forgotten the way he said that sentence. My father's syntax was often peculiar, as though he'd absorbed the Victorians whole when he made them his area of expertise, taken them in as you do an oyster. But for once it seemed to me he could have said "I want" or "I need." He could have paid me the compliment of necessity, or indispensability. But no: "It seems to me another woman is what's wanted here."

We looked at each other and I thought I saw something relax in him, in his eyes and shoulders, and I knew that he knew I would do what he wanted. "We'll see how it goes," I said.

"Ellen," he said, "this is not something that can be decided piecemeal. It's important that we settle this for the duration. Your mother will need someone to take her to the hospital for chemotherapy. I have no idea how debilitating that will be or how many other things she will no longer be able to manage. The doctor says she will need someone with her during the day. And a sabbatical is out of the question for me right now."

"A sabbatical is out of the question for me right now, too."

"Ellen, will you do this or will you not?"

"I don't know," I said. "I'll be back on Tuesday." And I turned to go.

"Ellen," he called when I was at the door. I watched as he passed his hand over his jaw. "This is a difficult time," my father said, and the effort of that sentence, within it the shadow of an apology, seemed to shake him. We were not in the habit of apologizing to one another. There had never been the need; neither of us ever disappointed. He sat down in a chair and let his head fall back, his hands slack along the upholstered arms. He looked old.

"I need to get the broom," I said. "I broke something." And I went to the kitchen and stood for a time, my head against the broom-closet door, a dustpan in my hand, and then went outside to clean up.

And so it was that I came back to Langhorne on a Tuesday morning, drove back in a rented car with a burgeoning sense of claustrophobia worse than if I'd been caught in an elevator between floors. I turned off the highway and drove through the more modest parts of town, the parts where the small houses were only an arm's length apart and the bigger ones had been chopped up into apartments for students and staff.

The green in front of the Town Hall was planted thick with asters in an early autumnal rusty orange. I always thought the town green looked best in spring, glorious with daffodils, hundreds of them. When a breeze moved across them they bowed, together, like dancers in a Busby Berkeley musical.

It seemed a long time until April, that day I drove back into town.

My few New York belongings were in the car—the futon, an old trunk, and a portable electric typewriter. As I pulled into the empty driveway, our house looked as though it was abandoned. Next door I saw a curtain rise, then fall.

I had quit my job at the magazine and sublet my apartment. The people I worked with had tried to be sympathetic, but they were incredulous. "My mother is sick," I said to the managing editor, a stout, short man named Bill Tweedy, flushed from high blood pressure and hard drinking, who had worked in newspapers and had contempt for himself and for the rest of us because we had the luxury of having six days from start to finish in which to put out a publication.

"Ellen," he said, "not to be crass, but a sick mother means three weeks off and a very nice arrangement of flowers sent by the staff. You were doing good here. You did that nice short thing on the gay cop, the story on the girl who got murdered on Madison Avenue, that was a good piece. You did all the research on that kids-and-summer guide. If you quit, there's no guarantee."

"I have to," I said.

"How about if I gave you a promotion?" he said. "More money?"

"Mr. Tweedy, do you honestly think someone would come in and say their mother was dying of cancer to get a raise?"

"Ellen, this is New York."

My friend Jules, my only real friend at the magazine or in New York, took me to lunch. Jules was fragile, physically and psychologically, too, but no one ever noticed because of the enormous aureole of black curls around her small pointed face, and the resonant timbre of her deep rich voice. Both made her seem like a big person, invulnerable and sure; the misapprehension that we shared those qualities had drawn me to her when we first met.

But I came to know the real Jules, the one who pulled that hair back from her face and leaned forward to peer suspiciously at herself in the mirror, who fell in love, was broken by it, sat alone for weeks feeding herself on yogurt and show tunes, and fell in love again. I knew the Jules whose mother from her earliest memories had told her that she should never be disappointed by failure because failure was all you could expect.

"This is a woman who would have told Abe Lincoln not to pursue a law degree," Jules told me once.

Jules loved me as I'd never been loved by a friend before, with full knowledge. She'd once been told by someone who had been a year ahead of me at Harvard: "Ellen Gulden would walk over her mother in golf spikes to succeed." "Well," Jules had replied, "I'm not her mother." After I'd cleaned out my desk at the magazine she took me out for lunch and held my hand across the table.

"Let them think we're dykes," she said disdainfully, glancing around at the buttoned-up men in deceptively wide and wild ties eating something tartar at the tables around us. "With the guys I meet, I only wish we were." When I started to cry she passed me Kleenex filled with lint from her leather backpack. There was a green M & M stuck in one corner of the tissue. Jules was incredibly, proudly disorderly. There were often odd bits of old food and half-empty coffee cups on her bedroom nightstand. "Eat it," she said of the M & M. "It will make you feel better."

"You have to do this," she added, rubbing my fingers as though I was a child who had come in from the cold. "You would want your daughter to do it for you."

"Jules, what about my life?"

"What about it? It's not forever. Look, Ellen, I understand. Do you think in a million years I would want to move back into my mother's apartment in Riverdale and listen to her go over all the ways in which Marvin and the floozy screwed up her life? But the truth is that she's your mother, and she needs you for a while, and you get your life back at the end and you've done the right thing."

"My mother and I—"

"Please," said Jules, "okay? Just please. Your mother and you have a difficult relationship? Excuse me, but why wouldn't you? Why should you be different from every other daughter in the world? Besides, she sounds like the only halfway decent mother in the world. Has she ever told you you need to lose weight?"

"I'm a good weight."

"You see, there you go. The fact that you would think that you have to be overweight to have your mother suggest you need to lose weight shows the ways in which you are clueless about how bad this relationship can be. The fact that you could say that you are a good weight is a measure of what a sane upbringing you had."

"You don't know my father."

"I don't need to know your father. I know Jonathan."

Jules did not like Jonathan. It was one of the only sore spots in our friendship.

"Don't start," I said.

"Agreed," said Jules, pushing her curls back with her fingers.

"I'm just afraid."

"I know you are. But when you come back here you will have done something really important."

"If I come back."

Jules squeezed my hand so hard I winced. "This is not *Peter Pan*," she said. "Your brothers are not the Lost Boys. They can learn how to run a microwave. Your father can learn where the Goddamn dry cleaner is. But no one," she ended, and her eyes filled, "can help your mother with the shit she'll be going through but you."

"Hire a nurse," Jonathan said when I called him at the data-processing job he worked two nights a week to pay for law school.

"She didn't hire a nurse when I had bronchitis," I said.

"Oh Ellen, did Papa George come up with that line? It's so—so self-sacrificing. It sounds just like him."

"Fuck you, Jon," I said.

"Oh, you will," he said, his voice silky, and he described in detail how I would when next he was in Langhorne, which seemed like years from now.

That was what I was thinking of as I tugged the futon from the back seat of the rental car—all the times we'd laid atop it and worked away, trying to find the places that would drive one another half mad, feeling half mad when we succeeded. Like a mummified prom corsage or a lock of hair, the stains on the futon were the memoirs of our life together. There was no place I could possibly imagine putting it that would not disturb the perfect prettiness of my mother's house.

It would be conspicuously out of place in my room, which was sponge-painted a pale blue, its windows veiled in flowered chintz. Over my desk were my diplomas, framed and matted, and the certificate from the state essay contest, handed to me hastily by the commissioner of education as the cameras made their *nick-nick* insect sounds. I had written a glib and self-righteous defense of euthanasia, and the conservative Catholic governor, who usually awarded the $1,000 prize, wanted nothing to do with me.

I spent the money on a hiking trip in Colorado and a leather jacket for Jonathan.

So I rolled my futon into the garage. Whenever I saw it there, over the next few months, whenever I went out to get a can of oil or a screwdriver, its misshapen bulk in the corner made me tingle, like a spinster peeking into the master bedroom of the house next door, all grim mouth and warm crotch.

I don't know how much my mother knew about my sex life, or the rest of my life, for that matter. I don't know how typical our relationship was, either. Perhaps I know the wrong sort of woman, overcerebral and nervous. I only know that I can tell from the timbre of Jules's voice on the telephone, edgy and a little higher than usual, that she has just seen or spoken to her mother. I only know that one day I went in to see my adviser at Harvard, a woman who had appeared on television news programs more than once in the role of a Valkyrie, brandishing her almost incendiary intelligence, and found her with her head in her hands. "The tenacious umbilical cord," she said lightly when I asked if I should come back another time, but her posture had given her away.

When I considered her dispassionately I knew that, as my friends said, I was lucky in my mother. It was simply that I rarely considered her at all. My mother was like dinner: I needed her in order to live, but I did not pay much attention to what went into her.

My father was dessert. He exhibited the kind of dim general interest in my brothers that fathers had in the television shows of the 1950s. But he did not play catch, and he did not fish. He read, and he taught. Sometimes he let me correct his blue books for freshman English. Sometimes I think he got his reputation as a savage grader from me, although I might have inherited my pre-dilection to judge harshly from him as well.

The most potent memory of my childhood is the sound of the door opening in the evening as he came in. It always reminded me of that moment in *The Wizard of Oz* when Dorothy opens the door of the house and the black-and-white world of Kansas turns Technicolor.

As I opened the same door, that Tuesday morning, the house was dim and gray, quiet, seemingly empty. The air smelled of some flower, very sweet, and I saw a pitcher filled with freesia on the gateleg table in the hall. In the living room there was a slender glass vase filled with blue iris, bright against the yellow-and-white striped walls. On the silver tray on the piano were the cards: "From the faculty and staff of Langhorne College," "Get well, Kate—Skip and Caroline Byers," "From the Buckley family with our love."

And then I turned and she was there, on the stairs, in blue pants and a shirt, the color lighting up her red hair like a flag. "Ellie," my mother said, in surprise and gladness. "You're home!"

I did not know whether it was my imagination, but her shoul-der blades seemed sharper, little wings jutting from her back as I pressed her close. She smelled of bath powder, but of something more chemical, too, and when I squeezed her I thought I felt her wince, although it was I who pulled away first, as I always had.

"I'm fine," she said, sitting down in one of the big wing chairs. "I am. I weighed myself this morning, thinking I'd be pounds lighter, but I'm still the same. It must be all this water I'm hold-ing. But the water's supposed to calm down, and meanwhile I have to take it easy. 'NO painting,' said Dr. Cohn, my new doctor, who is, you'll love this, a woman. 'NO papering, no stenciling, no upholstering.' I had to stop her and say, 'May I needlepoint and sew?' 'Yes,' she said, 'if it doesn't include a ladder or a staple gun.' "

She went on like that for so long that it seemed she would run out of air; she talked about the doctors, the flowers, the food in the hospital, the food her friends had brought to the house in casserole dishes. And then suddenly her face stilled, sagged. Her eyes lost their shine, and she took a deep breath. She seemed to marshal her strength, and then her eyes lit up again like lanterns that had momentarily guttered in the wind of her thoughts.

"I don't know why I'm talking about all that," she said. "The important thing is that I'm all right. That's why you're here, isn't it, to make sure I'm all right? And I am. I never want you or the boys to worry about me. I feel good. I feel fine. I sleep more than I used to. But I'll be myself before you know it. It would kill me if I thought you were worried. I can live without a staple gun." And we both laughed.

"You look great, Mama," I said, and it was almost true. She looked so good that I remember wondering whether, by the end of the month, I could throw out the grad student who'd sublet my apartment and get my old job back.

"Well, I didn't know you were coming or I'd have something in the oven," she said, touching her hair. "I don't know how good any of these things people brought over will be. Like bringing coals to Newcastle, I thought, to bring us food. So we'll have dinner out tonight at the Inn. Jeff drove Brian to school and your father has some meeting or other. So the two of us will have an early dinner, and then we'll go to Duane's and get some books. You'll tell me what's good and I'll read instead of paint. I have to have something to read anyhow while I'm having the treatments. You know how the hospital is—two hours waiting for five minutes pricking the end of your finger for some blood. Or whatever they're going to do to me now. How long can you stay?"

I looked at her, at her long-fingered hands with their nails kept short for the sake of her projects, and I realized that she did not know why I was there. It was how it had always been. My father made the decisions, and she learned about them later and lived with them. Improved on them, usually.

"I'm home for a while, Mama," I said. "I'm back in my room upstairs for a while."

"Home?" she said. "Here?"

I nodded.

"Oh, no, Ellen. What do you mean? What about your friends and your little apartment? What about your work?"

"I've taken some time off," I said, but I could not keep my eyes from giving me away.

"Oh no," she whispered. "No no no no no. Not to be a nurse-maid to me, to take care of this house, to take care of my house. You'll hate me."

"That's absurd," I said.

"Oh God, Ellen," she said, as though I had not spoken. "You have to go back. We can have dinner and then you can take the train in the morning. Or the last one tonight. There's one tonight late, isn't there?"

"Mama," I said. "Mama, you're going to need help. I can sit with you while you have the chemotherapy"—and when I saw her lips begin to work I added—"the treatments. I can take care of the house and do some of the things the doctor says you can't do until you're feeling better."

"Oh Ellie," she said sadly, "I'm not a fool. Don't talk about it as though I have the flu. I said to Doctor Cohn, 'Well, I can't do this and I can't do that, but can I at least commit to doing one of the Christmas trees around the green for the caroling evening?' And she says, 'Well, Kate, it's a long way until December.' And of course your father starts to hum that song about it being a long time from May to December. And Dr. Cohn shot him such a look. 'Well, Doctor, I'll make you a Christmas ornament,' I said. 'I'm Jewish, Kate,' she said. 'Well, then I'll make you a menorah.'

And I will. Doing that does NOT include a ladder or a staple gun."

My mother looked around the room and slowly came back to me. "I know why you're here," she said. "I know what's going on."

"I'm staying."

"I see that," she said. "Whose idea was this, your father's?"

"Both of ours. All of ours. Mine. It's just for a while, Mama."

"This will never work," she said. "He should have known it would never work. He knows you."

She was only saying what I'd already said to Jules a hundred times. But I wanted her to think better of me than I'd thought of myself.

"That's not fair," I said. "I can help. I can do things here for you. I can do things with you. I come home and you're not even happy." I sounded petulant but I did not care.

My mother put out a hand lightly to touch mine. "Ellie, I'm always happy when you're here. But I don't want you out of pity."

"It's the right thing," I said.

"For who?" she said, and when she saw my face she sighed. "This is hard for your father."

"Him? What about you?" What I really wanted to say was: what about me?

"I'm fine," she said. But her smile was bleak, without light or warmth. And for the first time I thought of what it must be like to know that you were going to die, that the trees would bud, flower, leaf, dry, die, and you would not be there to see any of it. It was like standing too close to the fire; my mind leapt back.

My mother's face was calm but empty; I realized she looked like my Grandmother Nina, who never showed anything on her face, even, my mother said, when her only son was killed in Vietnam and the chaplain came to the door of their apartment on Broadway.

My mother liked to tell the story of how two men—"boys really, kids"—had come into the dry cleaners her parents owned one day and demanded the money from the register, and how her mother had spit Polish curses from between her clenched teeth, her face expressionless, while they reached across the counter and stuffed bills into the pockets of their jeans. I imagined that my mother's face now was much as my grandmother's had been then.

"Do you want some tea and a piece of cake?" my mother asked evenly, as she had asked so many times before. And without waiting for a reply she got up, tentatively, and went into the kitchen, and soon I heard the kettle whistling.

W ell," my mother said the next day as we sat at the oak table in the kitchen drinking tea, "what should we do?"

"Do?" I said.

For of course I thought we would not do anything much except drift, that she would feel sick, although she did not look or act sick at all, and I would be miserable, although I would hide it and deny it. That we would see one another, as we always had, across a divide.

But when I first arrived home she still behaved as though she was Kate Gulden in her own safe haven. And Kate Gulden had always had something to do, some project, some plan, dozens of them at once, so that it seemed a sin, if she was knitting, for her not to have a pot of something or other simmering on the stove.

"We need a project," she said that morning. "Something the two of us can do together."

Had there ever been such a thing? I was the one who ran in and out of the house; she was the one who stayed inside it. Somehow it made the peculiar intimacy of our situation so stark, that Kate and Ellen Gulden were finally together, alone, searching for something they could do in tandem.

"I guess I could use the staple gun and you could guide me," I remember saying in a lukewarm fashion.

"No no no," my mother said impatiently, and she bent her bright head down to the mug of tea, blowing into it, a wreath of steam around her face. "Something different." She looked off for a moment, and then slowly she said, "A book group."

Then and now, there was something about the tone of her voice that made me know that she had come up with the idea earlier and was pretending that it was new. "A book group?"

My mother laughed, an artificial trilling sound that had a certain impatience about it. "Ellie," she said, using the diminutive that only she gave me, "are you going to repeat everything I say as though it's the most startling thing you've ever heard?"

"No, I—I'm sorry. A book group. Fine. Who else should we have?"

"Oh, no one else, I don't think, do you? The two of us will read books and talk about them. I've always wanted to belong to a book group, but there are only two of them in Langhorne, and I never really fit into either one. One is that group of younger women from the country club who read junk, and the other is the one the faculty wives have. They always seem to be reading books I've never heard of, by writers I've never heard of. I suppose they're relevant."

"Relevant?" I said.

"There you go again."

So that became our project, what my mother named the Gulden Girls Book Group. We went down to Duane's Book Store that afternoon, one of those September afternoons that feel like deepest August, warm and dank and slightly overcast, the trees dipping to meet the dusty sidewalks. We bought two paperback copies of each of three books: *Pride and Prejudice, Great Expectations,* and *Anna Karenina.* And when we came home we arranged them carefully on the shelves in the den, both of us stepping back for a moment to see how they looked, as though they were a sort of still life.

Those books gave shape to our days, those first few months. They were distinct from the chemotherapy regimen, although we always took books with us when we went to the hospital to wait, and my mother often read while she was lying on the recliner as the chemicals dripped slowly, tiny raindrops into the tributaries of her body. And when I had spent sufficient time each day on the small everyday chores of laundry and vacuuming I found so tedious, she would call out to me: "Time to read."

"What a great thing," said Jules when we talked on the phone. "She trumped you at your own game. Not to mention the professor."

"Jules, the thing you do that I hate is that you read a hundred times more into everything than it deserves. We bought books. We're reading books. We'll talk about books. So what? I never said she was stupid."

"Thanks for sharing that, hon. I never thought she was. And what I meant was that she probably figured you'd be bored and she'd look at you being bored and it would remind her of why you were there. But instead she found something that will guarantee that you won't be bored. Very smart. Very smart."

I wish Jules had met my mother, but somehow I had never arranged for them to get to know one another. Both of them were smarter than I was about people. But they only spoke once on the phone when I was out grocery shopping. I remember afterward that I asked Jules what they'd talked about. "Tie-dyeing," she said. To this day I am not sure whether she was kidding.

One afternoon my mother and I packed our books, took a picnic up to River View Park, and spread an old quilt on the grass on a rise from which you could see all of Langhorne. The Montgomery River ran below us, a sluggish strip of brown with ailanthus trees growing on its banks. Off to one side, behind a stand of pines, were the public tennis courts, always cracked, always crowded. Across the river was the campus of Langhorne College, concentric circles of construction—the stout Gothic of the thirties, the characterless hotel architecture of the fifties, the newly built science building a blinding wall of glass. At their center was the enormous red brick turreted mansion that had once belonged to Samuel Langhorne, where he had lived with a stout and rather jolly-looking wife whose portrait, black satin and pearls, hung over the mantel in the reception area of the administration building. Her name was Minnie, and they had no children, which, as a child, I had thought rather sad. But that was how the college came to exist, its motto being something in Latin that, in translation, meant "all our children."

The classroom buildings hung over the river from a high and stony bluff. Behind them the campus fell away to the dormitories, a scattering of ugly little houses, and a rock quarry out of sight just beyond the back gates. Two footbridges and a one-lane bridge for cars linked it to town, and when the admissions office gave directions to prospective applicants and, more important, their parents, they always brought them that way instead of the direct route off the highway and past the quarry and a truck-storage depot. Langhorne was a fine but somewhat obscure small liberal arts college, a kind of poor relation of the Swarthmores and the Haverfords, and driving through Langhorne proper was more calculated to win hearts and minds.

Sitting cross-legged on the quilt, we ate chicken sandwiches and cucumber salad with red onion. Except for the hint of scalp beneath her sunlit hair and some lines that had appeared around her mouth, my mother looked fine. She took my arm when, as now, we had to walk over rougher ground, but she did it lightly, affectionately, to make it seem companionable rather than necessary. When we'd eaten blueberries I lay on the blanket rereading *Pride and Prejudice* and my mother worked on a needlepoint design of sunflowers on a blue background. Then she took out her book and I took a nap.

It was a beautiful day, the day of that picnic. The sun warmed our arms and legs, but there was a breeze, too, that ruffled the pages of my book. A tennis ball, bright against the tumbled browns and deep greens of the hillside, skittered by and bounced away over the edge of the outcropping, down toward the river below.

I woke as it went past, sweaty and cramped, curled on the quilt in the fading sun. I thought of the time Jon and I had gone skinny-dipping just below this spot one summer night, then made love beneath the low-hanging branches of some bush. There had been a full moon, and after I was finished but before he was, as he still moved above me, his half-breath half-grunt the only sound in the still night air—*uh uh uh uh*—I lay with my head turned sideways and saw stray balls all around, tennis balls, a Wiffle ball with its plastic scored by plastic bats, even a golf ball from the driving range past the tennis courts.

There was nothing erotic about the memory. I had had twigs in my hair, and an old knotty root made a tear on my thigh, and when I mentioned the balls afterward Jon became sulky, accused me of being sexually remote. But I felt lonely remembering it. I looked out across the river to the college and wondered where my father was now, and knew that if I asked my mother she would know, would have memorized his class schedule as she did every semester.

But she was the one who brought him up and broke the silence. She was staring across the river, her eyes vacant. Then she said, "I remember this book. I was reading it when I met your father. I remember admiring it but being a little put off by it, too, because it does that cheap thing that people do, it makes the sister who is sweet and domestic and good a second fiddle to the one who is smart and outspoken. Jane and Elizabeth. I remember them now. It didn't seem fair to me, that Jane was so good and yet Elizabeth is the one who is admired."

"I suppose that's Austen fighting back. She was that kind of woman and she knew that it was the sweet and good girl who was esteemed in society, not the one like Elizabeth who speaks out."

"But Jane Austen should have known better than to make women into that kind of either-or thing—"

"Do you really think she does that?"

"Yes, I do. It happened in another book, too." She looked out over the river again. "*Little Women,*" she said after a moment. "There was the sister who was the writer, and the one who had babies."

"Jo and Meg," I said.

"It's all the same," she said. "Women writers of all people should know better than to pigeonhole women, put them in little groups, the smart one, the sweet one. Women professors do it at the college, too, at faculty teas and things." My mother pitched her voice low and looked from under her brows. " 'Oh, you keep house—how turrrribly innnnterresting.' " She laughed, but I did not.

"Perhaps Austen just meant them as prototypes," I said.

"No, they're real enough, both of them, Jane and Elizabeth. Jane admires Elizabeth, and Elizabeth admires herself."

"Not true," I said. "Elizabeth admires Jane plenty."

"Really? Where? When you're reading it this time pay attention to that, show me where, tell me if you still believe it when the book is done."

"I thought you'd said you'd already read this book."

As though I had not spoken she went on: "I remember how relieved I was to see that they all had names I could pronounce. I'd just finished reading some Russian novels and the names drove me crazy. There'd be these long names in *War and Peace* and I'd just skip over them. Does that surprise you?"

"I think most people do that."

"I didn't mean about the names. I meant that I read the Russian novelists."

"No," I said. It did.

"When I was your age, or a little earlier I suppose it was, because when I was your age I already had you, I used to go over to the library at Columbia when I wasn't working at the dry-cleaning shop. I'd read for hours. My parents gave me off from ten to two most days and I went over there and studied. I think in the back of my mind I thought it would be a substitute for not going to college. I found a reading list for freshman English once and I read all the books on it, although afterward your father said most of them were no good."

"But you didn't meet him in the library."

"I met him at the cleaners. He had one sports jacket, a navy blue blazer, and he brought it in. It had a big spot of tomato sauce on it from the Italian restaurant on Amsterdam Avenue, and my mother made that clicking noise with her mouth she used to make when a customer brought in something really dirty. He told a funny story about taking a girl to that restaurant, the daughter of his thesis adviser I think it was, and having her father walk in the door and hitting his fork with his elbow and getting sauce all over them both. That episode killed the romance. Or I did."

"Grandma and Grandpa must have been wonderful chaperones."

"All your grandmother said when he brought the jacket in was 'Ready Tuesday.' But I kept reading in the library until he recognized me and then I kept reading in the library until he took me out to the Hungarian bakery for coffee and I kept reading in the library until he took me to the Italian restaurant. His hair was all black then, and he was thinner, but not much. He was very handsome."

"Still is."

"Yes." My father's regular features had lost flesh in some places, sagged in others, his rather thin mouth becoming more of a liability as the parentheses of middle age appeared around it. He was the male equivalent of that handsome woman about whom people say, "She must have been a beauty when she was younger."

"And he was so smart," my mother added. "The moment he opened his mouth you knew how smart he was." She looked from the river to me and she smiled, a smile so full of remembered joy that it hurt my heart to see it. "I leaned across the restaurant table and said, 'I would be the ideal faculty wife.' And when I leaned back, all red in the face, or at least that's what George said, hair red, face vermilion, he said, I leaned back and the entire front of my pink turtleneck was covered with tomato sauce."

"You never told me this!"

"You never asked."

"Oh, Mama, that's a smartass answer," I said.

"Was it?" my mother said, brightening. "Smartass?"

"Definitely smartass. And are you saying that that's it, that that's why he married you, because you asked him?"

"Oh, Ellie," she said ruefully, as though she was surprised I didn't understand something so simple, "I imagine he married me because I reminded him of his mother."

I thought back to my Gulden grandparents, who had run a summer camp in the mountains of New York State. Both of them were dead now, but when I was a little girl I had gone to them for the two weeks before school started, after the children from Long Island and Manhattan and Connecticut had gone home from camp, sunburnt and covered with mosquito bites. I had wandered through the reeds around the horseback-riding paddock picking up the arrows gone astray from archery and bringing them to my grandfather, a strong, quiet man with forearms that stretched the seams on his short-sleeved Banlon shirts so the stitches showed.

My grandmother was different. She looked like my father, lithe and fine-featured, and she sat on a rock while I hunted for crayfish in the creek and let me bake baking-powder biscuits with a thumbprint filled with jam in the center of each one. She smelled of roses and flour, sang Christmas carols at bedtime, braided my hair each morning and tied it with bits of yarn left over from arts and crafts.

"I guess I can see that," I said.

"I remember liking what I read of *Pride and Prejudice,* only wishing that it could be told from Jane's point of view. Your father said that would have made for a very dull book. Your father never really liked to talk shop when he got home. Except with you, of course, but that's different. I think he thinks of that as part of your education. Sometimes when I listen to the two of you I feel like a Little League player listening to the Yankees."

"Oh, come on."

"I don't mind. It's interesting."

"That's not how I would describe it."

"How would you describe it?"

"It's tiring," I found myself saying, "staying on top of your game."

The breeze was stronger now, blowing the pages of the book and lifting one corner of the quilt. Downstream I could see two children playing beneath the footbridge as I had done when I was small, pitching stones into the water.

"It's a mistake to base your entire life on one man's approval," my mother added quietly.

"It was the way women lived when you got married," I said.

"I was talking about you, Ellie," she said.

"Jonathan and I don't have that kind of relationship."

"I wasn't talking about Jonathan," she said.

We grew quiet again. The carillon across the river that Samuel Langhorne built to foster a sense of spirituality on campus rang out "Amazing Grace." When it stopped, "was blind but now I see," hung in the air for a moment like a cloud.

"Why didn't you finish the book the first time?" I finally said, the notes dying like the sun going down.

My mother wrapped her hand around the paperback in her lap and held it to her chest. Her knuckles gleamed like four round white stones in the pale yellow light. "I left my copy at City Hall the day I married your father," she said. "It was a library book, too. I had to pay to have it replaced."

"I'm not sure how this book-club thing works," I said. "When we're done, do we set up some time for discussion?"

"Wasn't that what we were just doing?" my mother said.

"No, I mean about theme and character and that sort of thing."

"Wasn't that what we were just doing?" she repeated.

"So we talk as we go along?"

"Why not?" my mother said.

"And when do we move on to the next one?"

"Ellen," she said, laughing, putting the book down and picking up her needlepoint, "for an intelligent girl you need an awful lot of direction. We'll go on to the next one when we're finished with the one we have."

My parents met and married in 1967, and though we later came to think of the 1960s as a time of great upheaval and liberation, the truth was that for them the upheavals came later, in their everyday lives. They were married at City Hall, took the subway downtown to Chambers Street, and were back in time for my father's four o'clock tutorial.

My mother went back to work in her parents' dry cleaners on Broadway, but after she locked up that night she went up to my father's one-room apartment at 135th Street, climbed into his bed, and next morning began to make curtains out of sheets. She cooked casseroles on a hot plate. They even had dinner parties, my mother once told me, chili and garlic bread balanced on the laps of half-a-dozen starving students.

By the time the Upper West Side was rife with consciousness-raising groups and faculty members were shedding their twin-set Smithy wives in favor of graduate students with short skirts and long hair, my parents were on their way to Princeton and then Langhorne, one a place in which change came slowly, the other a place in which it came hardly at all.

I was a clever child, with the ceaseless goad stabbing away deep inside me that comes from being the eldest child of a clever parent. While my mother drove us to swimming lessons and taught us to string stale cranberries for the Christmas tree and scolded us for using vulgar language and laughed at our knock-knock jokes, my father's distance was as seductive as his smile.

Nothing changed when my mother became sick. If anything my father was more distant than ever, and more mannered in his manner when he arrived. "What ho, crew?" he would say, putting his briefcase on the bench near the door. Or "You've never looked lovelier," he would say to my mother, bending over her hand, and she would reply, as she always did, "Oh, Lord, Gen," the pet name she had invented years before, shorthand for Gentleman George. Often my mother was already in bed when he got home. Sometimes, when I heard him quietly close the kitchen door long after night had fallen, I felt as though I was losing both my parents at the same moment, although I did not feel in the slightest like a child. I saw them with the cold eye of the adult now.

One night shortly after my mother and I had had our picnic and formed our book club, my father and I found ourselves together in the dark and sweet-smelling living room, with its bowls of homemade potpourri. Looking up from *Pride and Prejudice* and the circle of golden light cast by the reading lamp, I finally said, "Why am I doing this alone?"

"Doing what alone, may I ask?"

"Tending to your wife."

His mouth got very thin, and his voice very English, a prelude to meanness. "My wife? My wife? That woman is your mother. I have sat here hundreds of times watching her do for you, care for you, cook for you—"

"And for you," I said, refusing to be shamed.

"Ellen," he said, "I have to earn a living. To pay the mortgage. To pay the medical bills. Your mother understands."

"Is reconciled, you mean."

"You know nothing about it." He picked up my book and raised his eyebrows. "Haven't you read this a hundred times?"

"Apparently this is the book your wife gave up to marry you," I said.

"You've lost me."

"We've formed a book club. Mama wanted to read *Pride and Prejudice*. She started it at Columbia and stopped reading it the day you two got married."

"I don't recall that she liked Austen very much."

"That's not really accurate. She thinks Austen is condescending to women. Especially women with more conventional characters and expectations than those of Elizabeth Bennet."

My father shrugged. "Jane Bennet is as satisfied with her lot as any young woman in nineteenth-century fiction, as you well know."

"I'm not sure I remember," I said. "Now that I'm a housewife I've got other things to think about. Floor wax. Ironing. Which brings us back to our original discussion."

"Which seemed to me particularly futile. You and I have different roles to play here."

"I don't like mine."

"It won't last forever."

"That is a low blow," I said.

"Ellen, there is no reason for the two of us to be at cross-purposes. Your mother needs help. You love her. So do I."

"Show it," I said.

"Pardon me?"

"Show it. Show up. Do you grieve? Do you care? Do you ever cry? And how did you let her get to this point in the first place? When she first felt sick, why didn't you force her to go to the doctor?"

"Your mother is a grown woman," he said.

"Sure she is. But wasn't it really that you didn't want your little world disrupted, that you needed her around to keep everything running smoothly? Just like now you need me around because she can't. You bring me here and drop me down in the middle of this mess and expect me to turn into one kind of person when I'm a completely different kind and to be a nurse and a friend and a confidante and a housewife all rolled up in one."

"Don't forget being a daughter. You could always be a daughter."

"Oh, Papa, don't try to make me feel guilty. What about being a husband?"

"That is none of your business. That is between your mother and me." He rubbed his eyes with the flat of his hands. "These days at the beginning of term are very tiring. And I don't have the energy for anger." And he disappeared into the dark of the hallway and up the stairs. His voice came out of the black, disembodied, a kind of Cheshire Cat without the smile. "Don't forget," he added, "I take the night shift."

As I stood up to turn out the lights and go to bed I glanced at the picture of the three of us on the piano. I saw my mother's glowing face, and thought of how she had made it possible for my father to believe that his world would be effortlessly cared for because she had, seemingly effortlessly, cared for it. I was beginning to understand the effort in the care now, and that made me angry, to know how she had pretended that he had a job and she had something so much less. And it made me fearful, too, of the future. The essential differences between my mother and me seemed less essential, now that I could see her sitting in the library at Columbia, reading her way through the classics. She had given that up for my father, and she had deferred to him ever since, it was true. But now I understood how easy it was to do what he required, particularly in the service of what seemed a worthy cause.

I looked down at the three of us in the photograph, frozen in brilliant color beneath a sunny blue Cambridge sky. And I wondered how much I, too, had made possible my father's unthinking primacy. Or was it their marriage I safeguarded, my mother ever sweet-tempered without the demands of my father's intellectual arrogance, my father still enamored of his wife because he had another companion for his life of the mind? How providential that most children left home when they did, before they were wise enough to understand their parents.

"You'll feel better in the morning," I said aloud, and as I stared at the picture it became abstract, a blur of color and light, subject to a hundred interpretations. Then I stepped back and it rearranged itself into what it had always been, a still life of happiness. My eyes were dry and sandy. I felt tired and sapped, as though I had been living here like this my whole life. As indeed I had, looking for myself in the space between the two of them.

I felt undone by that night's exchange with my father, as undone as I had been the day, years before, when I first began to understand that it was not only his work that kept him on the Langhorne campus long after classes were done for the day. Langhorne, too, had a library, though not as large and distinguished as Columbia's. There was something churchlike about it, with its long and narrow stained-glass windows commemorating Shakespeare's heroines and its plain benches flanking the big oak tables. I, too, went there to fill in the gaps in my public school education with ambitious social studies projects and papers on Conrad and Melville that were half cribbed from literary criticism texts.

I don't know what brought my father to the library one afternoon when I was working there, at a table with a gaggle of girls doing a group project deconstructing T. S. Eliot's *Four Quartets*. But I heard them clearly once he had stalked down the center aisle and into the stacks: the divine Professor G, one said, and who is it now, said another, since his teaching assistant went to Colby?, and I'd do him, said one with curly black hair and a big gap between her front teeth.

No, they squealed, and a boy scratching away at a legal pad with a stack of reference books in front of him turned to glare at them. He's old, he's married, he grades so hard, they whispered.

He's my father, I thought.

I could imagine the man he was to them, because I had seen that man myself, though rarely at home, where, it occurred to me, he rested up for the hard work of becoming that George Gulden, the lover, the dazzler, the charmer. I find it difficult to talk about my father's charm today without reducing it to something akin to a snake in a basket and a fakir with a flute, talking about it the way you talk about drinking when you've been sober for years and all you can remember about a beer is what it was like to wrap your arms around the toilet at three A.M. and catch the sanctifying smell of bowl freshener as you threw up.

But it was a real true thing. My father was cordial to men, albeit intent on making his word known, his word law, but to women he was courtly and so warm he appeared to be courting even the elderly and the very young. "My dear Mrs. Duane," he would say as he stepped to the counter in the bookstore, "where might I find *In Cold Blood*? Your help will serve, not only me personally, but an entire generation of impressionable students who think of Truman Capote as a guest on *The Dick Cavett Show*. And, by the by, if the jacket of that new Norman Mailer stacked in the window fades, will you consider pitching them all as a service to mankind, or, in deference to the head of women's studies, who buys those copies of Germaine Greer you persist in ordering, a service to humankind?"

Mrs. Duane was a sophisticated woman, the widow of a former State Department official who had remarried and moved to the country from an apartment on one of the museum blocks off Fifth Avenue. But she was helpless before the stream of pleasantries that my father could pour from the pitcher of that personality. I had watched her once shift a huge stack of *The Canterbury Tales* from

one wall to another because my father had complained about finding them in the short-story section. "I would say, George, that
you had the gift of blarney if only you were Irish," she had said
more than once. "I have gemütlichkeit," said my father, "that's
what it is, whatever it is, be it some rich fruit dessert with clotted
cream or a disease of the pancreas, I have it and it is yours. Have
you the book?"

"I have," Mrs. Duane said. And if she hadn't, she would have
gotten it.

He did this with me, too, when he remembered, although never
once after I had come home to care for my mother. I can still
remember how he taught me the ABCs in the evening before bed,
when we were living in a small two-bedroom apartment on a back
street far from the university in Princeton and I saw him on weekdays only when I was bathed and brushed and perfect in my long
eyelet nightgowns. (My mother made those nightgowns. "I cannot for the life of me find a decent nightgown for a little girl anywhere!" she would say to her small group of faculty wives, who
were perfectly satisfied to put their own children into Mickey
Mouse pajamas or Doctor Dentons.) "*A* is for Aaaah-aaaah-aaaah-
CHOOOOOO!" he would sneeze. "*B* is for blunderbuss. *C* is for
cancan dancers kicking up their heels for Toulouse-Lautrec in the
fin de siècle." And so on until we got to *Z*, which was for Zsa Zsa
Gabor. No one said Zsa Zsa like my papa.

Sometimes, particularly if one of my girlfriends was in the car,
he would sing "Let's Call the Whole Thing Off" or recite slightly
dirty limericks or compliment the girl extravagantly on an ACT
LOCALLY, THINK GLOBALLY T-shirt ("Can human understanding
surpass the sentiments now beating within—whoops, atop—your
breast?") Of course, they loved it all. "My father sits in the car and
farts and tells me to shut up while he gets the sports scores off the
radio," said Jennifer Buckley, whose father owned a company that
built supermarkets and public schools. "Your father knew one day
that I was wearing Giorgio. Excuse me, but no contest."

But a man who can identify perfume on an eleventh grader sitting in the back seat of his car may have certain shortcomings as a father. One night in December, home for Christmas my first year at Harvard, I went to his office, high in one corner of an old limestone building that houses the English department and its classrooms. Grandma Nina had called from Florida, telling my mother in Polish that Grandpa had had a stroke and that the doctors believed he was going to die. The phones at the college were out of order because of a winter ice storm, some cables down, and so I took the footbridge, holding tight to the railings as the wind made the walkway sway, trying not to look at the cold river below, the water high on its banks.

The guard waved me through, and when I got to the fourth floor the office door was closed, but I could hear sounds from within, moans, the thump of the old springs on my father's shabby leather couch. "God, Beth," I heard, even through the closed door. "Jesus Christ, Beth." Beth was the name of a fierce feminist American history professor who was visiting from Rutgers. This is so banal, I thought to myself, using one of my father's favorite words, so banal, people do this all the time. Carefully and quietly I took a sheet of stationery from the desk of the department secretary and wrote "Your wife wants you." But I stood there and listened for a long time before I slid it under the door. Even now, all these years later, it gives me a sick feeling to think of it.

I don't know whether my father knew I knew. Our relationship underwent a change after that. I was less supplicant, more judge, and I was a person who, when called upon to judge, always judged harshly. A girl once dropped out of our creative writing seminar at Harvard because we had to read aloud and then talk about one another's work, and after four sessions she could not bear, she told the instructor, to hear what I would do to her stories, based on what I had done to others. I was unrepentant when the instructor told me this. "That's her problem, isn't it?" I said.

I judged my father just that harshly, or maybe more so because I'd imagined he had adjudged me wanting for so long and in so many ways. But nothing seemed to have changed between my parents, then or ever. And it was much later that I made the connection between what had happened and my enduring love affair with Jonathan, in which I wanted and hated him in relatively equal parts. When we went back to Cambridge after that Christmas vacation, Jonathan was amazed to discover the things I had now decided to do when we were in bed together. And not just in bed—I once slid my hand into his lap and inside his fly during an art history lecture, an explication of the Arnolfini wedding portrait, those two whey-faced people in elaborate robes preparing for a tedious eternity together. It is amazing to me now how far I was willing to go to mimic my father. It would make an interesting case for any psychiatrist.

We never spoke of what had happened, my father and I. The closest we ever got was when I came home six months later for summer vacation. I told my father of an encounter I had had with a professor in the Harvard graduate English department, who was also a novelist of some note, after I sent him some stories of mine. He had not liked the stories, I could tell by his careful and rather empty comments, although he had told me he had never seen brown eyes quite as dark as mine—"really, truly black!" he fake-marveled. I knew after only a year at school that this was clumsy code for "Be friendly and I'll take you to dinner and to bed."

I told my father of how, looking at my name at the top of each page, he had said, "There was a George Gulden in my grad school group. He was a smart guy but kind of a pain in the ass. He just dropped off the face of the earth after he got his degree."

We both knew what that remark was code for, my father and I, as we sat eating vegetable lasagna and Caesar salad, but he did not flinch and I told the story casually. My mother turned away, turned to the stove, and Jeff and Brian gaped. My father smiled thinly and said, "He's a very poor writer, and he was a very poor doctoral candidate. Did he like your stories?"

I didn't answer, and my father smiled again, knowing what that was code for. I remembered I had answered the writer in my mind, had imagined saying, with hauteur, turning away his offer of another beer, "He's my father. And you're an asshole." I imagined myself stalking out and leaving my manuscript on the table. Instead I had ducked my head and said nothing, took my stories and walked home in a driving rain, so that the manila envelope was the consistency of cereal by the time I got inside my dorm room. Jon was waiting on the bed in his underwear, reading a biography of Jefferson. "Did you sleep with him?" he asked. "You are a pig, Jonathan," I said, dumping my ruined manuscript in the basket. "Yeah, but I'm your pig," he said, crooking his finger at me, and over I went again.

Hospitals are a little like the beach. The next wave comes in, and the footprints of your pain and suffering, your delivery and recovery, are obliterated; the sheets are changed. But transient as it all is, if I went to Montgomery Medical Center today it would be a kind of homecoming, although one of the small desires of my life is that I never ever see the place again, its awkward red-brick bulk, its tiered parking garage and automatic double doors.

For four months it was our sometime world, where my mother saw her doctor and had what she still preferred to call her treatments. Its floors were covered with gray linoleum speckled with white and black so aggressively ordinary as to be offensive; its intercom interruptions and the glass-fronted cabinets filled with pointed things became the backdrop of our life together.

Off one of the corridors that fanned out from the lobby we waited in molded plastic chairs to be ushered into a cubicle where the closest thing my mother had to salvation, before morphine became her saving grace, could flow slowly into her veins and try to kill off the cells run amok. They'd wanted her to check herself into the hospital for the chemotherapy but she'd refused, and so I brought her every three weeks and we spent the day amid the sharp smells and clamor of the outpatient unit.

They'd made it pretty, the chemo cubicle, with flowered wallpaper and a bright blue leatherette recliner. Even the chemicals were somehow decorative, the crystalline bags glimmering silver in the overhead light of the windowless room. It took almost the whole day to get it all in, drop by drop by God-please-let-it-work drop.

Oh yes, I prayed in that cubicle and in the hallway outside and in the cafeteria, where I went as much to shake off the feeling of being buried alive that I felt in that tiny room as because I really wanted another cup of coffee. But I prayed to myself, without form, only inchoate feelings, one word: please, please, please, please, please.

My mother made me wait outside when she was examined by her doctor. She was a rather fierce-looking woman, Dr. Cohn, with the strong and handsome face that you see on old coins. She wore simple sheath dresses of slate blue or taupe or dull prints, as though they were bought mainly because they were unobtrusive beneath a white coat. I remember how firm her handshake was, so definite, like everything else about her. I thought she was rather cold, but since then, since I've gotten to know more oncologists, I realize that she only had the slight wariness that so many have, faced as they are so often with certain failure.

Certainly Dr. Cohn was kind to my mother. She always came downstairs to visit during her chemotherapy, took her hand, and talked with her quietly about her symptoms as the chemicals did their methodical drip-drip dance.

"There's platinum in this stuff, Ellen," my mother said, smiling, during the second round, "just like in my wedding ring. That's why my mouth tastes like tin."

"Is it working?" I said.

"I can't say how well it's working yet," Dr. Cohn said. "I'll be doing some tests and I'd like to hear how well you felt, Kate, after the first time."

"She threw up the entire next day. Everything. Every bit of food she ate. And when that was gone she had the dry heaves. Plus her hair is starting to come out all over her pillow."

Dr. Cohn's smile was so faint that it was little more than a pucker at the corners of her mouth. "Those aren't unexpected side effects. But I'd like to hear from Kate about how she's feeling."

"It's not too bad. I do hate the tinny taste. I'm losing weight, although I never thought I'd see that as a problem. And my hair looks pretty awful." My mother ran her fingers through her thinning red curls.

"Oh, come on, Mama. You must have thrown up ten times the last time."

"Any pain?" said Dr. Cohn.

"Nothing to speak of," said my mother.

"Are you sure?" I said.

"Ellen," said my mother.

When Dr. Cohn left I followed her out into the hallway. Her stride was long, and I had to hustle to catch up with her.

"Doctor, I really feel at a loss here. I don't know enough about what they found during her hospital stays. I don't know enough about her prognosis, about what to expect. I really need ten or fifteen minutes of your time."

She put a hand beneath my elbow. "Come," she said, and walked me back down the hall.

"Privately," I added.

"I won't do that," she said evenly. "This is your mother's illness. She deserves to be part of any discussions we have about it." She pushed open the door and walked over to the cubicle.

"Kate," she said, and my mother opened her eyes and smiled. "Ellen has some questions about your condition and I wonder whether you'd like me to answer them now or to see you both upstairs later?"

"What kind of questions?" my mother said, and for a moment I could not answer.

"About where the cancer started. About whether it's spreading. About what comes next."

My mother looked into Dr. Cohn's eyes and not mine as she answered. She recited like a child called to give an answer in class. "The scan showed it was in the liver. And maybe in the ovaries, too, although they can't find that on the scans. There's something in the blood test that makes them think maybe the ovaries are involved. The doctor in the city who looked at the pictures and the slides and gave us a second opinion said that's highly unusual but not unheard of. Do I have it right so far?"

"Exactly," said Dr. Cohn.

"What else, Ellen?" my mother asked.

"I just feel as if I need to be filled in."

"On what?"

I knew what I would have said if the doctor and I had been in the hallway together. I would have said: how long? I would have asked: how bad? I would have wanted a blow-by-blow of disintegration, the road to death. But I could not ask the questions with my mother there. I suspected she already knew the answers, that she'd wanted the same ones I did, and wanted to keep them to herself.

"That's all," I said. "I'm going down to the cafeteria for coffee." Dr. Cohn followed me out.

"I'm the kind of person who likes to know things," I said.

"So is your mother," the doctor said. "Why don't you ask her about some of them?"

Suddenly I stopped and snapped my fingers. "I just thought of something," I said. "My mother's parents owned a dry-cleaning shop. Do you think the chemicals there could have caused this?"

"Your father asked the same thing," Dr. Cohn said.

"And?"

"And your mother said 'What does it matter now?' "

The only time I saw my mother break down during those weeks was when we were passing through the lobby just as a woman was rising from a wheelchair at the automatic doors, turning to take a sleeping newborn from the arms of a nurse to carry it out to a waiting car. The baby's hand was splayed on the swaddling, a pink star, and my mother's mouth began to work as she stood and watched mother and child move through the doors. "Ah," she breathed, and she pressed a tissue to her face.

Within weeks she knew the names of all the nurses, their family backgrounds, the ages of their children. As she waited they would smile and say her name: Good morning, Kate, how are you? Just a moment more and we'll get you in. And naturally, the county being what it was, they knew us. One of them had a son who had gone to school with my brother Jeff. Another had a daughter on scholarship at Langhorne. "She says your father is one of the best professors there," she said. "She says when you get an *A* from him it really means something."

"She is absolutely right," my mother said.

"I remember when you won the essay contest," said a nurse named Gina as she ran a needle into the catheter the doctors had implanted just above my mother's heart so that the nurses wouldn't have to hunt around for veins. "The Port-A-Cath will be a lifesaver later," she'd said to me. "For the morphine."

"The morphine?" I'd asked.

"Well," she'd said, looking down at a tray of instruments, "maybe not."

Usually the two of us were alone, but one morning, I remember, there was an elderly woman who described in detail her hip replacement and the subsequent convalescence which had cast a long shadow over her life. Finally, almost as an afterthought, she asked my mother why she was there. "I need a chest X ray for a life-insurance policy," my mother replied.

"If I had told her the truth, I would have been there forever," my mother said after her treatment was done that day.

The woman could not have been from Langhorne, or she would have known about my mother's illness. Everyone in town did. They were all a little too bright, a little too chatty when she went to Phelps's hardware or the supermarket. "How nice that Ellen's home," they said, but no one asked what I was doing there, because they already knew. "How well you look, Kate," they lied. Lord, I thought, what a shock it would be if any of them ever had the guts to lean across a counter and say, "How's the cancer?" But despite the scarves and hats my mother began to wear over the ruin of her pretty curls, despite how thin she became, I never heard the word "cancer," not ever, until after the cancer was gone.

The only person who used the word was Mrs. Forburg, my senior English teacher. One day soon after I came home I received a note in the mail addressed to me in her angular vertical script. It was short and straightforward, just as she was. "Ellen dear," she wrote, "I think of you fondly and often, not only because of your mother's illness but because of your own responsibilities. Would you come to dinner soon? My own mother died of cancer when I was young and perhaps we could be of help to each other. All love, Brenda Forburg."

I tucked it in a corner of my desk blotter and took it out from time to time to call. But there never seemed to be the time.

For despite the chemotherapy, and the days afterward when I could hear her heaving pitiably in the master bathroom, despite the weekly blood tests and exams, I suspect that my mother would have said that those were wonderful and full months for her. She and her daughter finally had the relationship she had always imagined would accompany the canopy she had made for the four-poster bed in the attic bedroom, the scrapbooks she kept of report cards and literary magazine poems, the hours she spent on birthday parties and Care packages to college and camp.

We went to the movies, took a day trip to the beach, ate lunch a few times at little restaurants whose ads she had clipped from magazines and newspapers. She got tired very easily, and once or twice the way she breathed made me frightened. But she refused to be housebound, or to let me be.

"What exactly are you doing all day?" Jules asked one night

when she called to regale me with the stupidity and arrogance of the Yale man who had my former job.

"I'm being a girlfriend," I said.

"Picking over the perfidy of men?"

"Shopping," I replied.

I suppose today that I should say that those months were wonderful for me, too, a chance to make amends for a lifetime of taking for granted. The truth is that while it was happening I tolerated it, and when I thought about it I hated it all. In the beginning I thought it was because of all that I was missing, because of the life just an hour away that was passing me by, in the city where you could become yesterday's girl in a weekend.

But it was more complicated than that, and simpler, too. As my mother guided me to the right sort of wax for the cherry bowfront chest or sent me out to buy cheese or berries, I felt as though I was sinking beneath the weight of a life I had always viewed with something even more dismissive than contempt, a life I had viewed as though it were a feature in *National Geographic,* the anachronistic traditions of a distant tribe.

It was a world without men, too, with my brothers gone away and my father scarcely there, letting my mother take care of her own disintegration as she'd taken care of her house, her children, the life which she had devoted to him.

"I know what you're saying," I told Jules. "I know someday I'll be able to walk away from this. But what if I just get back into it again? What if I marry Jon and it turns out that what he really expects is a suburban matron who knits sweaters for his children?"

"What Jon will want in his first wife is the kind of woman who runs charity luncheons and hires good staff. His second wife will be the trophy wife, the one who designs jewelry or something and wears leather pants."

"You've just reduced three lives to a set of clichés," I said. "And one of them is mine."

"True clichés, El. And I'm betting that one of them won't be yours. I know you don't like me to cast aspersions on Jon, but how often has he called you? How often has he written? When will he come to visit? Your mother needs you and you need him and he's nowhere to be found."

Jules was right; Jon had called only twice since I had come home. But I did not care much. The Ellen Jon knew was the other Ellen, the one who always shone with the luster of success. The Ellen who sat in the hospital corridor with Kate Gulden was inevitably a loser; after all her triumphs, this endeavor was doomed to failure.

One afternoon in early October we went to the big mall outside of town and across the racks at one store my mother saw a woman who had once been part of the group that decorated the village green for holidays—the Minnies, they called themselves, after the childless Mrs. Langhorne.

"Oh, Ellen, do you remember Sheila Fenner? She was in the Minnies when you were in high school."

"And I miss it," said Mrs. Fenner. "But I'm a working woman now, and there's no time for anything but the grandkids and Bill's dinner, and even that comes out of the microwave. But look at you, Kate, you're a shadow. When did you lose so much weight? You're a bone."

"Oh, you know," said my mother shrugging. "Running around. Keeping up with Ellen."

"Weight Watchers?" said Mrs. Fenner archly.

My mother looked at me sideways. She knew what I would say if left to my own devices: "No, Mrs. Fenner, it's the chemotherapy plan. A delicious shake for breakfast, one for lunch, an IV in your chest at teatime, and before you know it you weigh ninety pounds."

"No," said my mother, "I hate those plans. The food is just awful."

"Well, it's nice to see you," Mrs. Fenner said. "And Ellen. Jill said she saw your byline in a magazine a while ago. That must be terribly exciting." I smiled. "Jill's husband is at Cornell Medical

School. I wish he'd finish up so they could get out of the city. I just worry terribly. Where do you live?"

"Greenwich Village," said my mother.

"Lovely. And how are the Minnies?" added Mrs. Fenner, in the slightly condescending way we speak of the lives whose usefulness we have outlived.

"I'm having them over for lunch next week," my mother said.

How I remember that lunch for the Minnies. Years later, when I was on call at the hospital, when my scalp began to feel rank and gritty and my face slack after a night of screaming and suffering and pleas for painkillers on the medical wards, I would try to gauge my fatigue and always I would come back to the same basis for comparison: I was as sweaty and drained as I had been at the end of the day I cooked for those women, the day I learned how much work it took to make lunch for ten, or at least to do it the way my mother did.

The day before, she sent me shopping, and when I returned she laid her ingredients out on the kitchen counter: the chickens, the zucchini, some cream, some carrots, I can't recall exactly what else. I was in the basement loading the dryer and I heard her making clanging noises, pulling pots and pans out of the lower cupboards, the tympani of my childhood. I could conjure up winter evenings at my desk, writing in my journal or taking notes on index cards, hearing that *crash-bang* and knowing that the engine of my world was running smoothly.

"I can do that," I said, as I came upstairs. My mother was squatting, the top half of her inside a cabinet, looking for a lid in the back. When she emerged she was clutching it triumphantly. "I should have redone this kitchen years ago," she said, getting to her feet, using the edge of the counter for support, panting a bit.

"I can do that," I repeated.

"You can make a chicken paillard and zucchini soup?" she said. She lifted her big stockpot onto a back burner and began to fill it with water from the tea kettle. "I should have redone it years ago," she said, as though to herself. "At least I would have had a sink deep enough to put a pot in." Then she turned, hand on her hip, narrowed her eyes and looked at me.

For just a moment she looked hard, calculating, as though she was sizing me up. Then she wiped her hands on a dish towel and sat down in one of the chairs at the oak table. She was wearing a big blue butcher's apron; she untied it, pulled it over her head, and handed it to me.

"The torch is passed," she said. "Take the chicken and put it into the pot with a carrot, some peppercorns, a stalk of celery and a handful of parsley and cover it with water. And put the kettle on for tea. You can't cook without tea."

It took me all afternoon to make that meal. She sat and gave instructions. I leaped back and screamed the first time I fed zucchini into the food processor and it let out a *chi-chi-chi* sound that made me think it would chew up my fingers. I mistakenly poured a mug of hot tea into the chicken stock. My mother just laughed. "At least it wasn't sugared," she said. "Leave it alone. They'll think it's some exotic new recipe if they notice at all."

At some point, I remember, I dropped into the chair opposite her, my face damp from the heat of the stove. "If you don't mind my asking," I said, "isn't there an easier way to do this? Don't people buy chicken broth in cans? Can't you get prechopped zucchini or something?"

"I don't think you can get prechopped zucchini, although you can certainly get chicken broth in cans," she said. "But I've always liked doing it this way. It tastes better and it makes me feel productive."

"Lord, Mama," I said. "You're the most productive person I know."

"Well, if you think that, it's because of all the things like this I did."

"But how did you do this when we were little? How did you have the time? Didn't we get in the way?"

"Not so much," she said, sipping at her tea. "You and Jeff were usually off someplace outside. And Brian would sit right here, on the floor, and cook with me. I would give him some flour and some water and he could sit here for hours and stir the whole mess together and sing 'Waltzing Matilda.' "

"I remember that," I said.

"The only problem I had was that you used to run away so often. That was mostly when we lived in Princeton. I'd be making stew or something and a squad car would pull up. After a while I got to know all the policemen. Do you remember that?"

"Not really," I said. "I remember you talking about it."

"One of them said to me, 'Well, Mrs. Gulden, this little girl is just on her way to somewhere else.' " She turned and looked at me, her eyes so bright, and then she smiled ruefully. "But Brian just sat and stirred his mess." There was a popping sound from the top of the stove. "You've got your stock too high," she added, and I sighed and got to my feet.

"I like the book club better," I said.

"So do I," my mother said.

"The Gulden Girls Book and Cook Club," I said, and she laughed. She looked so happy. But I noticed that when she lifted her mug of tea her hand trembled. You could hear her breathing a room away. And often, almost unconsciously, she rubbed at her lower back as though she had a pain there.

It was a good lunch; I remember that, too. Someone said that the soup had an unusual taste, and both my mother and I choked. "It's Ellen's secret recipe," my mother said.

The annual plan for the Christmas trees was made at that meeting; it took almost as much time as my stock to simmer and settle. Each year the Minnies decorated the twelve blue spruces that stood in a cluster at the end of Main Street. Each year they made dozens and dozens of balls and figures and garlands, and then they rose on ladders, all those women, like a construction crew, and turned the trees into the focal point of the town green. The mayor lit them and a choir sang carols.

The trees were a Langhorne tradition and were taken very seriously: if you lived in Langhorne and did not attend the tree lighting ceremony, everyone assumed you were too sick to stand, which is what I sensed the Minnies feared would happen to my mother in the six weeks before Christmas. One year a group of high school boys had picked the trees clean of their decorations in the middle of the night, and when school was dismissed that day there were two squad cars outside in the circular driveway. By next morning all the decorations were back on, and back on exactly where they had been when the Minnies had put them on.

"Now, what are our colors?" Linda Best, the district attorney's wife, said as she leaned her shelflike bosom on our mahogany dining-room table.

"I think red and gold this year," said Isabel Duane, eating her chicken in the European fashion, the tines of her fork turned down and her knife pushing bits of food onto their sharp silver points.

"Oh, not again," said Mrs. Byers. "Wasn't it just the year before last that we had red and gold?"

"You always do this, Caroline," Mrs. Duane said. "You always lump them all together. We haven't had red and gold for years."

"Oh, Kate," said Mrs. Byers, turning to my mother at the head of the table, "wasn't it just two years ago? Remember, because you used those angels with the big red robes and the gold trumpets? It was the year before last."

"Isabel's right," my mother said, a hand atop Caroline Byers's to cushion the blow. "Last year blue and silver; the year before was red and white. We haven't had red and gold since the year Ellen left for Harvard. I remember because I was making angels the first Thanksgiving she was home."

"How many years ago, Ellen?" Mrs. Best said.

"Five. Or six."

"So red and gold it is," Mrs. Duane said, with a little nod that said she'd known it would be so. Mrs. Byers frowned. "It seems done, somehow," she said with a sigh.

I could almost feel my mother relax at the other end of the table. She loved the tree decorating, and she had been deeply unhappy one year when some Minnie, now gone, moved to Florida or somewhere equally distant spiritually and physically, had prevailed upon the others to embrace a color scheme of blue and green. "Ugh," she had said whenever she sat down to work on her decorations that year.

My mother had one tree to do by herself, as she had for many years; she would not be moved by faint suggestions that she oversee the entire project. I thought of Dr. Cohn and her menorah. She would get one, I knew, made by my mother from a pattern in some magazine. Or she would get some other token, a sampler or a needlepoint pillow. I could imagine Dr. Cohn telling people who came to her office that a patient had once made it for her.

"Is George taking some time off?" Mrs. Best asked as they stood to leave after coffee and dessert.

"George?" my mother said. "He has more work than ever, with this new faculty tenure committee. And he's working on an article. You know how he is."

Mrs. Best's mouth narrowed to a thin line of bright coral lipstick. "Well, yes, so is Ed, but under the circumstances—"

"Linda, you will be late for the library meeting," Mrs. Duane interrupted. "And so will I, and I just won't." Mrs. Duane hugged my mother, and I saw my mother wince and wondered where it hurt. "Lovely lunch, Kate," Mrs. Duane said. "Lovely lunch, Ellen." And she cut her blue eyes toward Mrs. Best and made a horrid face. Then they all were gone.

"I'll clean up, Ellie," my mother said, but ten minutes later I found her asleep in the living room and I cleared the table and did the dishes myself. It had been a lovely lunch, but it had tired her. I hated Linda Best.

The leaves turned and floated down, commonplace to all but the children, who scuffed through them along the curbs in their school shoes on the way to the bus stop. We made Halloween treats, a quarter and a Tootsie Roll and a plastic witch riding a broom, all tied up in an orange napkin with a black ribbon. I learned how to make beef burgundy, although I nearly ruined it, and to fold napkins into swans. The tasks were both tedious and challenging, like diagramming complex sentences. "In the unlikely event that I become the overseer of an elegant household," I said, "I will have one company meal."

"Don't forget your zucchini soup," my mother said.

She told me stories of going to public school in New York when the schools were still good there, about riding a Schwinn her father bought secondhand in Riverside Park, about being forbidden to go to City College, which was all the dry-cleaner's daughter could afford, first because her father wanted to protect her from the Jews, then the blacks. She took out her past lives as though to look at each, fold it carefully, and put it between tissue paper in some cedar-scented bottom drawer.

She told me of how her brother Stevie, older by two years, had gone to Fort Benning on a bus to join the Army and how she had envied him the excitement, the trip down south, the communal life instead of the airless apartment with the tiny spotless kitchen, and finally the tissue-thin letters with the strange exotic stamps. She told me of how they finally brought him home from Vietnam in 1965.

"My mother said to the funeral-home director, 'Open the box.' Stevie's dress uniform was perfect, I don't think he'd worn it more than once or twice, but his poor face was so swollen that it was hard to tell it was him. And they'd powdered it over, but you could still see that it was a funny blue color, like a bruise. My mother looked at him and she said 'Steven' very quietly, and she touched his hand."

That was the only time my mother cried during October, that and in front of the television. At night sometimes we went through the television listings with a pencil, picking out old movies. We watched them with a bench in front of us, bowls filled with Styrofoam balls, pins, ribbons, sequins, so we could work on the Christmas decorations.

We watched *Waterloo Bridge,* saw Vivien Leigh jump to her death after descending into prostitution. We watched *Dark Victory*—Bette Davis blind—and *Now, Voyager*—Bette Davis beaten down. We watched *Stella Dallas* three times.

And cried and cried and cried and cried, blowing our noses into the tissues that stood amid the finished decorations. Or sometimes we cried at tragedies on the news shows, toddlers, as yellow as young pumpkins, who needed new livers, girls who left home to become Broadway hoofers and wound up as decapitated hookers, former child stars photographed with hidden cameras as they picked food from dumpsters. Mass murders, earthquakes, floods, fires—all took our minds off real tragedy for at least a little while.

We finished *Pride and Prejudice* and turned to *Great Expectations.* My mother thought Pip's admiration for Estella was unconvincing. "It's the weak link in just about every book I've ever read," she said one day, lying on the couch with the book on her lap, her raspy breathing punctuated with a barking cough. "They set up a very smart, very thoughtful, very nice character, and then have him fall in love with someone that anyone could tell is a horrible human being."

"But in real life nice smart people fall in love with horrible people all the time. More often than not, in my experience."

"Well, you should know," my mother said, and then immediately added, "I'm sorry."

"Apology accepted," I said.

"Believe me, Ellie, I understand sexual chemistry. Understand it perfectly. From experience." My mother's face began to turn a deep rose color against which her eyes looked very brown, but she seemed determined to go on. "It's a powerful thing."

"Mama," I said, "are we about to have that little sex talk we never had when I was thirteen?"

"I beg your pardon! We did have that little sex talk. For God's sake, I practiced for it for two weeks. And we had it when you were eleven, when I first noticed that you had"—she made a pointing motion with her index fingers—"poking out the front of your swim-team tank suit."

I frowned. I vaguely remembered something about tampons and fertilization, but it was as murky as the water in the pool where we practiced for swim team, with its yeasty smell of overchlorination, a smell I had realized some years later in Jon's car was second cousin to the smell of semen.

"Please don't tell me you don't remember," she said.

"I kind of remember."

"I even had a little pamphlet about the female sex organs, and then all you cared about was the math. What about twins, you said, and I explained that there were two eggs. What about triplets? I think you got all the way up to octuplets. That was the first time I'd heard that one, octuplets. And finally I told you how the egg and the seed got in the same place at the same time and you said, without missing a beat, 'How does it feel?' "

Suddenly it all came back to me. I remembered how on that day, too, my mother's face had flushed bright, and she had run a hand distractedly through her hair, and then my father had come into the hallway unexpectedly, noisily, ebulliently, with some great news—a sabbatical? a publication in some scholarly journal?—and she had never answered the question. But I had known the answer by her face, and, later, by her manner some Sunday mornings at the breakfast table, bemused, sleepy, and self-satisfied.

"Of course I told you the truth," she said now, completing the memory the way it ought to be. "I don't think you were a bit pleased. You just looked at me in that sizing-up way you had when you were young and went upstairs. I wondered what you were thinking. I always had a hard time figuring out what you were thinking."

"I know," I said.

"I didn't do a very good job of dealing with that," she added, looking down at her hands and turning them in her lap. "Figuring out what you were thinking. Your father was better at it. Much better." She looked at me and added, "I'm sorry."

"That's all right," I said, a little mystified because I was not sure what the apology was for. For so long I'd thought about myself as a girl who'd walked away from her mother's life that it would be a long time before I would start to think about the other part of the bargain, how easily she'd let me go.

One morning I awoke confused from a dream in which Jonathan and I were biting at each other at the front of a large lecture room filled with students. I heard high cries from the bedroom below, and for just a moment I thought that there was a baby somewhere in the house, waiting to be changed and fed. Then my father called my name. When I got to their bedroom he was sitting on the edge of the bed, a towel around his waist, and my mother was crying without tears.

"She's in horrible pain," he said. "She says it's her back." And he turned to her. "All will be well, Katydid, shh, shh, shh. All will be well. Shhhh."

"A heating pad," my mother said, her voice shrill.

"She's been up most of the night," my father said. "I couldn't find a heating pad but she insisted I shouldn't wake you."

"Let Ellen sleep," my mother said querulously, as though she had been repeating it all night long.

I brought a heating pad down from my room and together my father and I pulled my mother upright, one on each arm. With the quilt rolled back and her nightgown slipping off her shoulders and twisted up around her thighs I could see how much she had hidden from me until now. The skin on her upper arms hung down in wrinkled sacs; her collarbone stood out like the beams that hold the house up. Her legs were narrow stalks, bruised. I was reminded of a girl in our house at Harvard whose diet consisted only of bananas and Evian and who left at midsemester, still insisting as her size three leather skirt slipped down her bony hips that what she really needed was to run another mile each morning.

Six weeks we'd lived so close together and yet she had insulated me from much of the disintegration she saw whenever she removed her nightgown each morning. Insulated me when she kept me out of Dr. Cohn's office, when she talked to me in gentle code of works of fiction and past lives, when she shut the door of the bedroom and bathroom and mustered her gay smile on our excursions. "Let Ellen sleep," she had insisted, and I knew why. She was not yet ready to let her child be the grown-up in the house. She had had one great calling, as a mother, and she would not be forced from the field.

When we laid her back down on the heating pad, my father and I, she was breathing as though she'd run up the stairs herself.

"You have a nine o'clock," she said to him, without opening her eyes.

As I was calling the doctor I heard the door open and close, and knew that he was gone. I wondered what he thought when he looked at the wreck of her body, whether he was sad or repulsed. I wondered what she thought as she watched him look. I wondered what life was like on the night shift, whether she was able to say and feel the things in the dark of their bedroom that she kept from me in the light of day, whether he was a better man than I now thought him.

I called Dr. Cohn at the hospital. "I know you guys don't make house calls anymore," I said, and before I could go further she said, businesslike, "I'll be there in half an hour." And in half an hour the blue Volvo with its MD plates and baby seat in the back was in the driveway, and I made a pot of coffee.

"Oh, Doctor, I've done something to my back, a disc or something," my mother said plaintively. "The pain is awful."

I watched Dr. Cohn fill a syringe, feel softly around the lump in my mother's upper chest, then inject something into the catheter lodged beneath the skin. Almost immediately my mother relaxed, and her lids began to droop.

"Better," she said, lying back with her arms at her sides.

The doctor rolled her over and lifted the blue flannel nightgown with its pattern of tiny flowers. I held my hand to my mouth and turned away, my head against the cool white jamb of the door.

"Ellen?" my mother said faintly, half asleep, and I tried to reply but my throat had closed around the knot of my fear and grief and no matter how I worked I could not make it open and let my words out. Although what I could possibly say, except "Mama," like a baby, a good child, I did not know.

"She went downstairs to fix me another cup of coffee, Kate," said Dr. Cohn.

"Oh, wonderful," my mother replied, and in a minute I heard her breathing slow and deepen. The doctor had pulled down her gown, rearranged the quilt, and was taking her pulse.

Downstairs we sat together at the table, that old oak table, with its golden surface. Dr. Cohn drank her coffee without speaking. After it was finished, she took a pad out of her bag and began to write. She had nice even script, and when I said so she laughed dryly. "People have been thrown out of med school for less."

She handed me the prescription. "She didn't throw her back out," she said.

"I'm not stupid, Doctor."

"I know that, but as you may have realized by now, intelligence is not what's needed here. Empathy is. Your mother seems to be in a great deal of pain. It's hard to tell how much because, as you well know, she is an uncomplaining patient. Perhaps to a fault. Her cancer is progressing far more quickly than I think any of us would have suspected. I wouldn't be telling you that if I hadn't already told her during our last visit. One of the most important things at this point will be the management of her pain. I've given you morphine pills. Depending on how she does, we may go to a pump that will dispense morphine directly through her catheter. Have you and your father discussed hospice care?"

"Doctor, I can't predict the future, but I can tell you this. No hospice, no hospital. I had a good job in the city and a nice apartment and friends and places to go and people to see and I junked it to take care of my mother. And I am going to take care of my mother. I will do what is required."

She began to write on her pad again. "Are you seeing someone?" she asked as she wrote.

"A shrink?"

"Actually, we in the trade prefer to call them psychiatrists. But yes. I think you need someone to talk to."

"I talk to my mother."

"You need someone to talk to *about* your mother. And about how your mother is making you feel about yourself. And your mother could use someone to talk to about how it feels to be dying."

"My mother is fine. My mother can talk to me."

"Can she? Has she said she's terrified to go to sleep because she's afraid she'll never wake up? Has she told you she imagines sometimes how the rest of you will go on with your lives and forget her? Has she told you that she wants to have sex with her husband but she's afraid he doesn't want her? Look at the stenciling around the ceiling of this room, at the quilt on her bed. Look at the trees outside this house and the wreath on your front door, which I assume she made. Has she told you how it feels to lose it all?"

Doctor Cohn pulled the second sheet from her prescription pad. Side by side they lay on the oak table. "Morphine sulfate," said one. "Jessica Feld," said the other, with a phone number under it.

"You need to talk to someone, Ellen," she said, standing up.

"You need to talk to someone and you need to give her the pills every eight hours to help her get through this next part. Don't let her chew them and don't crush them. I'll send over a wheelchair. She may experience difficulty walking soon. I'd like to see her tomorrow if she's up to it. I'll let myself out."

Before she'd even pulled out of the drive I took the two prescriptions upstairs and stuck one under the edge of my desk blotter, beneath the note from Mrs. Forburg I hadn't answered yet. When I went to the pharmacy with the other, Mr. Sellinger filled it without pleasantries, except to say as I left, "Give our love to your mother." And I did, and the pills. For a while, they helped.

My brothers came home the Tuesday before Thanksgiving. Brian burst into tears when he saw her. But she only pulled him down next to her. He knelt by her chair and put his head on her chest, next to her heart. "No, no, Baba," she said as she had so many years ago.

Jeff stood looking down at them, a crooked smile on his freckled face. "Ma, you look like hell," he said.

"It's Ellen's fault," she replied.

"Nah, it's not. You haven't been eating your vegetables. You've been out dancing all night long. There's an empty six-pack behind the shoe rack in your closet. I know your kind."

"Oh, Lord, Jeffie," she said, and he ruffled her hair.

But I think our mother's appearance was not as big a surprise for either of them as mine was for Jonathan, when he arrived at the house unexpectedly on Wednesday. I heard steps behind me and there he was, handsome in a blue sweater and gray flannel pants, his eyes hidden by his mirror sunglasses. It was when he took them off that I saw the surprise in them, saw him look me up and down in a way that, under different circumstances, would have been flattering. I was wearing a red-and-white checked apron that said KISS THE COOK on its bib, and I had pushed my hair up into a haphazard bun on the top of my head. I was making biscuits, and my hands and the front of my apron were covered with flour. I hugged Jon and kissed him hard, and when I finally pulled away I had left him blotched with white, his sweater, his pants, even the part of his hair that hung heavy like a butterscotch parenthesis over his forehead.

"Oh, hell," he said, looking down at himself.

"Love you, too," I said, and playfully—or spitefully, I'm not certain which—I put a floury thumbprint in the center of his chest.

"Ellen!" he yelled. After I'd washed my hands and taken off the apron he wrapped his arms around me and kissed me for a long time in the quiet house. "You smell like butter," he said, but he didn't sound that happy about it.

Both of us pulled apart as we heard slow footsteps on the stairs. My mother came into the kitchen. "Jonathan," she said brightly, and he bent to kiss her cheek, pale yellow skin stretched over sharp bone. I left them talking about law school. But after I had taken a shower, when the two of us were out in the car, he leaned back against the seat and let his breath out, long and hard: *Whhhhhooooo.*

"How do you feel?" he asked.

"As little as possible."

"I see what you mean," he said.

He didn't, of course, because instead of putting off feeling, Jonathan never really felt things at all. I liked to think he loved me in those days, but loving a woman was not truly part of his constitution. No Jessica Feld, no "what we in the trade call psychiatrist," was necessary to explain this to the laywoman. Jonathan's mother had left when he was just two and she just twenty, had decided her spur-of-the-moment teenage marriage was a mistake and left behind its most tangible asset, the little boy who, once grown, would never be able to say "I love you" without believing that the sentence was a prelude to a farewell, an abandonment, a kick in the teeth.

She lived in California now, had another family, a house with a pool. Once, when he was twelve, he had managed to get his mother's phone number out of his grandmother and had called her and heard a little boy answer the phone. "How could somebody just leave their kid?" he told me he asked her when she came on the line, and she replied, still with a broad streak of Brooklyn in her voice, "I just did."

"You could almost hear the shrug," Jonathan said.

Not long ago I saw Jonathan on Madison Avenue with a really lovely-looking woman, with blond feathers of hair around her face and sharp intelligent eyes. I knew that she was smart and interesting, someone you could take anywhere. Jonathan appreciated her, I'm sure, just as he appreciated me, appreciated my quick mind, the determination and ambition, the ardor and the lack of inhibitions. But love? I don't think so.

His father had been a police officer in New York City, taken retirement after the requisite twenty years and what the cops called a tit job as chief of security at Langhorne College. He and his son moved into an ugly modern house just outside town which was, Jon once said, four times the size of the Brooklyn apartment they'd shared with his grandparents.

He had stared openly at me in English class, and afterward I heard him ask Jackie Belknap who I was. "Gulden?" said Jackie. "Study, study, study, bitch, bitch, bitch."

"Just what the doctor ordered," said Jonathan.

He was good-looking in an odd kind of way, with eyes a little too close together and dirty blond hair, a strong jaw and surprisingly full and feminine lips, very red. These last gave him a powerful aura of sexuality which was not in the least misleading. But we were a match as well, both of us quick and anxious, driven and oblivious to the effect we had on other people. Hungry puppies, as Jeff would have said. Jeff would have said that someday we would wind up eating one another up. But I wouldn't have listened.

Jonathan's father had remarried when we were in college, to a secretary at Langhorne. That Thanksgiving, he and his wife—"call her my stepmother and die," Jon said to me early on—were three hundred miles away at her daughter's. We walked in the door of the house and began to remove our clothes before it was even closed.

In movies there is always something sexy about such a thing, about the sight of gray flannels, red turtleneck, flowered panties, gray socks, in a Hansel-and-Gretel trail leading to the bedroom. But as I was struggling with hooks and eyes as though it was the most important thing in the world that I be naked, there was something so driven and desperate about it that by the time I was on my back on the bed all pleasure had vanished. I almost said aloud, "All I really want to do is sleep." But not to Jonathan. Not ever to Jonathan.

It had been a long week leading up to the holidays. Sometimes my mother would twist in the chair and I would know that something was gnawing at her belly and her lower back. Certain lines about her mouth, once only smile lines, began to deepen with her grimaces. Her hair was wispy, the thin and awry fuzz of an infant, and each morning she wrapped her head in a scarf and pulled a few strands from beneath it to soften the sharp bones that showed so clearly now in her face.

And the rages began. The worst was the day when I brought the wheelchair out. Once the pain came in earnest she was like that, turning from time to time into a person I had never seen before. She raged against several members of the Minnies who wanted to make her honorary chairman of the tree ceremony and spare her the work of decorating. She raged at the way Mrs. Duane had rubbed her back in the bookstore, "petting me as though I were a dog." The outbursts seemed so different from her usual self that I sometimes felt as though the cancer itself had a voice, and I was hearing it. Or it was the voice of the morphine.

"I am not an invalid," she cried when she came down from a nap and first saw the wheelchair folded in a corner. "First you dope me up and then you want to turn me into an invalid." She sat down heavily on the living-room couch, holding a pillow to her belly like a shield, and raged at the wheelchair and at me. "Put it away right now, Ellen. Put it away or I will roll it down the street." She picked up a Styrofoam ball and with shaking hands tried to push a gold sequin into it with a drawing pin. "It's humiliating," she said, and the sequin dropped to the floor.

"I just want you to be comfortable," I said.

"You want me to be dead. You want me to die so you and your father can get on with your lives."

She was wrong. I had hoped the wheelchair would give her back some of her dignity, not take it away. And I'd hoped I'd get her back, too, for a few weeks more, another book perhaps, another series of lessons in her old familiar domestic life. But I knew the only thing that would restore her to her old self, bouncing on the balls of her feet, baking the day away with flour in her hair, keeping her dark feelings inside, was the clean slate of death. Then that Kate Gulden would live always in my mind. I was frightened of this other Kate, this enraged and dessicated impostor. She was right about that; I did want that angry stranger gone. For so long I had wondered why she was not angrier at my father, at her lot in life, at the bargain she had made. But as I saw her rage, felt it like a black thing with teeth and claws, I blessed her tranquillity, and yearned for it.

I tried to tell Jonathan all this. Dr. Cohn was right; I needed someone to talk to. After we made love I lay staring up at the ceiling fan, tears running down the sides of my face, and said, "If I had any guts at all I would hold a pillow over her face."

"Don't say things like that," Jonathan said.

"Oh, Jonathan, you don't know. You're drinking coffee in the cafeteria and working on your moot court arguments and I'm watching this woman start to slowly disintegrate before my eyes, and all I can think is, this is my last chance to know her, to be her, to not kiss her off because she doesn't work or she didn't graduate from an Ivy League school or she doesn't think the world rises and falls on whether or not there was really a Dark Lady behind Shakespeare's sonnets. And the days slip by. She hates Elizabeth Bennet, can you believe it? Just hates her."

"Who the hell is Elizabeth Bennet?"

"*Pride and Prejudice.*"

"Oh, well, then, that explains it," Jonathan said, leaning up on one elbow, his face caught in the last bit of daylight shining through the blinds in his bedroom. "Listen, Ellen, you need some rest. You are going to go crazy with this. Can't Papa George give you a break so you can spend the weekend with me?"

"I can't go anywhere, Jonathan. I can't tell from day to day whether she'll be all right or not."

"I think you're being too hard on yourself."

"There's no such thing as being too hard on yourself, Jon."

"Is there such a thing as being too hard?" he said, moving quickly from death to sex, his favorite subject, as he pushed my head down.

Afterward we dressed and drove back to my house. "Do you realize that during the entire thing we never kissed?" I said.

"Oh, Christ, Ellen, calm down," Jon said, sated now and irritable.

I spent the rest of that evening creaming onions, peeling yams, making stuffing exactly as my mother directed, producing a great groaning board of dishes just as she always had. After Jonathan brought me home, as I stood in the kitchen in my nightgown slicing celery, I realized that I was doing it all for the sake of stability, to make it seem as though this Thanksgiving was no different from any other. I was maintaining, abetting, creating a kind of elaborate fiction, just as my mother had, with gravy and pumpkin pie and heavy cream. The fiction that everything was fine, that life was simple and secure, that husbands did not stray and children grow, that the body did not decay and finally fail, that the axis of the earth passed dead center through the kitchen and the living world and the world kept spinning, our family unchanging, safe and sound.

My mother looked horrid on Thanksgiving morning; she had made up her face elaborately, as though somehow she could create her own fiction with blush and eye shadow, the fiction that she was well, that she was blooming. But my brothers did not collaborate; instead of making the rounds of friends' houses that afternoon, they stayed at home, wandering in and out of the kitchen, talking of school and asking about home. They settled into the couch with Jonathan for the football games. My father sat with them, reading and making derogatory comments. "The greatest single collection of future car-dealership owners and fast-food-restaurant franchise magnates in the United States," he said.

"So Rod Laver is a teaching pro at a country club right now," said Jeff. "Big difference."

"Tennis has finesse," said my father. "Tennis has style and grace."

"The sport of kings," said Jonathan.

"Come off it, Jon," said Jeffrey. "You love football. The only thing I've ever seen take your mind off yourself is the Super Bowl."

"And Wimbledon," Jonathan said. "And I wasn't agreeing. I was commenting."

"Sucking up," muttered Jeff.

"God, I hate that expression," my father said. He turned to me, then looked into the kitchen. "Where's your mother?"

"She's upstairs with Brian."

"Don't make her feel superfluous, Ellen," my father said.

"And don't make me feel guilty."

I basted and rearranged the cheesecloth that was draped around my turkey like a shroud. I was beginning to talk about food the way my mother did: my stuffing, my yams, my turkey. My zucchini soup. It would always be my zucchini soup, with a cup of tea in it.

Upstairs my mother was settled in the big chair by the window in her room, her feet up on the ottoman. She was wearing a handsome plum-colored dress with big brass buttons which I had bought her at the mall; when she saw that the label had been cut out she was so pleased. "A bargain!" she said. "How much?"

"None of your business," I said with a grin, as though I had gotten the dress for next to nothing. In fact it had cost seventy dollars, and I had taken the label out because it read MOTHER AND CHILD. Maternity clothes, my mother needed now, to accommodate her poor swollen belly.

When I went up to check on her, Brian was sitting crosslegged next to the ottoman, a book in his lap, reading aloud. As I came in he slid the book beneath the ruffled skirt of the chair.

"What have you got there, Bri?" I asked. "*Tropic of Cancer? Peyton Place? Story of O?*"

"Much worse," my mother said.

Brian slid the book out again and held it up. It was a Gothic novel, with a cover illustration of a woman in ruffled petticoats being pressed to the highly defined pectoral muscles of a man wearing only jodhpurs. "Your father will call the police," my mother said, giggling.

"The thought police," said Brian. "They would all be wearing tweed jackets and they would deprogram you by making you read the *Oxford English Dictionary*."

"Oh, honey," said my mother, giggling again, "don't make fun of the *OED*."

"They take you in a room and put headphones on you and make you listen to Orson Welles read *Silas Marner*," I said.

"Now, there's a real mystery," my mother said. "How someone wrote a book as good as *Middlemarch* and then wrote a book as boring as *Silas Marner*. Jeffrey would say she was all over the map."

"Oh, Ma," said Brian. "The person who wrote *Silas Marner* was a guy. George Eliot."

My mother and I screamed and held our heads. "Oh, my God, Bri," I said, "if Papa heard you you'd be on the road with your thumb out, on your way back to Philadelphia. George Eliot was a woman. It was a pen name. Her real name was Mary Ann Evans."

"Are you sure?" said Brian.

"Honey, it's okay," I said. "You're going to major in political science. Just don't let Papa hear you. That and this"—I nudged the paperback with my foot—"would finish him off. I can see it: PROF KILLED BY BAD LITERARY TASTE: SON HELD."

There was a knock at the door and when my father looked in, we all began to laugh.

"What's so funny?" he said.

"A case of mistaken identity," I said.

When the food was on the table in the dining room, on the mahogany table with its matching breakfront and china closet and chairs that had once belonged to my grandparents, my mother took Brian's and Jeffrey's hands and said, "I want to say grace." And for the first time in years we did:

"Thank you for the world so sweet, thank you for the food we eat, thank you for the birds that sing, thank you, God, for everything."

When I raised my head and dropped my father's hand I looked at him and there were tears in his eyes.

For dessert I had made pumpkin pie, and as I was in the kitchen cutting it my mother came in. She looked tired and she'd eaten all her lipstick off, leaving only the edge of it, like false wax lips from Halloween.

"I need a pill, Ellen," she said.

"Mama, I gave you one just after lunch. It's only been four hours."

"Ellen, I need a pill. Where are they?"

"They're in the cabinet in the powder room. Can't you wait until after dessert?"

"Get me a pill, please, Ellen," my mother said, so loudly that all conversation stopped in the next room. "And remember that this is still my house." I could hear the edge of one of those rages in her voice, and as she returned to the table I went to the medicine cabinet.

I heard her say to Brian, "Now—I want a full report on the roommate and any suitable girls."

"And you can tell me when we go out later about all the unsuitable ones," Jeff said.

But Brian did not go out with the rest of us. He helped my mother to bed after we'd had our coffee in the living room; he sat in her room after she'd dozed off, listening to her breathe in the dark. "Don't fall asleep here," I whispered, but he didn't reply, and I knew he'd be there until my father came up. I remember thinking that if they gave any of us an aptitude test for taking care of Kate Gulden when she was mortally ill, Brian, sweet and earnest Brian, would have aced it. Jeff once had described us all: "The food chain is that Ellen lives up to Pop, and I live up to Ellen." A little plaintively Bri had said, "What about me?"

"You don't have to live up to anyone, kid," Jeff said. "You and Mom just have to get up every morning and be present on the planet."

So predictable, that it would all begin to unravel in a bar. That was where we went after the dinner dishes were done, Jonathan and Jeff and I, to a bar called Sammy's, named in honor of Samuel Langhorne, who was about as much a Sammy as Thomas Jefferson was a Tommy or John Adams a Jack. The place was one of those dark English-pub imitations, with cheap, mass-produced stained-glass windows and a big dark wood bar with heraldic nonsense fixed to its front. It was full of town kids home for Thanksgiving break and the community college kids, who wished they were. Jeff had to wade through a sea of glad hands and big smiles. One girl ran her hand up his khaki leg from knee to thigh and said, "Come over to see me."

"Who was that?" Jonathan asked.

"A very happy woman," said Jeff. "Name of Jennifer."

"They're all Jennifers," I said. "When our mothers were young, they were all Kathys and Pattys. In ten years they'll all be Ashleys and Taras."

"Aren't you tough!" said Jeff.

"My middle name."

"Yeah, you put on a good show, El. But I see through you."

"Deep down inside a romantic?"

"Deep down inside a softie."

"This conversation is like a Kahlil Gibran sitcom, for Christsake," said Jonathan. He smiled over at Jennifer, who smiled at him. I slipped my hand into the back pocket of his jeans.

"I'll cut it off, Jon," I whispered as we sat down at a table, a slab of heavy varnished wood with a round red votive candle winking at its center.

I hadn't had a drink since the day I'd come back to Langhorne. It didn't feel right; it didn't parse. Neither had the seal of sex I'd felt between my legs as I'd cooked and cleaned the night before in my mother's house. I thought about it as the need to be in control, to be there for her in every way, in case of some crisis, some emergency. I thought about how terrible it would be if she was left to suffer alone while I took my forays into pleasure in Jonathan's boyhood bedroom with the pennants still tacked over the bed, if she called out and I was too muddled by wine to hear.

But now, when I analyze my own behavior, I think I felt obliged to deny myself anything carnal, a frisson of lust, the blur of a shot of vodka, to help pay for her pain, as though pleasure was an affront to her.

That night in Sammy's, with Jonathan smiling that promising smile across the table at me, the red light making amber shadows on his face, I forgot all that. I had two beers, then something called a Samuel Sling, fruit juice and a muddle of different liquors, one of those drinks that go down so easy and make your head swim so fast. Under the table I ran my foot up the inside of Jonathan's thigh. The two men talked about the football, their course work, their professors. In the middle of a sentence I cut Jeff off.

"He just kills me," I said.

"Who?" said Jon. But Jeff knew.

"My father. He just kills me. He sat there and let you guys clear the table. He didn't say a word to me about dinner. And he goes off before she's even asleep and says he has work to do in his study. As though we were servants. As though we're there to serve him. Jesus." I signaled the waitress across the room. "We need another round," I called.

"The hell you do," Jeff muttered.

"This is what it's been like from day one, Jeffie," I said. "He is literally never there. I literally do everything."

"Does your mother complain?" said Jonathan.

"That's not the point," I said loudly.

"El, the entire bar doesn't have to share this with us," said Jeff. He shrugged and looked at Jon. "My mother never complains about anything."

"Exactly," I said. "And now she can't because he's never around."

"He was never around before," said Jeff.

"She was never dying before," I said.

"Everyone deals with bad stuff in their own way," Jon added.

"Well, that's the point, isn't it, Jon?" I said. "Whenever one of you guys says people deal with bad stuff in their own way, it means you don't deal with it at all. You just wait for it to go away. You don't help. You don't listen. You don't call. You don't write. WE deal with it in our own way. WE deal with it. We girls. We make the meals and clean up the messes and take the crap and listen to you talk about how you're dealing with it in your own way. What way? No way!"

Jennifer at the bar was staring at our table. So were her friends. I gave them the finger and Jeff pulled my hand out of the air. "Whooa,' he said. "Should we get out of here?"

"I am not your father, Ellen," Jon said as the waitress brought our drinks. He took my glass from the tray and put it down on his side of the table.

"No you are not, Jon," I said, reaching across the table to get it. We pulled in opposite directions; the glass toppled and my drink ran into his lap. "Jesus," he said, standing up.

"Let's go," Jeff said.

"I'm ready," Jon said, "and Ellen sure as hell is. Do you want us to drop you at home?"

"I'm going with him, Jon," I said. "It's been a long day. A long week. A long month. It's very tiring, being my mother."

"Ellen, you have lost it. You are not your mother. You have never been your mother. There is no one in the world more different from your mother than you are."

I took my jacket from the back of my chair. "That was the stupidest thing you've ever said, Jon. And I am leaving."

"I haven't seen you in almost three months."

"Whose fault is that?"

"Oh, Christ," said Jon.

"Cool it, Jon," said Jeff. "You got laid yesterday, you'll get laid tomorrow, and you'll probably get laid Saturday."

"Hey, Jeff, my sex life is none of your business. And neither is hers. She's a big girl."

"Ah, hell, she's not as big as everybody thinks."

"If everyone could stop talking about me as if I wasn't here, I'd like to go home and just go to sleep," I said. "I'm drunk and I'm tired and I'm sick of all of you. And I don't want a ride because I want to walk home just so I can be alone for a change."

And I was alone, walking home in the cold November night with my nose and eyes running, leaving Jonathan angry, locking eyes with Jeff and with Jennifer, whose lip gloss and tousled bangs seemed a world away to me. I felt like a very tired housewife, and I looked like one, too, in my corduroy slacks and cotton sweater. When I got home my mother was sitting in the living room, reading. "You didn't have to wait up for me," I said.

"My back hurts."

Next morning the boys left me to sleep late, and when I woke up and heard war whoops from outside the window I looked out to see Brian letting my mother roll down the street in the wheelchair, with Jeff stationed down the gentle slope to stop her. The look on her face reminded me of the first time we ever put Brian on a sled at River View Park, the commingling of fear, excitement, joy, and terror. "Go for it, baby!" Jeff yelled as he put out his arms to catch her. "Bring it on home."

My head hurt and my tongue felt too big for my mouth. I climbed back beneath the quilt and slept until almost noon, and when I awoke and went downstairs my mother was sleeping on the couch in the living room, her hands beneath her cheek, a throw over her legs. A note from my father on the kitchen table said "Catching up at the college." In the den my brothers were talking, their voices rising, falling, breaking. I went out on the porch and sat hugging a sweater around me until the sun began to disappear and a chill to descend. Then I went inside to make turkey sandwiches.

Jonathan did not call that evening, and I didn't call him. When he called on Saturday it was to say that he was going back to Cambridge early to get some work done and that he wanted me to think again about coming up soon to spend a weekend with him. "There's no way, Jon," I said, and we hung up with no plans to talk, to meet, no "I love you," not even any salacious suggestions for the future. Jon, I remember thinking to myself, was not of this time and this place; he was something I would come back to when I came back to being the other Ellen.

It would not be until months later that I would learn, from both their sworn testimonies, that he had spent Thanksgiving night and most of Friday morning in bed at his father's house with Jennifer. So predictable, all of it. So unsurprising, so somehow apt, along with all the other things that happened that winter.

The first part of my mother's illness had been a kind of childhood for me, the kind of childhood I might have had, had I been a different sort of girl, my mother a different sort of woman, and both our needs to woo my father less overwhelming. Holiday cheer, Thanksgiving side dishes, stories of childhood, girlhood, and marriage—all of these were handed down to me, now, with a certain air of urgency, as though it was a school assignment on which she'd fallen behind, this chance to reclaim the daughter she might have had, the one who, like Brian, would have been happiest sitting at her feet, laughing up at her own laughter.

But once she began to use the wheelchair our relationship was reversed, she the child, I the mother. Perhaps it was why she had resisted it so strongly. It was difficult for her to get around the house alone; the doorways were narrow, the rugs a beautiful impediment in shades of crimson and deep blue. But although I moved the furniture closer to the walls, I did not even ask if I could roll up the old Orientals. What she needed now was for the things around her to be as lovely and familiar as possible. So much else was shifting and becoming ugly.

One day she decided we should go downtown on foot—"and on wheels," she added—to pick out three more books at Duane's. She put on a blue pea jacket that had always fitted her perfectly, sleek and elegant, and it concealed how thin and concave her chest was now, like the breast of a baby bird.

"What about a little makeup?" I said. "Just in case we run into someone."

"Somehow I don't think your father envisioned you having a career as a cosmetologist."

"And why not? I could wind up in the *Tribune* that way." My mother liked to say that every engagement announcement in the local paper was of a cosmetologist engaged to a man "associated with" a construction company. It drove my father crazy when she read them aloud, but crazier still when she read about the weddings, all the detailed descriptions of someone's point d'esprit dropped waist, bishop's sleeves, and cloudburst tulle headpiece.

"Oh, Ellie, you've been in the *Tribune* more than anyone except Ed Best and the mayor. Go look in my scrapbook upstairs. Girls' State, the Spelling Bee, the Essay Contest, your graduation speech. You're always in the *Tribune.*"

"It sounds like you're keeping a running count."

"You bet I am. And why shouldn't I? Now go ahead and put a little makeup on me, but don't get carried away."

It was more difficult than I'd imagined. When I had smoothed on foundation, penciled in eyeliner, and brushed on mascara and blush, my mother looked a little like the kind of pictures I'd drawn of her when I was five, all round red cheeks and eyelashes like spiky black spiders. I had not gotten the effect I wanted, which was the impossible illusion that Kate Gulden was just as she always had been.

"It's very difficult to do this on someone else's face," I said.

My mother leaned on the chest of drawers in the hallway and

peered in the mirror. "You've never worked on a redhead before," she said. "That's your problem." She took a small sponge from the bag of cosmetics I was holding and scrubbed her face for a moment.

"Much better," I said.

"Your career as a cosmetologist is over before it began," my mother replied.

"As a cosmetologist, I'm a great writer."

"You are a great writer," said my mother, my fan club, my burden, as I buttoned her pea jacket and pulled on her beret.

With her bony face and pallor, she looked like an aging fashion model. She'd always been a pretty woman, my mother. Unlike so many other women, whose wedding photographs are more like pictures of their daughters than of themselves, she had kept her looks and her bright eyes.

I put on my down jacket and brought the chair backward down the front steps—*clunk, clunk, clunk*—in a technique I'd learned from watching mothers in the city with their strollers. My mother came down the steps slowly and carefully and sat down.

"I feel stupid in this thing, but I want to go out," she said. "I feel like I've been a hermit. You too. You haven't been out since your brothers left after Thanksgiving."

We came down the street slowly because I was afraid of losing control of the chair on the slope and because I could tell, watching her head swivel from side to side, that she was looking around carefully, sight-seeing in her own neighborhood. "Look, Ellie, the Jacksons already have a tree up in their living room," she said, and "Claire Belknap had better put something over those roses or she'll lose them if there's an early frost," and "Why did the Bests paint their house that color? It was so nice when it was white." It was as though she was seeing for all it was worth that day, all of it, every single insignificant trivial marvelous detail of it, every one.

At the bottom of the hill we turned onto Main Street just below the green. The flowers that usually ringed the flagpole were gone now. The twelve big evergreens stood alone, the sweeping angel wings of their branches so beautiful.

"They never quite know what to do with that planting area after they take the asters out but before the trees are decorated," my mother said. "Our first year here, there was this new woman, I think she was the provost's wife, who donated dozens of poinsettias. Public Works put them all in, no questions asked. Not one person seemed to know that poinsettias are tropical plants and have to be kept indoors in a cold climate. Next morning it was the saddest sight you've ever seen, like a battlefield. All those plants had just keeled over. Your father came home thinking this was a wonderful story and I told him I had known when they were putting them in exactly what would happen. But we were new here and I didn't know who to tell, or if I should tell, and so in the end I just kept quiet. Your father thought that made the story even more wonderful, that he had a wife so clever that she'd known how ridiculous the whole idea was. So he told it around at every Christmas party, although in the telling I kept getting cannier and cannier and meaner and meaner. Your father got a very good story out of it. But the provost's wife was chilly to me for years."

It was cold that day, but we stopped at least a dozen times so my mother could talk to people she knew. It was difficult to maneuver the wheelchair up and down the curbs and over the uneven pavements, and sometimes she became impatient. When she wanted to go into the Langhorne Shoe Shoppe, I struggled with the chair at the door, holding it open with my hip, trying to steer and force the big rubber wheels over the ridged floor mat in the doorway.

"This is exactly like dealing with that damn double stroller I bought when Brian was born," she said. "I'd be heaving and hoing it through the door and you'd be halfway out into the street with me screaming after you."

She used the armrests to help herself stand up and walked inside, leaving me to back out and set the brake on the street. I watched her through the display window, glimpsed her profile between a pair of tassel loafers and some hiking boots. We had the same sharp noses. She was talking to one of the salespeople, and then she sat down. I stood on tiptoe and could see her slipping off her flats, and then someone emerged from the back room with a tower of boxes.

"Ellen?" a voice said behind me.

It was Mrs. Forburg, my English teacher. "Couldn't you call me Brenda now?" she said.

"To be honest, I'd rather not. I think you should remain Mrs. Forburg forever. It's a kind of honorific."

She laughed. In her parka and gray pants she was as small as a ten-year-old, but she had the dried-apple skin and white-gray hair of a grandmother. "Is your mother inside?" she said.

I nodded. "She appears to be buying shoes. I didn't know she needed shoes."

"Does any woman really need shoes?" Mrs. Forburg said, looking down at her own gray walking oxfords. "Buying shoes always gives me a lift, like buying new stationery or a new purse. It makes you feel as if there's something to look forward to." She reached across the chair and touched the back of my hand. "Did you get my note?" she said.

"I did, I did, but I've been so busy I haven't had time to call you. Jeff and Brian were home for Thanksgiving, my mother and I are doing a lot of things together. The house. You know."

"I didn't mean it as a command performance. I just wanted you to know that I'd always be happy to feed you some spaghetti and listen to your troubles."

There was the high rattle of the bells over the shoe store door, and my mother came out with a bag. "Beautiful new loafers," she said as she sat down heavily in the chair. She looked up. "Mrs. Forburg!" she said.

"It's good to see you, Mrs. Gulden." My mother slipped the shoe box out of her bag and showed off the loafers, gleaming cordovan leather with tassels. She showed me how the black flats she was wearing were slightly down-at-heel. It was quite a performance, but I could tell by the look in her eyes that Mrs. Forburg recognized it for what it was. It was the same look she had once given me when she handed me back a B paper savaging Charlotte Brontë, a paper made up almost entirely of my father's opinions. "Original thought next time, Ellen," she had said quietly that day, but it had sounded less like a rebuke because of the sympathy in her gray eyes, and a certain tone to her voice, the same tone she had now. She saw things, Mrs. Forburg.

She had always been my favorite teacher—Jeff and Brian's, too, although neither of them had been as mesmerized by English literature as I was. Mrs. Forburg had deftly steered me through fiction and verse, gently edited my poetry, which was clever but not at all deeply felt, and made me keep a journal my senior year, although I think she sensed that she was getting the expurgated version of my life. "She is still the best English teacher I have ever had," I said one night when I was home during my last year at college. "Then you are taking the wrong courses at Harvard," my father had said dryly. I had been shocked into silence, but my mother had not.

"You're just jealous, Gen," she said evenly.

"Jealous? What do you mean?"

"Ellen can have more than one teacher," my mother had said without looking at him. There was a sharp scraping sound as he had pushed back his chair.

"You misjudge me, Katherine," he replied.

On the street outside the shoe store my mother smiled up at Mrs. Forburg and took her hand. "I'd like to invite Ellen to dinner, Mrs. Gulden," Mrs. Forburg said. "To get reacquainted. Would that make life difficult for you?"

"No! Absolutely not! She's cooped up in the house all the time with me and she gets antsy, although she doesn't say it. I'll make her call and arrange it with you." And so we continued down the street.

"I didn't know you needed shoes," I said.

"I don't," my mother replied.

It was a busy afternoon. We stopped at Phelps's and Mr. Phelps hugged my mother, swaying back and forth, his eyes glistening. "Oh, don't go getting mushy on me," my mother said, smiling at him brightly. He gave her the name and number of a young mother who had been in to ask about stenciling flowers on a crib. "I wanted to have you talk to her, but I wasn't sure how you would feel about it," Mr. Phelps said. "I'll call her when I get home," my mother promised.

At Duane's, both Mr. and Mrs. came from the back room to discuss what we should be reading next, and I saw Mrs. Duane drop a Gothic novel with a cover illustration of a tortured-looking woman in a hoopskirt into our bag. The wives of two faculty members came over to tell my mother how well she was looking, and she leaned down out of the chair to speak to their children, toddlers and one gangly girl of eight or nine who stared hard, perhaps remembering her parents whispering about something terrible—"Kate Gulden . . . so young . . . George's wife . . . just awful"—in the kitchen. A woman who lived several blocks over from us began to talk of homeopathy and herbal medicines, but my mother smiled and said, "Not now, Frances." Then we went down the street and got an ice-cream cone and I pushed the chair home with one hand while I licked away.

"Good thing you looked nice," I said. "I felt like I was with Jimmy Stewart at the end of *It's a Wonderful Life*."

"They're all just sorry for me," my mother said.

"Oh, please," I said. "That wasn't what that was all about. They were all so happy to see you. Everyone likes you."

"I know that. They just didn't have to think about it until now."

"That's terrible," I said.

"You can't judge, Ellen. People are different. People love in different ways. Sometimes hugs and kisses, sometimes something else. And sometimes they can't feel it, they're just made that way."

"Like who?" I said, afraid.

"My mother was like that. She was very poor as a child, and things were hard, and I've never been sure how she came to marry your grandfather, but it wasn't what either you or I would think of as a love match. And I think some part of her shriveled up and died from not being used, not being exercised. The closest she came was loving my brother, and look how that ended. The closest thing she has to a son is a flag all folded up into a triangle that she's never unrolled once, and a rubbing of his name from the Vietnam Memorial that one of her nephews sent her after he took a trip to Washington."

I turned the chair into the flagstone path to our front door. We never used it, always went in through the kitchen, but there were six steps there and here it was only three to the porch and a shallow sill into the hall. "It's almost time to decorate the house," my mother said, as I came around to face her and help her out of the chair.

And she raised her arms to me to be lifted up, and I wrapped mine around her. She pulled me closer and I could feel her body like sticks in a bag, the slightness of her now, her ribs like some fragile musical instrument beneath my hands.

"Thank you, Ellie," she said.

"We'll go downtown again next Saturday," I said. "You can buy some more shoes. Everyone will be so happy to see you."

"I'm happy to be home. I'm so tired I'm going upstairs to bed as soon as I have some tea." We walked up the stairs together, arm in arm. "I can make it myself," she said.

"Do you need a pill?"

"I'll get one myself. Ellen?"

"Huh?" I said, bumping the wheelchair back up the steps.

"Call Mrs. Forburg and arrange to go to her house for dinner," my mother said. She moved slowly into the kitchen, her fingertips feeling along the walls, itsy-bitsy spiders yellow-white against the wallpaper, as though she was blind as well as lame.

I lay on the couch for a while and finally I fell asleep, almost as tired from the afternoon as she was. When I finally woke I could see the streetlights shining amber through the looped drapes of the living room, and hear my mother in the kitchen. In my mind's eye I could see her sitting at the oak table, her upper arms as round, her skin as pink and clear, her eyes as serene as they had been six months before.

"Here's the most important thing to remember," I heard her say in her authoritative "Ellen, you will not wear that dress to play in Buckley's backyard" voice. "You must tap most of the paint off the brush before you begin. You want an almost dry brush, not a wet brush." And then: "It's definitely a girl? Oh, that's wonderful. I have one daughter and you can't imagine . . . twenty-four . . . yes, she is . . . well, I do, too . . . oh, I know, but you get used to it . . . well, that's wonderful. What design did you choose?"

The woman who wanted to stencil the crib. Of course. I stared at the streetlamp and thought I saw snowflakes falling against the scrim of its glow. Claire Belknap had better mind her roses. Ellie Gulden had better wax the runners on her sled. Ellie Gulden's sled was still in the garage, a Flexible Flyer with her name painted in red script on the crossbar, next to Jeff Gulden's sled and Brian Gulden's sled

Kate Gulden had painted the names. My father had never pushed us down the hill at River View Park and never pulled us up. There were no snow days at the college, where everyone could tumble out of bed and into classroom buildings. There were no weekends for a man who wanted to be a department head, or later for a man who was one.

But I could see her, standing at the place at the bottom of the hill where there was a dip and then a bump, yelling up at us, a cap pulled down over all but the smallest divot of eyes and nose and mouth, "Not so fast. Not so fast. Slow down. Oh, my lord, Jeffrey, you'll give me a heart attack." All of life like a series of tableaux, and in the living we missed so much, hid so much, left so much undone and unsaid. Jeff had broken his arm once on that hill, and she had taken her tempera paints and painted a toy soldier up the entire length of his cast. He had been mortified.

A few minutes later I heard my father come in the back door, and her cry: "George! So early." She sounded much as she had that day I first came back: "Ellie! You're home."

"Come outside and see the snow," I heard him say softly.

"There's snow?"

"Just a little." And then the kitchen door opened again, and closed with a click, and I went up to bed and heard no more. In the morning there was no snow at all, except in my mother's memory. "I caught it on my tongue," she said. She laid her hand on my father's at the breakfast table. "It was beautiful."

"Yes, it was," he said, and smiled back at her.

No one knows what goes on inside a marriage. I read that once; the aphorism ended "except for the two people who are in it." But I suspect that even that is not the truth, that even two people married to each other for many many years may have only passing similarities in their perceptions and their expectations. I think I read somewhere, too, that social scientists interviewed couples and found that they had vastly different ideas about everything from their spouse's favorite dessert to their preferred sexual position.

Sometimes I feel limited now by how much life experience I have to extrapolate from books and research articles.

But I know from experience that those least capable of truly assessing any marriage are the children who come out of it. We style them as we need them, to excuse our faults, to insulate ourselves from our own expendability or indispensability. I remembered the great relief I felt when I first read about Oedipal theory, the relief of knowing that the triangle in which I found myself was archetypical.

So that when I saw my parents together day after day during that winter I could not truly say whether their relationship was changing or whether I was really seeing it for the first time because I was seeing my father for the first time.

One day early in December he asked me to have lunch with him in a steakhouse several miles from campus, the kind of dim and faintly pretentious out-of-the-way place I imagined you would take someone for an assignation.

"Come here often?" I said, as the waiter brought drinks and steered us toward the salad bar.

"Most of the time I'm far too busy for lunch. I eat at my desk while I work."

"I'm flattered," I said.

"Ellen, I had several agendas when I asked you to meet me today. But one of them is certainly to find out why you are being so hostile. I know this is not the optimum situation for any of us, but you and your mother certainly seem to be managing well. I'm perplexed as to why I'm met with coldness or overt hostility whenever I enter the house."

"Give me an example," I said.

"Oh for God's sake," he said, "this is not a debating contest. You know exactly what I mean. Do you need more help? Should I have a nurse come in?"

"A nurse didn't take care of me when I had chicken pox."

"This is not chicken pox and if you need an example of what I'm talking about, the sarcasm in that sentence is sufficient. Do you want salad?"

"Not if it's iceberg lettuce and canned chick-peas."

"I'm quite certain it is."

The waiter took our order, and there was a long silence broken by the sound of someone in the kitchen throwing pots and pans around in a fit of temper or extraordinary clumsiness. The brother of a member of the college board of trustees stopped by our table to say hello.

"Look, Papa," I said. "I don't want to fight with you. I'm under a lot of pressure. I don't need any more from you. I'm just getting through this day by day."

"I understand that completely, Ellen. And I understand that whenever we talk about what is going on, we talk about you, about how you are feeling, about your unhappiness. I think this time should be about your mother. It calls for a little empathy."

"Empathy is the one thing I never really learned," I said softly. "You never taught me empathy."

"Learn it now," he said peremptorily.

"And you? Where is your empathy?"

"I told you before—"

"I don't want to hear about the mortgage. The college would give you a leave any time you wanted. You've taken sabbaticals to write books and you can certainly take one to participate in the most important thing that's ever going to happen in your God-damn life."

"Keep your voice down."

"Oh, fuck that, Papa. I'm the one who is behaving appropriately here, to use your expression, and you're the one who's not. She needs you to be with her."

"Did she tell you that?"

"She doesn't need to tell me that. She shouldn't need to tell you. Yesterday she sat for twenty minutes with the Goddamn Christmas wreath on her lap before I could put it on the front door. She kept feeling it as if she were blind, as if the meaning of life was in the pinecones she'd wired to that wreath. I asked her if she needed help putting it up and she just said, 'This is pretty, isn't it?' Sometimes she goes into her room and pretends to sleep and instead she goes through all these boxes of stuff she has, swim-meet ribbons and pictures we drew years ago and old papers from when she was in high school. She just stares and stares at them. Why should she have to sit by herself and look at pictures of her life when she could have the real thing? Why should she sit around conjuring up her memories of your life together when she could be with you making real memories? Everything has changed in that house, everything, from my level of empathy to her level of agony. But you don't know about either because you're behaving as though life goes on as usual. Life as we knew it is over. Done. Finished."

My father sawed away at a bloody steak without looking at me. Finally he said, "You're giving her the morphine?"

"And I'm going to keep giving her more and more. If the pills turn out not to be enough, I can get a little pump that will deliver it into the catheter they put in her chest. But I'm not you. And I can't deal with all the pain in her head. She can only go so far with me. She still thinks she has to protect me, or baby me, whatever. You're her husband. She needs to talk to you."

He stared at his food, making it into a kind of still life: a piece of dry gray-white baked potato, a red wedge of meat. Another. Another. It looked as though he was playing chess with his lunch as he moved it in mysterious patterns. As he cut and arranged he spoke quietly, so that he could not eat unless he stopped. And could not stop until he had finished.

"Sometimes I think about how I first saw her at Columbia, and how eager she was," he said. "But you know that because you know how she is. So eager, as though she wanted to see and understand and know everything, but not in that way the students had, to catalogue and dissect and then eventually dismiss or internalize it. But in the way she had of seeming to want—" he stopped sawing at the food, searching for a word in the still and murky air above our table—"wanting just to soak it up. There was a kind of life there, as though if you felt her cheek she would be warm. And she was. Still is. She's never changed much, all these years. There's still that, that—avidity. And I wonder sometimes where it will all go. It seems impossible that it will simply go out, like a light. All fiction takes as its great central mystery death, mortality, but it seems to me now that all of it misses the point."

He looked up at me, his empty fork poised in the air, like a small weapon or a signal of surrender. "I can't imagine the light going out," he said.

"You're talking about her as if she was already dead," I said.

"I've known her all my life," he said, and his eyes were puzzled, dull, like the eyes of a sick animal.

"Me too."

"Yes," my father said. "I suppose it's even truer of you children. But you'll go on. I have a difficulty imagining a life without your mother."

He ate then, slowly but with gusto, as though he'd completed some exhausting task. When he was finished he looked up again, his eyebrows sardonically lifted, his everyday self. "So much for the soliloquy," he said. "It's merely that I can't bear the thought that she's in so much pain. Sometimes at night she's awake for hours with it."

I sighed, and said what he wanted to hear. "I can take care of that," I said.

"I will try to give her more of an opportunity to ventilate," he said.

"Papa, we're not talking about an opportunity to ventilate. If she needed to ventilate, I'd send her to this shrink Dr. Cohn recommended. She needs you to talk to her, to listen to her, to let her know that it's all right to talk back to you, to confide, to unload. Tell her some of the things you've just told me."

"But she knows all that."

"Sometimes people need to hear things said out loud before they become real," I said.

Coffee arrived, bitter and tepid. A secretary from the English department bent over the table and told me that I was a very lucky person to have such wonderful parents. She twinkled at my father and waved over her shoulder as she disappeared into a dim corner of the restaurant, and I wondered if she had slept with him. The cheesecake tasted like heavily sugared spackle. I remembered I had to pick up strings of white lights to loop around the azalea bushes by the porch. I remembered we needed milk and toilet-bowl cleaner. I spilled coffee on the front of my sweater but luckily my mother had taught me the month before how to get coffee stains out with baking soda.

"I think we need to begin discussing funeral arrangements," my father said.

"Papa," I said. "You ask too much. You always have." I went to the bathroom and when I came back he was finishing his coffee and talking to the brother of the board member again. "Gotta go," I said, and I left for the mall and the supermarket.

When I got home my mother was asleep on the living-room couch, her mouth open, her lids fluttering as though someone was chasing her in her dreams. In the kitchen I sat at the table, littered with little notes—the one that said "lights for bushes" I threw away—and some stencil patterns of rocking horses and flowers. I telephoned Dr. Cohn's office and her nurse said she would call another prescription in to Sellinger's. But five minutes later, as I was still going through the notes—"shop for Xmas presents for J. and B.," one said, and I wondered how we would manage that—the phone rang.

"Ellen," said Dr. Cohn, without preamble, "how are we doing on that dosage? When does she get breakthrough pain?"

"First hour the stuff doesn't help, second and third hours she feels great," I said. "Fourth and fifth she dozes. About the sixth hour her back starts to hurt. Sometimes I cheat a little and give her something then."

"Good. You go ahead and do that. I think if we play around with this a little bit we can keep her comfortable and maybe lessen the sedation some, although that may be the disease and not the medication. Make sure she keeps taking it with the laxative. How are her spirits?"

"Depends. Quiet and thoughtful now, a lot of the time."

"Cogent?"

"Yes." I picked up the rocking horses. "Giving stencil advice on the phone."

Dr. Cohn laughed, a surprisingly deep and throaty sound. "I find your mother amazing," she said.

"Me too," I said, and I held my hand tight over my mouth so no noise would come out, no sobs.

"Ellen?"

"Fine, fine, I'm fine."

"I want to send you a nurse. Once a week. Blood pressure, heart sounds, that kind of thing. And to keep a watch on the catheter so that if we need it later for morphine it's in good shape. She can give you a break, let you get out, maybe help your mother bathe or dress."

"She can bathe and dress herself."

"Whatever."

"No nurse," I said.

"I insist."

"No."

"She'll come Monday."

"Ellie?" my mother called from the living room.

"I've got to go," I said. "I'll get the prescription later. Thanks for your help."

I sat at the table and looked down at a sheet of paper. Morphine, morphine, I'd written over and over. The phone rang again.

"El?" Jonathan said. "Guess what? I got the job."

Jonathan had applied to the district attorney's office in Manhattan for a summer internship. Sleek and full of himself in a gray double-breasted suit and red tie, he'd interviewed the Wednesday before Thanksgiving. He sounded more surprised than I was at his good fortune.

"We'll get a sublet downtown, near your old place. It'll be perfect for me and from there you can look around for something permanent. One of the women in my Con law class says she knows an NYU instructor with a one-bedroom on MacDougal who may be going on sabbatical. Maybe I can even get a magazine piece out of this." From time to time Jonathan threatened to write something to prove that he was at least as good as I was, a fact about which I had no doubt.

"Can you ask Jules whether she knows of anything or if she can ask around? She's got to know someone who's going off for the summer and wants to rent out their apartment or have someone house-sit their cat or something," Jonathan went on. "I am so psyched about this. The money is for shit but the contacts and the résumé value are great. And naturally the living arrangements will be superb even if the apartment's a pit."

"It's great, Jon."

"We'll celebrate at Christmas. My father is going to love this. Love it. It's the closest a lawyer ever gets to being part of the NYPD."

"It's great."

Silence. "Are you okay?" he finally asked.

"Just working on my morphine dosages here. I had lunch with my father and he wanted to discuss funeral arrangements, but before he could get to burial versus cremation I left to pick up toilet-bowl cleaner. And I'm reading *Anna Karenina*. I have this sneaking suspicion that this time around, she's going to stay with her husband and have a miserable life." More silence. "I'm pleased for you, Jon."

"And we'll get a place."

"I can't leave here."

"Yeah, but by June, El . . ." Silence again, longer this time.

"Jonathan, I'm not going to look for an apartment on the assumption that I can get rid of my mother in time to spend the summer in bed with you."

"I didn't mean that," he said.

"Yes you did. You thought to yourself, well, Mrs. Gulden will be dead by summer and then I can split the rent with Ellen and get laid in the process."

"Look—bottom line? Next time I have good news to share I'll call somebody else."

"Bottom line? That's a good idea. Because good news does not compute for me right now." I don't know which of us hung up first. I was the one who cried afterward. I'd been with Jonathan for nearly a third of my life and it ended over a summer sublet. Or at least that was what I would say when I made it flippant and amusing for Jules. I should have felt angry or bereft or heartbroken. But those emotions seemed luxurious to me, like a long hot shower or a bubble bath. I could not afford them.

I heard a shuffling sound and looked up to see my mother leaning on the doorjamb. She was wearing a pair of my old leggings and a shirt of my father's, its lower buttons pulling slightly over her distended belly. And for just a moment I thought to myself: you have ruined my life. You have ruined my life with your damn selflessness, your damn accommodations, your damn illusions, your damn husband, and now your damn death. Perhaps a shadow of all that passed over my face, for her voice was plaintive, almost childlike, when she spoke.

"I need a pill, Ellen," she said, the trace of a whine in the ebb and flow of her inflection.

I handed her the vial. "What would I do without this stuff?" she said, and she took one, her head tilted back and her throat working like a bird drinking from a puddle. "I'm so tired," she said after it had gone down. "I'd like some tea."

"I'll make it," I said.

"Please," she said as she went back to the living room. I put the kettle on to boil, and then, as though by rote, I put bread in the toaster and mixed sugar and cinnamon together in a small bowl and took the butter dish out of the refrigerator. It was almost like waking up from a dream when I finally looked down and saw, on the pretty lacquer tray, the mug of tea and the plate with two slices of cinnamon toast cut in triangles. It was the snack my mother always made us when we came in from sledding, playing in the snow, skating down at the pond behind the public library.

I carried it carefully into the living room and put the tray on the coffee table. The room was dim, and my mother was asleep on the couch, her breathing raspy, her eyes sunk into the concavities of her skull. One hand was held to the side of her face, as though to shield it from view.

"Mama," I said softly, but the only answering sound was the rattle of her breathing. I sat down on the ottoman and drank the tea and ate the toast and it was as though the house was breathing, too, all three of us breathing in tandem, dying in tandem, trying to keep body and soul together as the wind shook the storm windows in their metal frames. A leaf blew down the chimney and lay shivering on the stone hearth, and in a few minutes I took the tray into the kitchen and then came back into the living room to sit with her and watch her sleep.

By Monday morning I had forgotten everything about my call from Dr. Cohn except what she'd said about the morphine. Three or four hours after she took the medication my mother was groaning with pain, sometimes keening as though she was chief mourner at her own wake. More morphine given more often helped that, although it meant she slept more and sometimes she talked to herself in a monotone I could hear from her bedroom. Maybe there were things she needed to speak aloud that she could not say to anyone else.

So when the front door bell rang, the carillon of my childhood, *bing-BING, bing,* as it had not done for so long—"they all think cancer's contagious," my mother had said wearily one afternoon of her friends—I was unprepared for the slender dark woman who stood on the steps in a bright red jacket with a big canvas bag slung over her shoulder.

"Ms. Gulden?" she said, careful to use the more modern honorific, the dissonant sound of bees buzzing. She had a slight accent and her teeth were very white against her dark face and hair. Above the *V* of her coat a white tunic jumped out like a surprise.

"Yes," I said, pushing at my hair, which I had not yet found time to brush or barrette back.

She put out her hand. "I am Teresa Guerrero. I will be helping you and your mother."

It was so deft, the way she said it, and I wondered if they taught them etiquette in some hospice training class: do not say you are there to take care, to treat. Say that you are there for both the patient and the family. Make yourself an assistant; do not try to run the show until later.

"Oh, Ms . . ."

"Guerrero. I am Ecuadoran originally, although for quite some time I have been an American citizen."

"Ms. Guerrero, I told Dr. Cohn I didn't really need any help. I'm caring for my mother myself."

"I appreciate that, Ms. Gulden. For today I will do nothing but meet your mother and monitor her vital signs, her heart rate, her respiration, her blood pressure. Later you can decide whether and in what ways you wish to use me."

I looked at Teresa Guerrero for a long time, but unlike most people she did not attempt to fill the silence that grew between us.

"I don't know about this, Ms. Guerrero," I said.

"We will find out."

"I am Ellen," I said, unconsciously adopting her speech patterns.

"I am Teresa." I stepped aside and let her in.

In the living room my mother was working on her needlepoint pillow, the background half finished. Her clothes hung loosely from her shoulders, and I had been able to tell for several days that she wore no bra, although I was not sure whether it was because she could not put one on or because she felt, with her poor deflated breasts, that it was superfluous.

Teresa put down her bag, which made a clinking sound. "Mrs. Gulden," she said, "my name is Teresa Guerrero and I am the nurse sent by Dr. Cohn to monitor your vital signs." Vital signs, I thought, she keeps saying vital signs. Perhaps it is to make the patient feel vital. Will she ever say she is here to monitor dying signs? I watched my mother smile up at her, her bright company smile, and wondered whether she would offer refreshment.

"I appreciate that," said my mother. "Would you like a cup of tea?"

"No, thank you," Teresa said solemnly. "I never drink on duty. I don't eat on duty either."

"Do you laugh on duty?" I said.

"If something is funny," Teresa said. Turning back to my mother she asked her to push up her sleeve and unbutton the top two buttons of her shirt. "Knock knock," she said.

"Who's there?" said my mother.

"Banana."

"Banana who?"

"Knock knock."

"Who's there?"

"Banana." Her slight accent made the word sound exotic and very beautiful, almost erotic.

"Banana who?"

"Knock knock." She inflated the blood pressure cuff and consulted her watch.

"Who's there?"

"Banana."

"Banana who?"

"Knock knock."

My mother giggled. "Who's there?" she said.

"Orange."

"Ah! Orange who?"

"Orange you glad I didn't say banana?"

We all laughed. "I thought these children had told me every knock-knock joke under the sun, but I've never heard that one," my mother said.

Teresa was listening to my mother's heart. "Shhh," she said.

She moved the silver disc of the stethoscope from place to place, stopped to run her fingers gently over the catheter beneath my mother's skin.

"Is it still beating?" my mother asked.

"Loud and clear," said Teresa, who took a clipboard from her bag and began filling in a form.

"Do you have children?" I said.

"No," said Teresa. "I have not yet married."

"So where'd you hear the knock-knock joke? Not from Dr. Cohn?"

"No, not from Dr. Cohn. From the daughter of a woman I also visit. She is five and thinks that joke is very funny. I have heard it from her perhaps twenty times."

"What's wrong with her mother?" my mother said, buttoning her shirt.

"Mama, I'm sure they're not allowed to go from house to house talking about their patients."

"Her mother has breast cancer, Mrs. Gulden," said Teresa. "I have been seeing her for three months. Her own mother cares for her some of the time but she is not able to do certain things for her."

"And she has a five-year-old?"

"And a seven-year-old."

"Oh, Lord, that poor girl," my mother said, her mouth trembling.

"If the two of you were together in this room you would have a great deal to talk about," said Teresa.

"Yes?" said my mother.

"We can talk more about that. In the meantime what can I do for you? Is your pain under control? Can I help with your diet? Would you like help with bathing or dressing?"

"Oh, I'm having a terrible time getting in and out of the bathtub. But I can't have you coming to bathe me."

"Mama, you didn't tell me that," I said.

"Oh, there are so many things to worry about, Ellen."

"I can help you."

"No. Not with that."

"Oh, Mama, I've been in a million locker rooms."

"It's different," my mother said.

"Let's go upstairs," Teresa said. "I can show you some of the ways that coming in and out of the tub can be made more comfortable. And I would like to irrigate your catheter and you should be lying comfortably for that."

"Will it hurt?" said my mother.

"Compared to what I imagine you are used to, not very much."

My mother's lips quivered again as she replied, "What I'm used to is awful."

"Yes," said Teresa, and she took my mother's hand. "It is important that you not hurt." My mother's head dropped, an orange daisy in a drought. Tears fell, *plop, plop,* on their joined hands. I felt like a voyeur, a stranger. They stood together, Teresa helping my mother to her feet.

"Excuse me," said my mother, pulling a tissue from her sleeve and dabbing at her face. "I'm usually better than this."

"Better and stoic are two different things, Mrs. Gulden. You have a right, even an obligation, to express your feelings." She reached into her bag and brought out a folder. "You may want to read these," she said to me. "Not all of them are suitable for all patients but Dr. Cohn seemed to think you should have them, particularly the more technical information." Then she offered my mother her arm. Through the white bones of the banisters I watched them disappear, head, torso, knees, feet, as though they were ascending to heaven.

In the folder was "The Dying Person's Bill of Rights" and some pharmaceutical pamphlets about morphine. There were sixteen tenets to the Bill of Rights, and I got through "I have the right to be treated as a living human being until I die" and "I have the right not to die alone." I did not break until the last one: "I have the right to be cared for by caring, sensitive, knowledgeable people who will attempt to understand my needs and will be able to gain some satisfaction in helping me face my death."

"What satisfaction?" I sobbed, and the tears ran hot down my face and I cried into a pillow until my face was as swollen as I imagined my mother's stomach must be beneath my father's shirts.

I don't know how long Teresa was there, but she never touched me or made any noise. When I finally looked up, she was standing with her stethoscope around her neck. She began to rummage in her bag, to pull out instruments and swabs in sealed silver packages.

"This is why I told Dr. Cohn we did not need a nurse," I said to her, still shaking. "Having a stranger in the house is too upsetting. I cannot afford to fall apart."

"Falling apart is curling up into a fetal position and staying in bed for a week," she said. "What you were doing is having the emotional response an individual has to the loss of someone they love. We cry to give voice to our pain."

"That's very poetic, Ms. Guerrero, but it doesn't make me feel any better."

"You are not going to feel any better for a long, long time, Ms. Gulden, and you know that far better than I do. But I refuse to believe that keeping your grief bottled up makes you feel better than crying."

"Like a five-year-old," I said, blowing my nose.

"The five-year-old who provides me with jokes never cries, Ms. Gulden. She does not understand what is happening. But you do."

I shook my head. "I can help her," Teresa said, and went upstairs again. In a few minutes I heard a cry, a short sharp one, from the second floor, and then the long murmur of voices, and I got up and went to make two cups of tea. I sat at the table in the kitchen and drank one while the other grew cold on the counter, a tan skim of milk congealing on its surface. From above came another sound. I went to the living room and looked upward, and then I heard it again, the sound of a belly laugh. Teresa came downstairs swinging her stethoscope.

"What was that all about?" I asked.

"She'll tell you," she said, as she began to pack up her things. "I've taught her ways to sit on the edge of the tub and then slide in in stages, but it's going to make it easier if you buy one of those rubber mats with suction cups and fasten it to the side so she feels more secure. Then she will not slip."

"Should I help her bathe?"

"She is embarrassed by the condition of her body, but it may become necessary. Does she have an odor?"

"God, no."

"That may come and when it does you will have to talk with her again." She zipped her bag shut and for the first time since she arrived she smiled. She was very beautiful.

"How old are you?" I asked.

"Twenty-three," she said.

"Jesus. I'm twenty-four. Why do you do this kind of work? You could be working in the hospital nursery, bathing babies."

"Anyone can bathe a baby," Teresa said. "Not everyone can do this."

"You're good," I said.

"That's what Dr. Cohn said about you, Ms. Gulden."

"Ellen," I said.

"Ellen," she said. "I will be back next Monday, unless you need me sooner." She handed me a card.

I put the kettle on and brought my mother a fresh cup of tea. She was on the floor in her bedroom looking through a long brown box, the kind lawyers keep documents in.

"Do you remember the Halloween the boys went as a set of dice and Brian fell over downtown and Jeff wouldn't help him up because he got such a kick out of seeing him waving his arms and legs around. Jeff said he looked like a turtle on his back. Oh, I could have killed him, but the idea was very funny."

"Don't tell me—you've got the costumes in there."

She held up a picture of the two boys standing side by side on the front lawn, the light dying behind them so that there was a bright disfiguring star of last sunlight in the upper right corner.

Jeff was showing number two, Bri a five. Lucky seven. "I lent the costumes to someone and they never gave them back. It was a good one."

"Is that what you were laughing about?"

"When?"

"I heard you laughing upstairs when Teresa was here."

"Oh," my mother said, laughing again. "No. It's another joke: a little boy comes into the classroom and his teacher says, 'You're late. Where were you?' And he says, 'On top of Blueberry Hill.' And a second little boy comes in and the teacher says, 'You're late. Where were you?' And the boy says, 'On top of Blueberry Hill.' And a third little boy comes in and the teacher says, 'You're late. Where were you?' And he says, 'On top of Blueberry Hill.' And a little girl comes in and the teacher says, 'I suppose you were on top of Blueberry Hill too.' And she says, 'I *am* Blueberry Hill.' "

My mother giggled. "The five-year-old told her that?" I asked.

"The seven-year-old," my mother said.

"If I had told you that joke when I was seven I would have spent the afternoon in my room."

"*Autres temps, autres moeurs,*" my mother said, her fingers moving in a stroking movement to the bump of the catheter beneath her skin.

"Voltaire, I think," I said.

"Really?" my mother said. "I thought your father made that up." And she laughed again and looked back at the box. "Remember the Halloween when you were Bo-Peep?" she said.

"And I had to carry those sheep you made and kept spilling my candy?" I said. "How could I forget?"

"I remember it all," said my mother, "every bit of it."

On the morning when she went to decorate her tree we threaded red ribbon through the spokes of my mother's wheels, the way my mother had threaded red, white, and blue ribbons through the wheels of our bikes on the Fourth of July when we were children, ribbons and playing cards—but only the red ones, for the color attached to the spokes with clothespins so that we made a noise when we rode like old engines, Model Ts in movies.

But none of the Minnies, even Mrs. Duane, who talked to us for a long time about a little girl who'd been kidnapped in Texas—tragedies! Oh, we loved our secondhand tragedies!—mentioned the ribbons. I suppose if they had acknowledged them it would have meant acknowledging the wheelchair, and if they acknowledged the wheelchair it would have meant acknowledging my mother's fragile sloping shoulders and the way her hands shook when she lifted them from the armrests.

And that would have meant acknowledging the disease, and the fears, and the dangers, and the death. Better than anyone I understood why they didn't want that to happen. Better than anyone except maybe my mother.

Imagine having to dictate your prose to someone else when you are writing a novel, or telling someone where to place the cerulean and how to mix it with white for the edges of a cloud in your landscape, and you can understand what it was for my mother to have to sit in her chair in front of the blue spruce, grown now to twenty feet all these years after its planting as a seedling, and direct my clumsy efforts to place her ornaments exactly where she wanted them. There were hundreds of them; both of us had sore calluses and little pin dots of dried blood on our fingers from pushing in the sequins and aligning the hanging wires. All red. All gold. Gold and red striped, gold and red spotted, random patterns of red and gold. And big red ribbons shot through with gold and stiff with wire, to be cosseted into bows.

"No no no, Ellen," she called from below as I attached a bow to a branch. "It's supposed to ripple." With her hand she sketched a shallow wave in the air, and the winter sunlight seemed to illuminate the blue veins on its back like miniature rivers, tributaries from her heart.

"That ball right near your hand . . . no . . . no . . . there! It's hanging too low. It needs to be tucked under there more tightly . . . higher . . . that's it . . . and then there should be one just below it . . . no, lower and over a little." It was like trying to scratch someone's back, finding the right spot, except that it was bigger than any back and the effort seemed to go on forever.

Mrs. Best had the tree next to us; her ribbons were gold, her ornaments red and gold wooden soldiers. "Where does your mother get that ribbon that holds its shape?" she asked me with her lips pursed.

"She just seems to have things like that," I said. "She's the kind of person who can go upstairs to the linen closet and dig up some silver stars if you need them."

"Oh, Linda, don't worry," my mother called to the two of us on our abutting ladders. "Yours looks beautiful already."

The truth was that even with my shortcomings at spacing, grouping, and tying, I thought the Gulden tree was the handsomest, although Mrs. Duane was swathing hers in some gold stuff that looked like fourteen-karat insulation, which was magical if strange. "Some of them never learn that with a tree this size in a public park, gaudy is key," my mother had said when I remarked that our ornaments looked like plump chorus girls in a second-rate summer-stock production of *42nd Street*.

As I stepped back to look at her tree, I could see she'd been right. The more tasteful decorations, including Mrs. Best's, seemed to disappear amid the ice-blue branches of the big trees. And when the switch was thrown on the red lights the public works people had threaded through the day before, the quieter efforts would completely disappear. "These will reflect!" my mother had declared triumphantly, turning her sequins in her shaking hands.

"Ellie, there's a bow on the other side that's much too close to the end of a branch," she called, fingering the ornaments in a box on her lap.

It took us nearly three hours to decorate that tree. By the time we were done, though the temperature was in the low thirties, I'd laid my jacket on the grass and discarded my gloves, my fingers alternately numb and aching from the pine needles and the wire hangers. "My back is killing me," one of the Minnies said loudly, clinging to a ladder with one hand and rubbing the small of her back with the other.

Mrs. Duane went down the street to the deli and brought back coffee and sandwiches for us all, and I sat at my mother's feet, my shoulders sagging, and ate roast beef and drank my coffee black. She ate nothing at all, only sipped at a cup of milky tea.

"How are you holding up?" I said very quietly.

"There's a problem. I don't know exactly what it is, but I can feel it."

"What?"

"It's something about the bows. Maybe they need to face down a little more."

And back up I went, as Mrs. Best stood with her arms crossed on her chest and looked from her tree to ours and then back again. She sighed. "Kate, you do have an eye. You simply have an eye. And with an eye, you either have it or you don't," she said.

What a dope, I thought to myself as I tilted bows downward.

"Linda, you're being silly," my mother said, but from the gay tone of her voice I could tell that she agreed completely, with Linda Best and with me, too. "It looks beautiful, and the children will love the soldiers. Do you have any more?"

"Tons," said Mrs. Best.

"Load 'em on," my mother said, as I cut my finger on one of the wires. "More is more."

I wasn't sure why she seemed so indefatigable that day, whether it was the brilliant weather, the pleasure she took in making things pretty, the return to something she'd done for so many years, or the competition—"the Super Bowl of home decor aficionados" my father had called it that morning at breakfast. Certainly my mother seemed a good deal happier at Mrs. Best's chagrin than was charitable, and at the improvement in the Best tree as Mrs. Best hung soldiers from every bare inch of branch.

Or perhaps it had been that she had gone out with my father the night before, dressed in her cranberry shift, the gold brooch of a bow with pavé diamonds at its knot pulling down one shoulder of the dress, which had already grown far too big for her. She'd made herself up painstakingly, but because her hands were unsteady her lipstick was, too, and her eyeliner looked a little like the stuttery lines on some hospital monitor.

She timed her morphine carefully so that the hours when she got most relief and least sleepiness would come during dinner and the chamber music concert they planned for later. She wore her fur coat and bent her head to rub her cheek against its soft collar.

When she and my father had driven away I sat on the living-room couch with my hands in my lap and tried to make a plan for my own evening. I had been so busy arranging for her dress, her medication, where her wheelchair would go in the car, that I had forgotten that for the first time in many months I would be alone. I called Jonathan, but he was not home and I left a breezy message on his machine: "Just called to check in. Call me if you have a chance." When I heard the recording of Jules saying, "Can't come to the phone right now . . ." I hung up.

But after I found *All About Eve* on a cable channel, ate some ice cream from the container, and had a light beer, I felt more like my old self, the Ellen Gulden who had walked around her little downtown apartment touching things her first night—sink, stove, bathroom taps—thinking "Mine, mine, mine."

Jonathan was not coming home for Christmas. He'd be doing three fulltime weeks of data processing; it would pay for his summer sublet. He had plenty of schoolwork to do, too, he'd said. And perhaps he had a first-year law student who loved the way he ran his tongue over his upper lip and made impudent eye contact as they talked about torts.

The pressure and pain behind my eyes and in my jaw was intense, maybe from the beer, and I wondered how morphine would go down with alcohol. On the TV Eve Harrington became a big star but sold her soul to that dandy of a devil, Addison deWitt. I'd never thought it seemed like such a bad bargain, although I'd have known better than to cross Bette Davis, with those mean sleepy eyes and that hard fish mouth.

The next movie was *High Noon*. I hated Gary Cooper and Grace Kelly—"so white bread," Jules and I would always say in unison—and I turned the television off just as a car door slammed outside.

Even before they got in the house I could tell that my parents' evening had not gone well. I could hear my mother arguing outside in the drive, and when my father opened the door with her clinging awkwardly to his arm, his face was white, his eyes dark.

". . . they were all looking," I heard her say as he helped her over to the couch, where she lay down slowly, in careful stages, her pumps left on the floor like a memento.

"I'll get the chair," I said.

When I came back in, my father had turned on the lamps and was in the kitchen. I could tell from the sounds of cabinet doors and canisters that he was making tea. My mother's eyes were closed, but she was biting her lower lip. When she opened her mouth there was lipstick on her teeth. Mascara was gathered at the corners of her eyes, smudgy shadows.

"Disaster," she whispered.

My father came in with a mug and handed it to her. She raised her head and shoulders to sip, then put it on the coffee table and fell back.

"I am never going out again," she said.

"Oh, nonsense, Kate," my father said. "A thousand people have dozed off during chamber music in the chapel. The president has done it nearly every time in my memory. Why shouldn't you?"

"Because I never would have before and they all knew why I did it tonight. I remember the Vivaldi and a little of the Mozart and then the next thing I know I'm waking up with spit all over my chin and everyone staring—"

"No one was staring," my father said. "They were getting ready to leave and gathering up their things."

"They were staring. At the restaurant people stared, too. And then you made the fuss about the chair—"

"The doors should be wide enough to accommodate wheel-chairs. It's the law. The restaurant was negligent."

"—and you used that word," my mother continued, the pitch of her voice climbing. "You used that word!"

"I'm sorry," my father said.

"I am not handicapped, and don't you forget it. Either of you. I am not handicapped. I'm just weak. And woozy. I get woozy. That's why I need this thing."

"I said there were laws about accommodating the handicapped. I did not suggest that you were handicapped."

"Don't say that word," she said. "Don't say it."

"I'm sorry," he said again.

I went into the kitchen and made myself a cup of tea. But when

I went back to the living room, my father was kneeling beside the sofa with his head in my mother's lap and she was smoothing his hair. They were talking to one another, but I could not hear the words, only the plaintive tones of one and the murmurings of the other. I went back into the kitchen and poured the tea into the sink, threw away the empty ice-cream container, took two aspirin for the pain behind my eyes, and decided to go to bed. The house was quiet except for the faint hum of the furnace from the basement, just discernible through the floorboards.

I went through the hallway to the stairs, past the watercolor portraits of Brian at six, Jeffrey at eight, Ellie at eleven with serious eyes and mouth and a pink ribbon holding back her dark hair. But my parents were there ahead of me, my father three steps up, carrying my mother, who had her head on his shoulder.

"I'm so tired, Gen," she said quietly, without ever knowing I was there.

"I know, dear heart," he replied.

The next morning my father said the dinner had been a fiasco. "If she were a child she would have been described as playing with her food," he said, then drained his coffee cup, picked up his book bag, and left for his nine o'clock class before she could come downstairs. Yet when she did come down she was all lit up, dreamy, smiling, with the lines softened around her mouth and on her forehead. And she stayed that way all that day.

My father, before he went to work, had been merely distracted; his hair was awry, and there was a spot of blood on his collar to match the nick on the underside of his chin. All the lines on his face looked deeper, as though he'd had a bad portrait done, or an unforgiving black-and-white photograph. "What class do you have?" I'd asked as I handed him coffee.

"Women in Dickens," he said.

"Miss Havisham and Estella? Or the wimps, Little Dorrit and Dora and David's sainted mother?"

"All," he said, standing up.

"What about his wife and his mistress?"

"Only the work, not the biography," he said. "Ellen, the buttons have broken on the collars of two of my shirts. I put them on the chair in the bedroom. Could you see that they're replaced? And I'd rather we had the skim than the whole milk. Or get both and give the whole milk to your mother. Your brothers will be home on Thursday afternoon so they'll need plenty to eat."

"But how can you separate the work from the biography?"

"What?"

"Dickens. How can you illuminate the work if you separate the work from the biography?"

"You know the stock answer to that," he said, distracted. "The work stands alone. Does the nurse come again soon?"

"Monday."

"Your mother liked her. She said last night that she found her helpful."

"She's good," I said.

"The doctor has decided to discontinue the chemotherapy," my father said.

"What?"

"She spoke to your mother the other day at the hospital, when you took her over. She told me last night. Dr. Cohn decided that it's not having much of an effect." He went into the hall for his briefcase. "I'll meet you at seven here for the tree ceremony."

"That's it? That's all? No more chemo? End of sentence? End of discussion?"

"What more is there to say?" my father said, and left for work.

The night they lit the Christmas trees on the green was a perfect night of its kind in Langhorne. In summer there would be those dark nights with a cool breeze blowing faintly and the passing scent of petunias in the air, nights that veered between hot and not so hot so that when you went skinny-dipping in the reservoir you would get out and then jump back in because the water felt warmer than the air.

In fall there were the sweater days, football days, when the sun shone clear but light yellow, the color of white corn, and as you walked down the street a leaf would pirouette to the sidewalk right before your eyes, almost brushing your nose, and late at night the rumble of the furnace would suddenly shake the house like a snore.

And spring, what there ever was of it, was all beautiful, the pure smell of wet and fresh and the daffodils sashaying on the green, in our yards, in hidden wild patches on the hillside sloping down to the river amid the damp grass.

And in winter there were nights like the one when they lit the trees that year, when the sky hung down like black silk punched full of holes so that the bright light behind could shine out in tiny points, thousands of them. The air burnt your tongue a bit with its cold, and the bony fingers of the bare tree branches reached up to lay hands on a full moon. It was bright outdoors, silver-bright, with the long black shadows of shrubs, houses, people walking down the sidewalk and staring up at the moon as though it was moving the tides of their lives and they could feel the ebb and flow inside them.

Usually on a night like that in Langhorne you'd only know how perfect it was when you went to take the garbage out and were dazzled, or came in late from work or a movie and stopped to marvel. After dark people stayed home in Langhorne, not because there was anything to fear, but because our houses—our kitchens, our dens, our bedrooms—were where our lives took place.

If a stranger walked the streets, which had never happened in my memory, he would see from the sidewalk one imagined oasis after another of yellow light and easy love: a woman's head at a kitchen window, her arms moving in slow and steady patterns as she washed dishes; children passing to and fro in their rooms looking for pencils or turning down the stereo on command; men dozing in big comfortable chairs. Outside on the cold streets you would see no one, except perhaps some child walking home from a friend's house after working on a school project, the pyramids in papier-mâché, a disquisition on *Romeo and Juliet* and family discord. You would hear nothing except for the faint sounds from within those houses, of piano practice and the water running and the commentators from *Wide World of Sports*.

But the night they lit the trees was different. Whole families, their collars turned up against, not the cold, but the idea of cold, of how cold it ought to be in the shadow of Christmas, came down the street to the green. From inside our house we could hear the murmur of their voices outside, a drone like that of bees around the hydrangea bushes on one of the perfect summer days.

My mother was upstairs getting dressed, and I was packing a

bag with her pills, extra gloves, and four Christmas ornaments that we had not put on her tree, just in case, she said, although it was hard to tell what "in case" meant. She'd put on an old pair of wool slacks, cinched tightly under a red turtleneck and the red sweater with reindeer leaping across it that she wore every year to the tree ceremony. She came down the stairs slowly, holding tightly to the banister, then settled herself in her chair and pulled her beret over what little was left of her hair.

"No coat?" said my father.

"I don't need a coat," she said. "I'm layered. Besides, I want to show off my sweater."

I was wearing red, too, and my father a green loden coat, and together we made a festive group, with our beribboned wheelchair. My father pushed the chair and I walked alongside. The moon touched the handles and made silver pools of its own reflection. My mother tipped her head back to look up.

"Beautiful night," she said softly.

The road around the green was packed with people, the crowd so large that some stood on the streets that fanned out from the hub. But we were able to push right through because my mother and the other Minnies were given a place at the front, next to the podium from which the mayor gave the signal to light the trees.

"Hey, Mrs. Gulden?" said Hetty Belknap, who for all her childhood had been known as Hugh and Sophie Belknap's change-of-life baby, a scrawny little girl with freckles and sandy hair that looked as if she'd cut it herself, perhaps with manicure scissors.

"What, sweetie?" my mother said.

"I like how you decorated your wheels," she said, and her father gave her a stern look. "I didn't say anything about her being sick," Hetty whined as he led her away.

"Hey, Ellen," said a young police officer keeping the crowd back, whose name I couldn't quite recall until months later when I saw him at the municipal building.

"Well, how are you?" I said brightly. "Look at you in your uniform."

"Ellen's imitating me, Gen," said my mother, giving me a wink.

The Presbyterian choir stood in their red robes with songbooks under their arms, and Amanda Bollan, who'd been in Honor Society with me, waved and then turned to say something to the woman next to her.

"Is Brian home yet?" one slender girl with fur earmuffs asked me, ducking her head.

The mayor shook hands with us all. So did Mr. Best, wearing one of his MAY THE BEST MAN WIN hats.

"Linda says you gave her good advice on her tree," he said to my mother.

"Oh, Ed, she didn't need it," my mother replied.

"You're looking well," he added. "And you, too, Ellen."

The Minnies usually stood in a semicircle behind the podium, but this year they grouped themselves around my mother's wheelchair. The mayor read their names amid the sounds of mothers *ssshusshing* their children and one little girl wailing loudly, the sound fading, like an ambulance turning a corner, as she was carried away into darkness.

I'd been a little girl here once, riding on my father's shoulders, clutching at his hair while my mother held Jeffrey awkwardly against her hip, to one side of her bulging stomach. The year she had first been a Minnie I had looked every morning in the basket in the hallway to see what she'd made for her tree the night before. But I'd never helped decorate before that morning. She'd never asked. I'd never offered.

"Happy holidays, Langhorne," the mayor said, a change from the "Merry Christmas" of years gone by because of the complaints of a Jewish professor of economics at the college that had occupied page one of the *Tribune* for a week two Januaries before. He raised his hand and the trees came alive, sparks leaping from amid their branches, the sequins on my mother's tree winking red and gold. The crowd burst into applause and the choir began to sing.

There was a moment of silence as the last deep sonorous note of "Silent Night" died away. My father's eyes were fixed on my mother; his lips were held together tightly, one to the other, but when she looked over, he smiled broadly.

"Which one did she do?" he asked, as though the tables and countertops of his home had not been littered with sequined ornaments for weeks.

"Third from the left," I whispered, smelling the lemon of his cologne and the musty wool of his coat. "Papa smells," I called them when I was a little girl, along with the smells of shoe polish and leather shoes.

"I suspected as much," he said.

The choir bounced through "Deck the Halls," their consonants as sharp as could be, punctuated with little white bursts of warm breath on the cold night. The Minnies hugged one another, and the mayor thanked them, and the crowd surged forward to look at each tree closely. For a moment I lost sight of my mother as she disappeared amid a circle of neighbors. The young cop smiled across their heads at me, then turned away, his pale face a moon above the children pushing through the crowd to find their friends.

"Are you Ellen?" said a woman with blond hair held back from a high forehead with a red velvet band dotted with silk holly leaves and sequined berries. She had on a black wool cape that swung open when she moved. She was very pregnant.

"I'm Halley McPherson," she said, shaking my hand. "We just moved here from Atlanta. My husband is comptroller at the college. This is such a nice thing, isn't it?"

"It is, but it must seem sort of small town after Atlanta."

"Well, everything really is small town, anyhow, isn't it? My husband always says there are no big ponds. Although your mom says you're a New Yorker, so maybe you wouldn't agree."

I smiled noncommittally. I didn't.

"Well, I just wanted to meet you because your mother has been such a saint to me. I told the man at the hardware store that I was looking for a decorating book to do the baby's nursery and he said that I didn't need a decorating book if I talked to your mom."

"Oh, you're the crib person. How'd it turn out?"

"It's beautiful. Nobody can believe I did it myself."

The crowd around us moved aside and there was my father, pushing the wheelchair. My mother smiled and put out her hand.

"Oh Halley, there you are in person." She looked down at Halley's midsection. "You look wonderful."

"Fecund," said my father.

"I'm due a week from Friday," Halley said.

"Mama, how did you know it was her?" I said.

"She talked me through making the headband, too," Halley said, raising her hand to her hair. "That's how she was going to recognize me. And soon she's coming to see the crib."

"Very soon," my mother said.

As we walked back up the hill, children eddying around us, adults calling greetings across the street to all three of us, my mother looked up at the moon again and said, "I do love Christmas. It's always been my favorite holiday. I used to decorate the whole apartment with construction-paper things when I was little." She took my hand as we walked. "Ellen, we need to get a tree," she said.

"No, no," I cried, and people turned around to look. "Please, Lord, not another tree to decorate. Let this cup pass from me."

"Just one more," my mother said, laughing. "Only eight feet tall or it won't fit in the living room."

"One more," I said. "That's my limit."

"And the boys will be home in two days, and we'll have ham for Christmas dinner. Much easier than turkey."

"Turkey wasn't so bad."

"And it's good to know how to make a turkey, just in case."

"In case of what?"

"Oh, you," my mother said.

"The Gulden tree was the most beautiful one," my father said.

"I know," said my mother.

The moon was as perfect and bright as a dime, and from some of the houses bits of colored lights shone out, the lights on Christmas trees whose outlines were lost in the dark of sleeping houses, empty houses, houses whose people were still winding their way up the hill. There was a slight wind, and the outdoor evergreens made a sound like hands rubbing softly together.

My mother shivered. "You're cold," said my father sternly. "You ought to have worn a coat."

"I'm not cold," my mother said.

A little boy in a red cap pulled low ran past us, crying "Mommy!" and faintly, from the bottom of the hill we could hear a group of people singing "We Wish You a Merry Christmas" in stops and starts, searching aloud for the words.

"I love Christmas," my mother said with a sigh.

My father leaned down so that his head was close to hers. "And Easter," he said. "I have it on good authority that Easter comes early this year. Very early. And that nice young woman will surely need you to teach her how to paint eggs or weave baskets."

My mother put her hand to my father's cheek, and then she looked up again at the moon. "No, Gen," she said. "Easter was never my holiday. To hell with Easter."

The second time Teresa came to the house Jeffrey and Brian were home from school. They had climbed out of Jeff's leaky jeep sopping wet, caught in one of those dreadful soaking winter rainstorms just outside of Philadelphia but determined to make it home for dinner. Our mother was asleep upstairs when they first arrived; the night after the tree lighting she had woken up crying with pain soon after she went to bed and then had woken again, after I gave her more morphine, weeping incoherently about the babies and a thunderstorm and a tree splitting in the front yard and falling on the house. I stood in the doorway of their room while my father tried to calm her, undone by her blank eyes and senseless rant. He held her arms and repeated, "You are having a nightmare, Kate. It is a nightmare. A nightmare. There is no storm. There are no babies."

"No babies," she said.

"No."

"I'm here, Mama," I said.

"A nightmare," she said.

"Yes."

Finally he eased her back and pulled the covers around her shoulders. Like a light turned off, her lids went down and she began to breathe heavily, as though she had a bad cold. My father got out of bed in his boxer shorts. While I looked away, leaning against the doorjamb, he pulled on last night's pants and shirt.

"I cannot sleep after that," he said. "Are hallucinations a side effect of the medication?"

"I don't know," I said. "What if they are? I'd rather have her hallucinating comfortably than suffering from the pain."

"I'm not suggesting that she should suffer. I'm suggesting that we should not administer medication without knowing all its side effects."

"Oh, Papa, who gives a shit? Who gives a shit if it makes her skin turn purple and blood come out her nose if it stops her from hurting? This is not an intellectual exercise. This is day-to-day let's get through this."

"Just ask the doctor," he said, going downstairs.

"You ask her," I said.

But instead I asked Teresa when she arrived with her bag. Jeff had been out with his high school friends until nearly dawn, and he was in the kitchen in bare feet and running shorts when the bell rang.

"My public," he said, holding a peanut-butter-and-jelly sandwich in his fist and throwing open the door.

"It's Teresa," I said, looking over his shoulder. "Come in, Teresa. She's upstairs and the area around her catheter seems a little red. She was hoping you would look at it and at some lumps she has on her sides."

"Certainly," Teresa said as Jeff held the door and watched her pass. She laid her coat over one of the wing chairs in the living room, took the small pouch from her duffel bag and went upstairs. In a moment I heard her call, "Rise and shine."

"Give me a clue," Jeff said.

"The nurse."

"The nurse?"

"I told you. Dr. Cohn wanted to send a nurse once a week. That's her. Teresa Guerrero."

"Teresa?"

"Jeffie, hon, I have a floor to wash and three loads of laundry. Dr. Cohn sent a nurse, her name is Teresa Guerrero, and I too have noticed that she is extremely young and attractive."

"When you said a nurse I pictured someone who looked like a dinner roll. Round. White. Fluffy. Comforting."

"Well, this is what you get instead."

"My stars," said Jeff, eating his sandwich. "Sakes alive. Well I'll be."

Before Teresa came downstairs Jeff had put on a pair of jeans and a rugby shirt. "Even shoes," I said. "My stars."

"Put a sock in it, Ellie," my brother said.

"I'm really glad you guys are home," I said.

"Me too. Especially for Brian. He's having a really hard time at school. Hates his roommate, hates his adviser, hates his courses. I think it's basically because he hates not being here. He even talked about transferring to Langhorne so he could be near Mom."

"Dad would never stand for it. Besides, if he doesn't do it next semester, he won't have to do it at all."

"You think?" Jeff said.

"Yeah. Unless there's some kind of miracle, I think we'll be coming into the home stretch soon."

"Ah, shit," Jeff said. "How soon?"

"I'm like an alcoholic. I take it one day at a time. I can't tell you what next week is going to be like."

"I saw Jon in Cambridge a couple of weeks ago. I went up to see the guys at BU and had a drink with him. He told me he wasn't coming home for Christmas."

"I don't think he can deal with the idea of someone losing their mother."

"Yeah, well, that's very understanding of you, but I think he needs to play out his little personal psychodrama at some other time, when someone he allegedly cares about doesn't need him quite as much. I think his behavior sucks."

"And you told him that."

Jeff smiled. "Is the Pope Polish?" he said.

"And?"

"He's not the kind of guy you need in a tough time," Jeff said.

"No," I said.

"On the other hand," Jeff said, "a year ago I would have said the same thing about you."

Teresa was swinging her stethoscope when she came downstairs. She had on big gold hoop earrings and a dress this time, with a long full white skirt that almost swept the ground, and she was carrying a small box, wrapped in red with red-and-green striped ribbon. All week I'd been delivering gifts while my mother slept, to neighbors, to nurses, to Dr. Cohn, who took out the small needlepointed pillow on the end of a ribbon that said OY VAY and hung it on the doorknob of her office. "The oncologist's creed," she said. "I believe that was the thought behind the gift," I had said.

Teresa held up her little box and smiled. "What a lovely woman she is," she said.

"You have any more jokes?" I said.

"No, no more. Those children are fixated on Blueberry Hill, Blueberry Hill, I believe because we told them it was vulgar. The boy keeps repeating the word, vulgar, vulgar, as though he loves the idea."

Jeff stuck out his hand. "Jeff," he said. "Gulden." Recovering a bit, he added, "All County Soccer, All County Lacrosse, eldest son, power serve."

"I believe your mother already told me all that," Teresa said cooly. Turning to me, she added, "I don't see any real problem with the catheter site. I've irrigated it again, and taken a blood sample, which Dr. Cohn wanted. When was her last medication?"

"I'm not sure."

"She seems very very tired to me. I don't believe the adjustment on the dosage or frequency is exactly right. May I speak to Dr. Cohn about it?"

"Sure. She naps in the morning and the afternoon now, but she doesn't plan them so much as she just drops off. Sometimes she'll fall asleep on the couch while she's reading or in her chair when the TV's on. Then she'll be fine for a while and then she'll start to fade again. She's particularly tired this week because she had a bad night Tuesday. My father wants to know—does the morphine cause hallucinations?"

Teresa looked up the stairs, then at Jeff. "Can we sit down?" she said.

"There are a variety of opinions about hallucinations and the use of morphine," she said when we were in the living room. "Many physicians will tell you that it does not happen. Others will say that it is one possible side effect. Some nurses will tell you that what happens are not hallucinations at all. When did this happen?"

"The other night she woke up crying about babies and thunderstorms."

"Well. There are several possibilities. One is that it was a nightmare and she had a more acute reaction than you or I might have because of the medication. The other is that it was a true hallucination. But she also may be working out some matters mentally that would emerge in that fashion. I know that is very vague, but we think some people we see have things that they want to think about or talk about and that the people who care for them can only see those things as hallucinations."

"Like?"

"I have an older woman dying of cancer of the pancreas who constantly accuses her husband of infidelity with a variety of their acquaintances. Very vividly and in considerable detail, I might add. I've learned a few things I did not know about sexual congress."

"Oh, shit," said Jeff.

"Are we sure he's not?" I said.

"We are sure he is not," said Teresa with a slight smile. "It is

my theory that she is contemplating his life without her and that
her anger and fear leads her to rehearse it in that way."

"Babies and thunderstorms?" Jeff said.

"I am not a psychiatrist, Mr. Gulden, and I am told that Ellen
does not want to consult one. But perhaps you are the babies and
this"—she swept her arm around the house and brought her hand
to rest on her bag and its welter of medical equipment—"is the
storm."

"Maybe you should think about psychiatry," Jeff said. "That's
pretty credible."

"Perhaps you can discuss her dreams with her, Ellen."

"I wish I could just take your stethoscope and listen to her
heart. Really her heart, not the beating, but inside."

Teresa took the stethoscope from her bag and handed it to me.
"Maybe it will help. Any intimacy will help. I can get another
one." She stood up. "I think I will come again soon if you are not
opposed."

"Any time," said Jeff.

"Mind your own business, Jeff." I slung the stethoscope around
my neck. Sometimes, afterward, I've thought of that, how that
was the first time I'd ever handled a stethoscope and how I hung
it around my neck, just like the doctors and nurses did. I've
thought about how Teresa gave it to me and how I kept it even
though I knew I should offer to hand it back.

"My mother likes you, Teresa," I said. "Come as often as you
think necessary, or helpful, or whatever. I have a feeling she may
need you more often now."

"Yes," Teresa said, picking up her coat.

"How long?" Jeff said.

"I cannot say for sure," Teresa said. "It's more important that
you take advantage of the time you have than that you worry
about how much time there is."

And that was exactly what we did over the next week. The boys
took her out in the jeep, wrapped in scarves and blankets against
the cold, to see the Christmas decorations all over town, from the

austere white lights in the bushes and trees outside some of the largest houses in our neighborhood to the small Cape Cod on a narrow county road ten miles from town, which had big plastic choirboys with 200-watt bulbs inside their pink heads singing on the lawn, a sleigh and eight reindeers in tortured postures on the roof, and a blinking sign that said JOYEUX NOËL covering the garage door.

The three of them came in that night howling because of Jeff's description of what he called "La Maison de Billion Lumières" and the electric bill of the family that lived inside. I could hear them in the den as I made cocoa and set out Christmas cookies on a plate in the kitchen.

"How can we possibly turn in without calling them and, as politely as possible, saying, 'Monsieur, Madame, why French? Why?'" Jeff cried. "'To add a touch of class to the Little Rascals with their plastic choir robes? Because—get this, folks—it's not working!'"

I brought a tray in and Brian added, "Geez, El, if you could see this place. And Jeff is driving real slow, real slow, and doing this description of all the stuff they have, and Mom is saying, 'Jeffrey, they will hear you!' But he can't hear her because she's laughing so hard she's making little squeaky noises."

"He was very mean," said my mother, laughing.

"I was just as mean about how constipated the Byers' house looked, with the white candles in each window. I'm an equal opportunity mean person. No one can call me a snob."

"You're a snob," said Brian.

Jeff grabbed him in a half nelson. "You're toast," he said. "You're through."

My father stepped into the den from the hallway, his hand over the telephone receiver. "Will you all please be quiet!" he hissed. "I am on the phone to Cambridge!"

"Jesus," Jeff whispered. "Cambridge! I almost interrupted a conversation with someone in Cambridge."

"Jeff," said my mother.

"All right, Little Ma. The cookies are supreme, as always."

"Talk to your sister, dear. She made them."

Jeff stared at me. "Picture it," he said. "Ellen Gulden actually putting flour and water in the same place at the same time—using the Mixmaster—the spatula."

"What the hell do you think I've been doing around here all this time?" I said. "Who do you think runs the vacuum and does the laundry and makes all the meals? Who do you think shops and cleans and makes the beds?" My voice began to break and there were tears in my eyes. I stopped and turned away, back to the kitchen. "Shit," I heard Jeff say, and my mother did not reprimand him.

We watched all of the Christmas movies, *Miracle on 34th Street* and *It's a Wonderful Life,* and when George Bailey's brother called him the richest man in town we sat there sobbing, and even my father cried silently. On Christmas Eve I made shrimp and opened champagne. "Betty Crocker! Sit right here by me," said Jeff, and this time I did not lose my equilibrium. We watched *A Christmas Carol,* the old black-and-white English version with Alastair Sim.

"There has quite literally never been a good film made of one of Dickens's novels," my father said, peering at the screen over the top of his reading glasses, *The New York Review of Books* open on his lap. "It's not possible. The backbone of Dickens is physical description. It's the description that fails them. Look, now, here's the party scene when Scrooge is an apprentice and nothing, absolutely nothing they can do in the way of casting or dialogue for the character of, say, a Fezziwig, can touch what is in the book."

"I bet that's just what Mario Puzo says about *The Godfather,*" said Jeff.

"Listen to the dialogue, Ellen," my father said. "The rhythm's been completely eradicated."

"Oh, put a sock in it, Gen," my mother said, and we all burst out laughing, all except my father, who colored slowly, from chin to forehead. Jeff had gone to get a copy of the book from my room, and he was reading along with the movie dialogue, which was remarkably intact. "I'm sorry, really," my mother added, "but you can't be condescending about *A Christmas Carol*. Not tonight."

"My point was—"

"I know. But I want to watch the movie."

I think at any other time my father would have continued the argument, or perhaps at any other time my mother would never have begun it in the first place. But he fell silent and read while the rest of us finished one bottle of champagne and opened another.

"Are you still angry at me, Gen?" my mother said during a commercial break. "I was never angry at you," he said.

But when we discovered she had fallen asleep, after Scrooge had learned to keep Christmas, he would not carry her upstairs. Perhaps it seemed too intimate a gesture to make while his three children stood around. Or perhaps, I thought, remembering how happy my mother had been the morning after their disastrous dinner, carrying her upstairs promised something afterward that he did not want to give. We woke her—"It's over? It's over?" she asked, like a small child who'd fallen asleep at the circus—and Brian led her upstairs.

Next morning she was up at seven, earlier than she'd been in weeks, to lie on the couch and open her presents. Jeff gave her a silk scarf with big bunches of purple grapes all over it, enormous and luxurious, and she slung it around her shoulders. Brian gave her a copy of Gibbon's *Decline and Fall of the Roman Empire*. She said brightly, "I've been meaning to read this for years," and the two of them laughed until they choked and had to be pounded on the back. Brian leaned toward me and whispered, "It's another one of those romance novels. The Duanes gave me the *Roman Empire* dust jacket."

I gave her a set of walkie-talkies, so we could communicate when she was in a different part of the house. My father gave her a platinum band of small diamonds in one perfect circle. It caught the light and turned it blue and pink, and though it fell down to her first knuckle when she moved, no one suggested she get it in a smaller size.

"It's called an eternity ring," said my father, almost shyly.

"I know," my mother said, the small stones brilliant against the dark blue of her velour robe. "It's beautiful, Gen. It's the nicest thing I've ever gotten."

Jonathan sent me a datebook, one of those thick leather ones that very busy women take out and put on the table at lunches, filled with phone numbers and memos to themselves and a page for each day of the year and a map of the London Underground, as though they ever traveled by anything but cab. The whole year to come moved like playing cards under my fingers, empty and clean, February, July, November.

I paged through, sitting on the floor beside the tree. My birthday in August was on a Friday, my mother's a Tuesday at the end of June. Easter did come early, at the end of March.

"Subtle, isn't he?" said Jeff as he looked over my shoulder at the empty white pages.

I still own that datebook. I use it every day now; I'd be lost without it, without all the phone numbers, the slips of paper with scribbled notes about times and consults and medication, the notes about where I have to be next Tuesday, next Friday, next month. Sometimes I feel if I lost it I would lose the linchpin of my life. But of course I remember that in one way I lost the linchpin years before, not long after I acquired the datebook. It was not an even swap.

When the year is done I take its pages, its scrawled and sloppy and often unintelligible record—what did "11—DMC" on May 12 mean, anyhow?—and put them in a small manila envelope, seal it, and put it in a shoe box. Jules, who has things thrown in boxes in every closet in her apartment, bank statements and telephone messages and old junk mail and family photographs, says I am anal and do this to bring surface order to a spiritually chaotic life. But by now, five years after the habit began, it has simply become one of those things you do, like the way you fold or ball your socks or whether you eat corn on the cob from left to right or right to left.

I never open the envelopes to look at those old pages. And no one, looking at them after I am gone, will know much more about me than they've known before, except perhaps, if it was not already manifest, that I am a very, very busy woman and that I like to use a fine-tip marker pen with black ink, not blue.

But what would surely perplex anyone who ripped open the yellow envelopes and looked inside are the first two months of the first year. I remember well that they are completely empty.

The datebook sat on my desk through January and February. I wrote Jules's number in it, which was unnecessary, since I knew it by heart. I wrote in Jeff's and Brian's addresses at school. I did not write in Jonathan's address; he had done it himself. In blue ballpoint. The only blue ballpoint entry in the book.

"Do you like it?" Jon asked. "I was going to get you the one with a week on a page but I figured it would never be enough, with all your running around. The day-on-a-page version makes it pretty fat, but I figured the trade-off would be worth it."

"It's great, Jon," I said.

"It was calling your name," he said.

And it was, it was calling the name of the old Ellen Gulden, the girl who would walk over her mother in golf shoes, who scared students away from writing seminars, who started work on Monday after graduating from Harvard with honors on a Thursday, who loved the moments in the office when she would look out at the impenetrable black of the East River, starred with the reflected lights of Queens, with only the cleaning crew for company, and think of her various superiors out at dinner parties and restaurants and her various similars out at downtown clubs or cheap but authentic places in Chinatown and say to herself, "I'm getting ahead." That Ellen Gulden, the one her boss suspected of using the dying-mother ploy to get more money or a better job title, would have covered every inch of these pages with the frantic scribble of unexamined ambition.

For two months I wrote nothing in it. I had no need. The big event of January was when the hospital bed was delivered and we moved the furniture from the den into the living room to accommodate it. The home of Kate Gulden was being dismantled bit by bit, going to that place where past perfect lives dwell, perhaps to live there side by side with the former Ellen Gulden, who ate ambition for breakfast and anyone who got in her way for lunch.

The last good afternoon I remember was when I learned to make bread. I kneaded and folded and patted down and covered up with a dishcloth and my mother and I talked about Teresa and what she did. As the bread rose we sat in the living room with our fat copies of *Anna Karenina*. I lost myself in the book, in Levin's scything under the hot sun, in Vronsky's self-absorption, in the romances and the intrigues and Anna's palpable misery and obsession. It was only when the light died in the room and I could no longer see the letters properly that I looked at my mother, who was looking at me, the book held open with her hand.

"I'm glad we did this one," I said in a rush, "because I'd really like your opinion. The last time I read it was for a course on women in literature and we had this young woman professor who said that the fatal flaw of the book was that it was written by a man and that Anna would have left her husband for her lover but that she never would have left her son, that if a woman had written the book she would have known that. I tried to talk to Papa about it once, but he kissed the whole idea off—I think he said that Anna stood for the body and Kitty for the spirit or something like that, which I suppose is right. But what do you think? Do you think she was right, that Anna would have stayed for the sake of the child?"

There was a long silence, and I thought she was thinking about what I had asked. And then quietly she said, "I can't see the words."

"I know," I said, "it's getting so dark." I turned on the table lamp. "You should have told me to turn it on earlier."

She shook her head, a shower of red glints, and she let the book slip from her grasp and onto the rug. "I can't see the words on the page anymore. I can't read anymore. My eyesight is going.

Like an old woman." She sighed deeply and then there was a sound, like a bone caught in her throat.

We sat in silence and finally she said, "It's hard for me to believe that any woman would willingly leave her child."

"Not for love?"

"That is love," she said. She reached down and picked up the book.

"I'll get you a magnifying glass," I said.

"A pill," she said. "I need another pill."

Later I told Teresa about my mother's eyesight, and she told me she was not surprised, that it might be some unusual side effect of the medication and the deterioration. "We had a book club," I started to say, and then I made that same sound my mother had, that swallowed sob.

"You will have to move on to something else," Teresa said.

"I'm scared shitless," I said, putting my face in my hands.

"Of course you are," Teresa said. "You are doing all of the right things. And that is the right thing now."

"I can't stand this much longer," I said.

It was quiet, so that I could hear the hands of the kitchen clock clicking round their inexorable orbit. Teresa waited a long time, and finally she said softly, with the first hint of sympathy or real softness I had ever heard in her voice, "You will stand it as long as you need to."

If it had not been for Teresa Guerrero I am not sure that I ever would have bathed or dressed. Like Baby Jane and her poor sister, my mother and I would have sat in the living room, in bathrobes and greasy hair. But because of Teresa, because I needed to make myself seem all right for her, I rose early, showered, cleaned last night's detritus off the kitchen counter, the plate from the leftover meal my father had taken from the oven faintly warmed by the tiny blue pilot, the plate from the cherry pie I had eaten before bed.

I was getting heavy; the only pants that fit anymore were the ones with the elastic waists. But my father looked just the same, drawn and distinguished, although some days he seemed better than others, and I always wondered if those were the days after the nights when he had had some associate professor, some administrative aide, on the creaky leather couch in his office. When I wondered that an anger as powerful as pain jumped in my gut, but I put it down because I could not afford it. I needed all my energy to get through the days now, now that my mother had begun to die in earnest.

Perhaps I was being romantic, but I think she made it happen herself, the slide, after the boys left. I remember how she had said "To hell with Easter," and I think that maybe for a long time she had struggled toward Christmas, toward the old traditions and the time together, that she had made up her mind she would marshal her strength for that time, in its way the apogee of the kind of life she had tried so hard to construct in that small and pretty white house, the life of family meals and pleasant rituals and pretty things.

She was so often gay during those two weeks, that sort of feverish gaiety they say people sometimes wrap around themselves for a moment's warmth before they put a gun into their mouths or step into the long tunnel of air from roof to pavement. I think that when Jeff had loaded his army surplus duffel next to Brian's in the back of his jeep, after he grabbed the roll bar and vaulted into the front seat, both of them packed in down and wool against the gray January morning, after my mother had held Brian's head on her shoulder, smoothing his tears away with the flat of her hand, after we two stood and waved good-bye—I think it was then that my mother gave herself permission to give up.

"I think she's lost the will to live," I said to Teresa one day a week later. "Is it that simple?"

"It is," she said with that faint curve of a smile, which in the beginning I believed was distant and a little condescending and now I saw simply as a dignified expression of understanding. "Your mother has been able to lead at least part of her life these last few months in the way she is accustomed to and loves. Perhaps now she realizes that is no longer true, that more and more she will become an invalid. They teach us there are stages in terminal illness: denial, anger. At the end comes reconciliation."

"Fuck reconciliation, Teresa."

"Not for you, Ellen. For her. I would not expect you to be reconciled."

Teresa came three times a week by then. One day Jules called when she was there, and when I called Jules back I told her I'd been with the nurse.

"Oh, that must be a day at the beach," said Jules, who had just broken off with a painter who said she was too needy because she complained when he tried to pick up waitresses at the restaurants where they ate together.

"No, she's great, Jules," I said. "She's like a combination shrink-priest."

"Some combination," said Jules. "And she takes good care of your mom?"

"She takes care of me, too. She talks to me. She keeps me sane. Sometimes I wonder which of us is her patient, actually. You and she are my links to the outside world. Or maybe you're my link to the outside world and she's my link to the inside world."

"You sound like you're in therapy," Jules said, chewing on something on the other end of the phone.

"Oh, please," I said, imitating Jules herself, who always said you could tell the people in therapy by how crazy they were.

"I think I might be changing my mind about that," Jules said softly. "I think I might need someone to talk to."

"You can talk to me."

"I know, sweet. But I can't tell you my troubles because my troubles are no troubles compared to your troubles." In the silence I could hear Jules chew and swallow. "Relative troubles, that's what we're looking at here. Does Teresa listen to your troubles without telling you hers?"

"I don't really think Teresa has troubles."

"God bless her," Jules said. "What a life."

Instead Teresa told me about other people's troubles in a way that was strangely soothing, that made me feel part of a great sorority of pain and suffering. She told me of how the woman with cancer of the pancreas had died in her husband's arms in bed, how the woman with breast cancer and the two small children had had a remission and didn't need Teresa anymore. "Will you have to go back to their house someday?" I said, wanting, like Scrooge, to see some scene of happiness connected with a death, and Teresa said with her eyes suddenly burning, "I pray not." Sometimes I forgot that there were other lives entwined with hers as intimately as were our own.

"Do you see someone?" I asked her one morning.

"I am seeing a man who lives in the city," she said. "But it is difficult to have a relationship at such a distance."

"Tell me about it," I said. "How did you meet him?"

"At church. My mother knows his mother. Until two years ago, I lived not far from him in Brooklyn."

"You used to live in the city? I had no idea. How did you wind up out here?"

"There is a camp for disadvantaged children about thirty miles from here. It is called Camp Dream. I went there when I was a child. Once we came to Langhorne for the movies. When I looked at it from the bus window I thought it looked like the sort of place I would like to live someday."

"So you just picked up and came here?"

"There is a shortage of nurses everywhere."

"But why did you leave the city? I love the city. When I slept in the city for the first time in my apartment, I remember feeling as if I was home for the first time in my entire life. Sometimes people say, oh, how can you sleep, all the noise? I listen to the horns and the ambulances, and it's like, life. Real life, right out-side."

"Yes, I know."

"So why did you leave?"

"How you love New York? That is how I hate it. The noise, the dirt. The real life. I have enough real life. When I am in my apartment here, I can hear the trees moving in the night. I will never go back to the city."

"Not to visit?"

"There is no one to visit. My mother died when I was eighteen. And the answer to your question is no, not of this illness and that is not why I do what I do. She was hit by a gypsy cab on Nostrand Avenue while she was on her way to work. The driver was very, very sorry, and so was I, and I left the city and came here. If the man I am seeing is interested enough, he will follow. If not, not."

"We have something in common. Our mothers, I mean."

"My mother was a hard woman who had lived a hard life."

"In what way?"

"I think I will leave that alone for now. There is no good way to tell people that they are lucky in their relations."

"I know that," I said. I looked over the living room, the piano and the prints and the framed photographs on the piano.

"I have never met your father," Teresa added. "I imagine he is an interesting man."

"Don't you ever wonder why you haven't met him?" I asked.

"He is at work when I am here."

"But don't you ever wonder why he isn't here, why he doesn't at least come by to meet you?"

"It sounds as if you are doing the wondering for both of us. And one of the things that it is important someone in my job understand is that illness brings out different qualities in different people. Some are enriched by it—yes, I know, you do not want to consider the possibility, but it is true, and I have seen it. Some people have a talent for it and some rise to the occasion. And some are diminished by their fear. They often deny, or withdraw."

"Jeff is right—you should be a shrink."

"Your brother is a very interesting person. I imagine your father is much like him."

"You imagine wrong. My father is much like me. Or I am much

like him. Or at least I was. Right now I'm not much like myself, if you know what I mean."

Teresa smiled again, such a small smile that sometimes you saw it in her eyes before her mouth, like something on a hospital monitor. "Suffering transforms," she said.

"Suffering sucks," I said.

"I agree. With both conclusions, actually."

No one came to see us. No one, except for the UPS man when Jules sent me books from the office, and manuscripts, too, so I wouldn't lose my editing touch. I stacked them in the corner of my bedroom and continued with *Anna Karenina,* even though I knew very well how it ended. I felt as though I had an obligation to go on until the train thundered out of the station.

Sometimes, when I went out to buy groceries or some books or a bouquet of daisies, because such things gave my mother pleasure out of all proportion to the act, I would run into some old friend, one of the Minnies, a faculty wife, and I could almost see the sentence forming in their minds before they said it: "I've been meaning to stop by, but . . ."

Another small spark of anger would flare in my chest, then die through lack of oxygen, except for the afternoon when I went into the bookstore to buy a magnifying glass. Teresa said she thought it was the medication affecting my mother's vision. But I think it was just one more part of her too tired to go on.

When Mrs. Duane began to say she'd been meaning to stop by,

I looked into her clear blue eyes, the color of sky, wise and so aware of the duplicity of what she was saying that they darted away from my own, and without thinking I interrupted, "Then do it. Don't tell me about it. Don't regret that you didn't. What she has is not catching."

"Ellen—"

"Don't," I said, my voice getting higher and louder. I realized that people in the store had stopped to listen but I didn't care. "No one has come to see my mother since the week before Christmas. She's lonely and she's sad and she thinks that everyone's forgotten her, and all because it's too uncomfortable for anyone to deal with anything deeper than winter ski plans and shopping for dinner." And I picked up my packages and left without paying.

I came home and put the magnifying glass on the table in the living room next to *Anna Karenina*. But I saw no evidence that it was being used. Still, I would not put her book back on the shelf with the two others. I would not declare the Gulden Girls Book and Cook Club defunct.

The next day Mrs. Duane called and asked if she could come over for lunch. I fixed chicken sandwiches and she and my mother ate at a properly laid table in the dining room—"placemats, Ellen," my mother had said. Mrs. Duane scarcely met my eyes. She gossiped with my mother about whose children were doing what and the January slump on Main Street.

I noticed that she assiduously avoided discussing the shortcomings of men, perhaps the greatest talking point when Jules and I had lunch together. And I wondered whether that was yet another difference between women of my mother's age and women of my own, or whether it was a difference between women who were single and women who were married and therefore had much, much more invested in their men than we did. Or perhaps it was because of how her friends felt about my mother and what they knew about my father. I wondered whether Mrs. Duane and the women like her had always done that around my mother, or whether they did it as a matter of course, not certain that any of their marriages were safe from being served up with the spinach salads and the iced tea.

My mother let me help her from her wheelchair into the dining-room chair in which my father usually sat, the one with arms, and that was where she was when Mrs. Duane arrived. She was wearing a sea-green turtleneck with a crewneck sweater in the same color, but the collar of the one and the bulk of the other could not quite hide her frailty.

The morning after her "lovely lunch," as she called it when she spoke of it to my father, she slept late and I was in the kitchen cleaning when I heard her faint footfalls on the old pine floors above me. There was the sound of the water running, the faint wailing of our pipes like a small and halfhearted banshee, the muffled closing of drawers and doors and then silence.

I sat down at the table with one of my mother's magazines, looking at spring perennials, although where I was going to plant perennials and why, when gardening bored me so, I could not have told you. I read the recipes and the instructions for making a bedskirt for a crib. Perhaps my mother was saving it for Halley, whose daughter must be overdue. From above me I heard a sound that I thought at first must be the pipes again, or a child calling from down the street, or perhaps a sudden bad-tempered fit of winter wind whipping around the dormers. It came again and I lifted my head. Again, and I went to the foot of the stairs.

"Ellen," came the cry.

I ran up those stairs as I had not run up since I was in high school, running to see if my father was in early, to tell him news and make it real—"I got into Princeton!" "I won the essay contest!" "I'm valedictorian!" How many times had I run in, banging doors, breathless, to tell him something and had to settle for her instead? How plain had it been on my face?

"Ellen," came the cry again.

Her bedroom was empty, the covers thrown back. Before my mother was sick I think the only time I had seen my parent's bed unmade was when they were in it, when I came in frightened after a bad dream, when I stuck my head in to tell them I had gotten home safely at one in the morning. A pair of knit pants and a tunic were on the chair, which had been moved closer to the bathroom door so that my mother could walk, stopping for a handhold as she went, from bed to table to chair to bath. The bathroom door was closed, and I knocked softly.

"You have to come in," my mother said with a catch in her voice.

The room was warm and smelled rank, the smell of perspiration and something sweeter, deeper. My mother lay in the tub, her arm across her eyes, perhaps practicing the child's fiction of believing that if she could not see me I could not see her.

"I can't get out," she said.

Silently I picked up the towel that was on the bench just next to the tub—she had made the bench from a kit, I remember, then painted it and sanded some of the paint down so it would look old—and hung it over my arm. I took her by the hands and tried to pull, but her legs scrabbled helplessly in the water, slick with bath oil, finding no purchase on the smooth porcelain of the tub. Then I reached around her chest and, with one great tug, pulled her over the edge and onto the bench. I was panting and the front of my denim shirt was wet with bathwater and, perhaps, perspiration. She weighed nothing, but felt so heavy.

I had never before and have never since set about a task which required me so completely to act without thinking. My mother leaned her elbow on the edge of the tub and her head on her hand and wept as I toweled off her poor ravaged body. I took it piece by piece, bit by bit, because I knew that if I allowed myself to really look at her, at what she had become, I would be done for.

But she knew, and while I couldn't speak, she couldn't keep silent. Suddenly she wiped her face with her hand and said, "I never wanted you to see me like this. I should have just stayed there until your father got home. I couldn't figure out what was worse, having you see me like this, or him."

"I would have come up eventually," I said, drying her shoulders.

"I would have died before I would have let you see me like this. Just . . . rotten. That's what I look like now, like a peach when it's all rotten. Like bad fruit. Why can't I just die and be done with it? It's a crime for a human being to have to live like this. Rotten like this." And she let her head drop down again.

It was an apt description. Her skin was slack on her body in places, like soft fruit when it's past its prime, on the insides of her thighs, her upper arms. But most of her flesh was stretched tight over her bones, a faint shroud for the skeleton: the two long bones running parallel beneath the skin of her arms and legs, the cage of pelvis and ribs. In her face every bit of skull was visible where the flesh had gone, leaving only the clear outlines of the understructure, the yawning Os of the eye sockets, the sharp peaks of the cheekbones, the hinge of the jaw, from which all the padding had disappeared. Her breasts were flat and sagging, like those of old women I'd seen in pictures of primitive tribes, and her pubic hair was nearly gone.

I went behind her, and, hooking my hands under her armpits, pulled her into a standing position. She held my arm tightly and shuffled into the bedroom. I helped her on with her underpants and her pants, her tunic, as she held on to the edge of the dresser. But I never touched her, not really, never patted her, much less held her close. And if I told you today that I've wondered about that a hundred times since then, whether I should have wrapped my arms around her instead of the towel, whether I should have rocked her as she had done so many times for me, I would be lying about the number, because it has been many many more.

I never try to remember how she looked that morning. I remember that I never touched her, and I never looked her in the eye. When I was done she moved slowly to the bed, like a blind person in an unfamiliar room, and she lay down on her back, staring at the ceiling. For the first time I noticed that the scarf Jeffrey had given her for Christmas had been slung over the mirror atop her dresser, so that a spill of glossy purple grapes and green grape leaves and the sinuous twist of vines hung in place of any reflection.

"I'm going back to sleep," she said.

That January, when they delivered the hospital bed, leaving the den in disarray and the living room crowded with furniture, leaving a long scratch in the oak floor of the hallway because they were careless with a metal side rail, she didn't say anything. She just got in and turned on her side so that she was looking out the window, out the window that looked out on our driveway and the side of the house next door. It was as though something was broken, but I think it broke in the bathroom, on that bench.

At the end she was both child and mother, both teacher and student, both strength and supplicant. At the end she lay in the den, in the bed with the high bars on the side, so that she would not roll out at night. Sometimes I would stand in the doorway in the dark, quiet and observant as a Peeping Tom, and watch her thrash and cry and talk, bits of disconnected things, about my father, about her babies, always babies. About people whose names meant nothing to me, who might be ghosts, figments, or regrets and missed opportunities. When she talked to her brother Steven one night, her eyes open even though their glaze made their blindness as clear as a white cane, that was when I stayed until the sky outside began to lighten. Somehow I thought if she talked to her brother, dead so many years ago, it meant she was seeing another country in her mind's eye and that her heart was hammering toward its inevitable full stop.

Often I watched with tears dripping down my face onto the front of my nightgown, but it was as though they were an inert function of my body, like a runny nose. There were no sobs, none of the heaves that you associate with a crying jag. There was no sound but my mother's thick and arduous breathing as I stood across the room, bleeding tears.

Once, when I came downstairs, the side of her bed had been lowered, and my father was wedged uncomfortably next to her. He and I looked at one another in the darkness, but I turned and went upstairs and if he followed afterward I did not hear him.

That room had white pine paneling on the walls and flowered curtains at the windows, a rose-and-green print I can still evoke in memory. The green couch had been carted into the living room, the hospital bed positioned in front of the wall of bookshelves so it faced the television. But all of the light and prettiness evoked by the decor was negated that month by the light, which was dim and gray, the dour grudging clouded sunshine of January and February. Now, today, I feel my heart begin to sink on New Year's Day and lift only—inevitably, ironically—when Easter is on the horizon. My miserable anniversaries.

One night the branches of the Douglas fir at the corner of the house lashed my windows and hers all night long, and by morning the snow was falling thick and fast, so that there was no light in the room at all and I had to turn on the lamps in the middle of the day. The snow began to drift until finally it reached almost to the windows. My mother kept her head turned to the side all day, except when she drank her soup, lifting the spoon to her mouth in a long slow arc, dropping her mouth open when the spoon was only halfway there, as though she could no longer trust herself to coordinate her motions more precisely. "The snow is so beautiful," she said, handing me back the mug, and then she fell asleep.

Beneath the rich yellow light of the lamp I read and, when my eyes became tired, went into the kitchen to judge the progress of the storm by the thickness of the blanket in the back, ripples and hillocks where it covered small bushes, a rise in the yard that marked an azalea I had protected with an upturned peach basket and a burlap bag. The phone in the kitchen rang like a scream in the quiet house, and when I went to answer it I saw that the day had slipped away and it was nearly seven. Only the light told me the time, and the light had been disguised all afternoon.

"Ellen," my father said, "I cannot possibly get home in this. The security people have closed off both the footbridges and no one has been able to get out to plow. I will sleep somewhere here."

"In your office?"

"I don't know. Several of the other people in the department have pullout couches. If I can find someone who's already gone home, I'll use theirs. If you try me here and there's no answer, that's what I've done."

"Uh-huh," I said.

"How is your mother?"

"The same."

"Tell her that I'll see her tomorrow."

"Yes."

"Are you all right?"

"Fine."

I think I remember that when I put down the phone there was a flicker of the thought that if my mother died during the night, with the snow falling thick outside, while my father was marooned on a sofa bed with some erudite honors graduate of a Seven Sisters college with strong opinions on Henry James and a soft spot for narrow handsome married men, that he would suffer with the memory the rest of his life. Or perhaps that was how I remembered it afterward, when memory plays so many tricks.

In the den my mother's eyes were open, looking at nothing. "Who was that?" she said softly.

"Your husband," I said in what I thought was a voice without expression. "He cannot seem to find a way to get home, so he is staying at the college. He says he will see you tomorrow."

"It's a bad storm," my mother said, looking out the window again.

"It's not that bad," I said.

"Ellen," she said, and her voice was stronger than it had been in days, "put down the book." In fact her voice was stronger, sterner, than I had ever remembered it, except the day that I mocked the little girl with Down's syndrome who once lived at the foot of our hill and my mother turned cold and pitiless in a way I had always thought only my father could. She was like a sprinter now, at rest until those brief necessary moments when she would become herself for just a few minutes.

"What has happened between you and your father?"

"What do you mean?"

"You have been very angry with him since you came home. If you're going to be angry at anyone about all this, you should be angry at me. I'm why you're here, not him."

"Mama, this is not about you. And it's not something we should discuss. I have my own differences with Papa that have nothing to do with you."

"They do have to do with me, especially now. He's all you'll have."

"Stop. Just stop." I raised my hands, palm out, as though to push the words away.

"No, you stop. You and your father will need each other. And you and your brothers. And I hope he can have more of a relationship with the boys, too, if I'm not there to get in the way. But you and he already have such a bond. You're so much alike."

"Please don't say that."

"Why? Because he's not perfect? Because he's not the man you once thought he was?"

"Mama, I can't talk to you about this."

"Ellen," she said, struggling to turn toward me, her hands like pale claws on the railing of the bed, her legs scissoring away the white sheets, "listen to me because I will only say this once and I shouldn't say it at all. There is nothing you know about your father that I don't know, too."

The two of us stared silently into one another's eyes, and I think that after a moment she gave a little nod and then lay back.

"And understand better," she added.

"All right," I said.

"You make concessions when you're married a long time that you don't believe you'll ever make when you're beginning," she said. "You say to yourself when you're young, oh, I wouldn't tolerate this or that or the other thing, you say love is the most important thing in the world and there's only one kind of love and it makes you feel different than you feel the rest of the time, like you're all lit up. But time goes by and you've slept together a thousand nights and smelled like spit-up when babies are sick and seen your body droop and get soft. And some nights you say to yourself, it's not enough, I won't put up with another minute. And then the next morning you wake up and the kitchen smells like coffee and the children have their hair all brushed and the birds are eating out of the feeder and you look at your husband and he's not the person you used to think he was but he's your life. The house and the children and so much of what you do is built around him and your life, too, your history. If you take him out it's like cutting his face out of all the pictures, there's a big hole and it's ugly. It would ruin everything. It's more than love, it's more important than love. Think of Anna."

"Anna?"

"In the book." She gestured toward the end table where my paperback copy of *Anna Karenina* lay.

"But you didn't finish reading it."

"I'd read it before." She looked at the snow falling, tiny floating ghosts tapping against the window, spinning in and out of the blue-black beyond. "I'd read them all before. I just wanted a chance to read them again. I wanted a chance to read them with you."

I leaned over the rail of the bed, its metal cold and hard against my chest, and took her hand in mine, her grip strong, painful almost, and then lax. I slid the railing down and I put my head on the sheets, atop the cage of her pelvis, no fat or flesh to protect it. I cried until the sheets were wet, and she stroked my hair, over and over, the dry flesh making a faint sibilant sound, like the smallest whisper. Then in a softer voice, she began to speak again.

"It's hard. And it's hard to understand unless you're in it. And it's hard for you to understand now because of where you are and what you're feeling. But I wanted to say it, I didn't say it very well, I'm no writer, but I wanted to say it because I won't be able to say it when I need to, when it's one of those nights and you're locking the front door because of foolishness about romance, about how things are supposed to be. You can be hard, and you can be judgmental, and with those two things alone you can make a mess of your life the likes of which you won't believe. I think of a thousand things I could teach you in the next ten years, and I think of how everything important you learned the first twenty-four you learned from your father and not me, and it hurts my heart, to know how little I've gotten done."

"No, Mama," I whispered.

"Yes, yes, yes, yes, somebody let me speak the truth, somebody let me," she cried. "Your father says I'll only upset myself, and you say, please, no, Mama, and only Teresa lets me speak. Saying it is the only thing that makes me feel better, even the drugs aren't as good as that. All the things we don't say, all the words we swallow, and it makes nothing but trouble. I want to talk before I die. I want to be the one who gets to say things, who gets to think the deep thoughts. You'll all talk when I'm gone. Let me talk now without *shushing* me because it hurts you to hear what I want to say. I'm tired of being *shushed*."

"What do you want to say?" I said, lifting my head and pushing my damp hair aside. "Go ahead and say it."

"I just said everything I wanted to say, except that I feel sad. I feel sad that I won't be able to plan your wedding. Don't have a flower girl or a ring bearer—they always misbehave and distract from the bride. And don't have too many people."

"Mama, I don't know that I'll ever get married."

"Don't say things like that, Ellen. Think about what I just told you."

"All right. What else?"

"I feel afraid that when I fall asleep I will never wake up. I miss sleeping with your father."

"Should I tell him that?"

"I already have."

"What else?"

"If I knew you would be happy I could close my eyes now and rest." Her voice was beginning to sink and die, as though it was going down the drain, rush of words to trickle of whisper. "It's so much easier."

"I know it is. I wish you could."

"No, not that. The being happy. It's so much easier, to learn to love what you have instead of yearning always for what you're missing, or what you imagine you're missing. It's so much more peaceful."

"I'll try," I said.

"It doesn't work that way." And suddenly she was asleep. Her mouth hung open and her hair was scraped back from her forehead, lank because we had not washed it for several days, not since the last time Teresa had come. The lines across her forehead were cut deep, as though someone had done them with a ruler and a pencil. The sheet over her midsection was dark with my tears.

Everything you know, I know, she'd said, and it was true. I was the ignorant one. I'd taken a laundry list of all the things she'd done and, more important to me, all the things she'd never done, and turned them into my mother, when they were no more my mother than his lectures on the women of Dickens were my father.

Our parents are never people to us, never, they're always character traits, Achilles' heels, dim nightmares, vocal tics, bad noses, hot tears, all handed down and us stuck with them. Our dilemma is utter: turn and look at this woman, understand and pity her, like and talk with her, recognize that she has taken the cold cleanliness of the spartan rooms in which she grew up and turned them, within her considerable and perhaps wounded heart, into a life-long burst of cooking and cosseting and making her own little corner of the world pretty and welcoming, and the separation is complete—but when that happens you will have to be an adult. There is only room in the lifeboat of your life for one, and you always choose yourself, and turn your parents into whatever it takes to keep you afloat.

Just before midnight she woke. She licked her lips slowly, twisting and turning her arms on the sheets, then turned her head.

"Is it morning yet?" she said.

"No."

"I need pills," she said.

It was a new vial, nearly full. She gulped one down, her throat working; coughed and then sipped again, her whole body moving with the effort. She sighed and it rattled deep in her throat, half groan.

"Help me, Ellen," she whispered. "I don't want to live like this anymore."

We stared at each other in the half-light of the lamps.

"Please," she said. "You must know what to do. Please. Help me. No more."

"It'll be better in the morning."

"No," she said, and groaned again. "It will not. It will not." She sounded like a tired and irritable child. She wrapped her fingers around my wrist, the wrist of the hand that held the pills. Her grip was surprisingly strong, and for some reason I thought of those people who lift Volkswagens off babies pinned beneath, of people trapped in caves and found alive, saved by a diet of snow, long past the time when they should have died.

"Please," she said. "Help me. I don't want this." But I could tell that the pill was already beginning to take effect, or perhaps that the effort of the words, the request, the hand on my arm, had put her under. She looked at me sadly from beneath lids that began to drop like those of some wise old bird. "Help me," she whispered. "You're so smart. You'll know what to do." Then her eyes closed completely. "Please," she whispered once more.

I slept that night in a chair in the den, fell asleep as the snow continued to fall. It covered everything without any sound except the scratch of the pine branches against the side of the house. I woke to the ugly fluorescent brightness of a world deep in fallen snow, covered with pitiless whiteness. It was a world changed forever, a world in which I found it difficult to meet my mother's eyes.

It must be terrible to bury someone you love in early May, when the ground is beginning to thaw and stretch and turn bright green and the smell of lilacs tumbles down from the bushes like a little benediction. Or in September, when the noon sun is still warm on your face but the evenings are cool enough for flannel and an extra blanket dragged up from the footboard in the middle of the night.

Or at Christmas. It must be terrible at Christmas.

February is a suitable month for dying. Everything around is dead, the trees black and frozen so that the appearance of green shoots two months hence seems preposterous, the ground hard and cold, the snow dirty, the winter hateful, hanging on too long. At the beginning of the month I had bought my mother anemones at the florist on Main Street, paid fifteen dollars for a tiny bunch because they seemed, with their fragile lavender and bright red, to represent something that seemed as distant as the moon. I put them on the table next to the window, so that when she looked out she saw, not just the gray piles of old plowed snow at the edge of the driveway, like slag from some quarry, not just the side of the neighboring house and the big oak groaning in the winter winds, but those frail and beautiful things, bending their heavy heads toward her. But after only two days they fell, drooping almost to the dusty tabletop, their stems defeated, perhaps by a draft from beneath the sill. And I threw them away.

"Lovely, Ellie," she whispered sometimes, even when they were gone. "Lovely flowers."

Teresa came one morning and attached the little machine, like a tiny tape recorder with its red digital numbers, that would pump morphine into my mother's catheter whenever she pushed a button on its side. Teresa programmed it and taught me how to do it, too. "We will have to say how much is enough, and for how long," said Teresa.

"Could she overdose with this?" I said.

Teresa looked at me, one brow raised slightly. "Not likely," she said.

My mother winced when Teresa lodged the needle in the catheter, but when it was taped in place and the little box placed at her side she said she felt nothing except the pull of the tape on her tender skin. "I can retape it, Mrs. Gulden," said Teresa, smoothing her hair, held back from her face with a black band. "Perhaps it is too tight."

"No, Teresa," my mother said. "It's fine. Thank you."

We sat by her side for almost an hour without speaking, Teresa and I, she making notations in the small log she always carried, me finishing the background on the sunflower pillow. As she slept, my mother pulled fretfully at the diapers she now wore. Three times in the past week she had soiled the bed, and I had called Teresa, who was not supposed to do such things—they had a health aide to change beds, someone not as skilled or as salaried as a nurse—but had insisted that this was no time to have someone new and foreign in our home. After Teresa cleaned my mother and helped her onto the sofa, I gathered up the sheets with a great deal of bustle and carried them to the basement, holding my breath so that I would not gag.

"I'm so sorry," my mother said each time.

Finally Teresa had taken her hand and sat on the side of her bed. "Mrs. Gulden, I would like to catheterize you," she said.

My mother's hand came up slowly to touch the small mound on her chest, above her heart.

"A urinary catheter," said Teresa. "So you need not use the bedpan or depend so much on Ellen."

"Oh no, Teresa," she said. "I don't need that."

"I think perhaps you do."

"No, no."

"Then I think perhaps you should wear protective pants."

"Oh no," she said, and lay back on the pillows. Tears began to slide from beneath her eyelids down the furrows from eyes to nose and nose to chin. "This is too much."

"I know it is upsetting," said Teresa softly, stroking the back of my mother's hand. "But I believe it will be easier for you. And for Ellen, too."

But whenever my mother dropped off to sleep she pulled at the diapers as she did now, as though when she was unconscious they became the tangible reminder of the pain, the disintegration, the life that had become a half life.

She ate nursery food when she ate, which was not often. She ate oatmeal, applesauce, puddings, yogurt. Her lips were cracked and dry, and several times a day I smoothed petroleum jelly over them so that they would not peel or bleed. It had become difficult to tell whether she was awake or asleep under the thin blanket of consciousness, or simply lying with her eyes closed, thinking the unimaginable thoughts that anyone must feel when they are standing on the bluff overlooking the abyss.

"How are the boys getting on?" she said slowly after Teresa had gone.

"Fine, I guess. Jeff is his usual wisecracking self. Brian has a new roommate and seems to like him better than the old one."

"Good. I worry about Brian."

"Do you want me to bring them home, Mama?" I asked.

"No, Ellen," she said clearly.

That last afternoon I gave her cream of tomato soup for lunch, but after three spoonfuls she shook her head, perhaps because the act of moving the spoon from mug to mouth was so slow, so torturous, so messy that I had to put on a new top sheet afterward. She wore her velour housecoat, its nap flattened by the days in bed, and from beneath it her legs were sticks.

"I look like those people in the films about the camps," she whispered, looking down.

I tucked the clean sheet, with its nice fresh smell, in around her, and pushed back her hair. On the metal cart in the corner that held her pills, her water, a box of tissues, now her soup mug, was a tiny picture in a heart-shaped frame of a newborn, its face the color of your skin after a hot shower. Her tiny fists were balled up and thrown over her head as though she was surrendering, and her face looked like an uncooked biscuit with raisins for eyes. The dome of her head, atop which there was only fuzz, was off-center and misshapen. Halley had had her baby and had brought over the hospital picture to give to my mother. At the door I said that my mother could not have visitors, but then a voice had called faintly, "It's all right, Ellie," and I had brought Halley in for a few minutes at my mother's bedside. She was nursing, she said, and could not stay long because her milk was coming in. But at the door she hugged me and said, "I'm so sorry, so sorry," as she wept. There were dark circles under her eyes and her hair looked nearly as unkempt as my mother's. Ground down by maternity, the two of them, I thought.

"This must be so hard on you," she had sobbed, trying to muffle the sound with a tissue she pulled from her pocket.

"It's almost over," I said.

When I came back into the room my mother had been staring at the photograph. "That baby is no beauty," I said.

"Babies are never beauties, especially first babies. They're a long time coming out, and they get knocked up in the process."

"The little mother doesn't look so good, either."

"She'll be fine," said my mother. "It's hard work, but she'll manage. When I think of the people I've known who've had children who had no business even owning a cat—well, they all get raised somehow."

"You were a good mother," I said.

"I worked hard," she had said.

It was around four when she woke up and started to turn toward me. Then, remembering, she reached up and pushed the button that released the liquid morphine into her catheter and from there to a vein. She closed her eyes and her breathing became hoarse and very loud, like the noise a stick makes when you run it down the length of a fence and it hits the pickets, one by one, with that surprising carrying sound. I paced my breathing with her own, the two of us raising and lowering our chests in unison to keep ourselves alive. "That works better," she said after a few minutes. Her hand found the medication machine again and pressed, but I knew nothing would come out. Perhaps it had a placebo effect, for she slept again for another hour. I turned on the lamps around the room after I saw her eyes glittering in the half darkness.

"I love you, Ellen," she said.

"I love you, too, Mama."

"I've always known it," she said, and she smiled, the old smile, so warm and full that it was like the moon laid on its side. It was in her eyes, too, and her whole face, so that all the devastation of the last six months fell before it, her whole soul shining out at me.

I tried to smile back but my mouth and chin quivered uncontrollably and my eyes blinked as though I had a tic.

"Gen?" she said. "Is your father here?"

"He has a late class today, doesn't he?"

She closed her eyes and her forehead furrowed deeply. Then she nodded. "I hope he's home soon," she said.

"I'll call him," I said, as I'd said before, but this time she did not try to stop me.

Inside the kitchen I dropped down at the table, my hands shaking, and pushed the buttons on the phone. Twice I misdialed and when I finally had the number right it rang and rang and I could see it, the office with its wall of untidy bookshelves, the books shoved wherever they would fit, stacked atop one another, spilling onto the floor near the big heavy desk with the narrow drawers down each side, books under the two nondescript chairs where the students sat, books climbing one side of the scratched and creased brown leather couch on which there was one pillow, needlepointed by my mother, that said, CALL ME ISHMAEL.

"Come on, Papa, come on," I whispered, but there was no answer and something inside me said, of course not, of course, there never is, there never was, just the incessant ringing, come home, come here, talk to me, tell. Tell. Tell. But there was no answer.

"Gen?" my mother called with that plaintive tone in her voice again.

"I'm going to campus to get him," I called. "There's something wrong with his phone."

I took my down jacket from the peg near the back door and fished in the pocket for my keys. It was the first time I had been outside for three days, and the cold was shocking, the sort of still and bitter cold that freezes all the soft and vulnerable parts, the membranes inside your nose, the end of your ears, the tips of your fingers. At first the car coughed and would not turn over, and again I said, "Come on, come on." I could not have explained my urgency except that my mother had never before called for my father at work—"bothered him during the day," she called it—except for the day when her father had had his stroke. Good news or bad, we waited until he came home, until he had taken his leather case from the back seat of the car and come up the steps and into the kitchen, until the door had closed and he had joined the family.

At the green the streets were almost deserted, the store windows impenetrably covered with a gloss of steam, heat within and freezing air without. The gears made a grinding sound as I climbed the road along the river to the small bridge that led from the town to the campus. The bridge was slick with ice, and I downshifted when the back end of the car began to fishtail. But still I kept my foot to the gas, desperate to give my mother what she so clearly wanted. I was afraid that when I came back to the house she might already be dead. I knew that if that happened I would never forgive my father, nor he me.

The end of the bridge sloped down sharply to a set of stone pillars, each with a plaque: LANGHORNE on one, COLLEGE on the other. I drove past the parking lot of the new science building, past the stolid gym and the two nondescript language classroom buildings to the old gray stone building with the word ENGLISH in capitals square as shoe boxes above the double doors. As I parked the car in the fire lane out front, the campus lights, tall poles with vaguely Victorian globes atop them, came on, and yellow lights twinkled all over the dim walkways like something on the London streets in the days of Dickens.

"Name, Miss?" said the security guard.

"Professor Gulden's daughter," I said, and ran past him up the stairs four flights, until on the last landing my heart rang in my ears.

The door to my father's office was closed and the lights in the waiting area outside off. By the red glow of an exit light and a low-hanging fluorescent in the hall, I could see a piece of paper taped to his door. But it was only a sign-up sheet for conferences for freshman English students, those hapless dozen assigned to what had always been the class my father most loathed teaching.

The door of the office was locked. The rest of the hallway was dark and the only sounds were the faint ones of cars and the occasional calling voice from outside and below.

"Goddamnit," I said aloud.

Downstairs the guard sprawled, legs apart, in a chair next to the sign-in book. "You still need to sign in, Miss," he said unhappily.

"Have you seen Professor Gulden?" I said.

"He came down and left about ten minutes before you got here," he said. "I tried to tell you, but you went too fast."

Without answering I ran back out to the car and started the engine. The radio was on, perhaps had been on all the way over without my noticing it. There was an outbreak of civil war in the Sudan and a budget deadlock in Washington. In Texas a twenty-year-old man had been executed in the electric chair, and five children had died in a school bus accident. The forecast was for colder weather overnight. I hit the stanchion of the bridge with the right front bumper of the car, slammed on the brakes, backed up, and kept on going. The street lamps cast round moons of pure white light on the black asphalt of the streets. As I came around the circle, I could see the Duanes locking up the bookstore. It was such an ordinary night in Langhorne. From outside, through the lace cotton curtains, our kitchen looked as safe and warm as it always had.

Inside, my father's book bag was on the table. In the den he bent over my mother, lifted the small canister that fed the flow of morphine into her veins, smoothed back her hair. "Where the hell were you?" he said softly without turning.

"At the college, looking for you."

"Why?" he said, turning.

"She was asking for you. She wanted you."

He turned back and ran his hand over the surface of her hair and down her raddled neck to her collarbone, its line a shelf above the downward slope of her chest. "You and I must have just passed one another," he said. "I could have killed you when I arrived and the house was empty."

"You were on your way here and I was on my way there," I said. "Like an O. Henry story."

"Comedy of errors," he said. "I should have known. It was just the shock of finding her alone. How has she been?"

"Not good."

"Has she eaten?"

"Not much."

My father touched the machine with a fingertip, as though he was afraid of it. "This is a pump version of her medication?"

I nodded.

"Is it helping?"

"I think so."

"My poor Kate," he said softly, and as if she heard him she stirred, plucked at the mass of paper wadding at her crotch one last time, and slowly opened her eyes.

"Gen," she said.

"Yes, dear."

Both of them turned and looked at me, my mother slowly, as though it required great effort. She smiled. "Go take a rest, Ellen," she said.

I'm not sure, even now, even after I've been asked more times than I can count, exactly how I spent the next few hours. I only know that as long as I heard the murmur of quiet conversation from that room I did not intrude, and I heard them for longer than I could have imagined possible. Once I heard my mother's voice raised, thought I heard her crying, thought I heard the word "Please!," one soprano note of entreaty. Once I heard my father's voice raised, thought I heard him curse loudly and hit the surface of something hard with his hand. But much of what I heard was the sound of two people talking quietly a room away, that murmur that sounds like pigeons in the park, wood doves just beyond the line where the lawn meets the trees.

I did take a shower, and I lay on my bed, soaking my pillow with my wet hair, and I think I dozed off for an hour or so. The house was very quiet and a half-moon was visible outside my window, the clouds moving across its profile.

When I went back downstairs the door to the den was open and in the light, the floor and walls thick with shadows that rose and fell and wavered with slow synchronized movements, my parents were sitting facing one another. My father was in a straight chair, with a plain china bowl in his lap, and my mother had the back of the hospital bed canted almost all the way up, so she seemed to be sitting upright.

Her head was angled far from her chest, her mouth open, her

eyes dull, except when he finally finished his slow arc of filling the spoon, lifting it to the level of her mouth, and bringing it forward. Slowly she would bring her lips together and apart, and then with a visible movement of her neck and jaw muscles would swallow, her head falling back.

She looked like a baby bird and he like someone feeding a baby. The motion went on, head forward, spoon forward, spoon in, head back. Each time they made contact her eyes would blaze, but I believe now, having replayed the scene so often in my mind, in the sepia tones that I believe lit it even then, that she was looking not at the dollop of rice pudding but past it at him.

Over and over I would see him lift that spoon in the lamplight. It was the most vivid way in which I remembered my parents together after I had lost them both, and in memory I tried to decipher it, to deconstruct the movements, the motives, the emotions, the truth. Although my idea of truth now is not what it once was.

I passed on from the doorway of the den into the living room and sat there reading the same page of *Anna Karenina* over and over again, the one in which Anna rides on horseback in a black habit, her hair in curls. I still remember that, as though it's yet another picture on our piano: the horse, the habit, the dark curls. And I thought of how my mother had already read this book, and both the others, how she had formed the book club to break through the reserve of her own daughter, to find something that the two of us could talk about before it was too late for the two of us to ever talk again. How deft she had been. "Tell," she'd said, and I had. But she'd done it without ever saying the word.

After about an hour my father came into the room, pushing his hair back with his hand. His eyes were edged sharply in red.

"No one should have to live like that," he said.

"How was she?"

"No one should have to live like that," he repeated. "No one."

"That's what she said."

"I know," he said, his mouth working. "She's right. She

shouldn't have to live like that anymore." He rubbed his eyes with the flat of his hand. "She wants me to sleep with her in there," he added. "I can't. I can't. Not tonight. I'm going upstairs."

"I'll stay up for a while," I said.

"That's not necessary, Ellen."

"I can't sleep anyway," I said.

"Let her be," he said.

For another hour I sat in the living room, looking around at all her handiwork: the big brass bowl on the cherry chest of drawers against one wall, with the old map of Langhorne framed and hung above it, the pillows needlepointed with big blowsy roses on the velvet couch, the coffee table that had been a desk before she cut its legs down in the garage, cutting herself with the saw, holding her hand to her mouth as she came into the kitchen for the first-aid kit that was kept in the second drawer next to the sink. Her blood always looked so bright against her white redhead's skin.

I stood in the doorway of the den for a long time and watched her after that, tired as I was. But she was not restless that night. There were no sentence fragments, no muttered names, no pushing at her hair or the hated diapers with her fingers. Her mouth hung open and she breathed in and out through it with a deep soughing noise, almost like a growl, and between those breaths a great silence hung in the air, a silence like forever.

When I sat down at the side of the bed I took her hand in mine. It was cold, and I could feel the bones, like little brittle sticks in my own warm and sweaty palm. I began to breathe in tandem with her, and when I inhaled it felt as if whole minutes went by as I waited for her to let the air out again and let me do the same. In. Out. In. Out. Perhaps it was because the breaths were so far apart, perhaps I was faint, but after a long while I began to feel as though I was watching the two of us from some corner of the ceiling, looking down on this evaporated woman with her red hair thin and dull now, her hands lying palm up on the sheet as though in some gesture of entreaty, and her daughter next to her, her rather square face hung about with a curtain of dark hair, her free hand plucking at the knee of her old black pants.

In. Out. In. Out. They breathed in unison, and as I watched them I wondered which would stop first. And then one did, the mother, and the sound brought me back to myself, out of the daze into which the slow repetitive sound had allowed me to fall. There was a sound like that a car makes when it won't start on a cold morning, an *eh eh eh eh* deep in my mother's throat, and I held tight to her hand as though I would crush it in my own long strong fingers. A shudder shook her body, and then the sound once more: *eh eh eh,* and one last long inhalation of breath.

I waited for her to exhale, waited for so long, holding her fingers, feeling them small under my own. I laid my head down near the foot of the bed but I did not let go until I could tell by a faint shift of the black outside that it was almost morning. Her hand was cold when I finally laid it on the sheet. The sheets were still as the snow had been after it stopped falling, still and clean. And when I looked at her face there was nothing of her there, nothing at all, as though she'd tiptoed out in the middle of the night when I'd dozed, just as she used to do when I was a little girl and fell asleep while she crooned "Safe and sound."

I was still sitting there at sunup when my father came down the stairs heavily and stood in the doorway, shivering, with cold or something else. "How is she?" he said.

"She's dead," I replied. "I'll go make the coffee."

PART TWO

I had not acquired much during the five months that I had lived in my old room, tracing the marching flowers of the stenciling around the edge of the ceiling in the dark, lulled to sleep finally by the familiar shape of the dormer window, awakened sometimes by the crying from the floor below, living and breathing and finally dying in tandem with my mother. There was the datebook, still on my desk, still empty. There was the bulky oatmeal-colored sweater my parents had given me for Christmas: that was how our presents were always labeled, although we always knew our mother bought them. There was a pair of jeans Jeff left behind at Thanksgiving that I had pirated, and a new pair of boots I bought at the mall because my mother had so wanted me to buy myself something one day in October.

And there was the navy-blue suit I bought for the funeral, to wear with a pair of old black patent pumps I found in the back of my closet, left over from high school graduation. I would not be taking that suit with me. I would not be wearing it again.

So when I packed my duffel two weeks after my mother died,

a week after she was buried, there was little more to put in than I had taken out—less, actually, because two pairs of cords were too snug now and I left them in a drawer.

I didn't prepare to go right away. I stayed one morning to oversee the dismantling of the hospital bed and the return of the wheelchair, folded like an empty suit, its plastic leather seat slumping dejectedly. On another I rearranged the furniture and called someone in to shampoo the upholstery and the rugs. The silver needed to be polished. I finished the background of the sunflower pillow and took it to a shop where they would fill it and sew on a velvet back; they knew what to do from all the other times my mother had picked out the shape, the fabric, the edging. As I was turning to walk out and heard the little bell on the door jingle above me, like the one Jimmy Stewart hears at the end of *It's a Wonderful Life,* my umbrella half opened against a cold and heavy winter rain, I stopped and told them to send the pillow, when it was done, to Jules's address in the city. I had decided I wanted to keep it.

One morning as I made coffee I told my father that I would be willing to clean out the closets in his room. He did not look up from his bran and his *New York Times* as he said, "No. Absolutely not."

But after he had gone to the college, wearing the same turtleneck he'd worn for three days, I went upstairs and pushed aside the white louvered closet doors, running my hands over the rainbow of clothes, the bright blues, the summer whites, the tartans, the purples and reds. And then, without thinking, I reached out my arms and hugged them. I smelled lilac eau-de-toilette and Jean Naté and Joy and attar of roses all jumbled together, the day perfumes and the night ones, the bath oils and the face lotions. Over them all was the smell of something else, but remote, musty, so dead that it was worse than it had been when I stood in the cemetery next to the oak casket, so clean, so shiny, like the table in the kitchen.

"This house is terribly empty," my father had said as he ate his breakfast the morning of the funeral, and it was true. Just as my mother's body had seemed inconsequential to me when I realized that the heat and light that lived within it had disappeared, so her house seemed hollow, a random collection of things, objects, as empty as a display room in a furniture store.

Jules called me so often that I began to laugh at her. "Just checking in?" I said, and she responded, "Oh, go to hell." She was all packed, ready to take the train down for the funeral, when I told her to stay where she was. I wanted to see Jules, to feel her fingers kneading mine, to tell her everything while the two of us curled up in opposite corners of the big old burgundy velvet couch in her tiny living room, our shoes on the floor beneath us. She would pick tendrils of horsehair out of the corner where the velvet had worn away; I would reach over and slap her hand. But not yet.

"I don't want you here now," I said on the phone. "I want to come back there and have it all be the same, different from this, not part of what's been going on here."

"Untouched by human hands," she said.

"Exactly."

"The magazine is sending a deputation."

"Please, Jules, tell them no. I just don't want it. All this is one thing and my life there is something else and I want to keep the two of them separate."

"Can't I be the exception?" she said softly.

"No. Not even you."

"I have that nice black suit that we bought on sale in Bendel's."

"You'll wear it to dinner when we go out to celebrate my new job."

"What? What job?"

"Got me. But when I get a job we'll celebrate."

Jules was quiet for a minute. "I don't know," she finally said.

"Please, Jules," I said.

"What are you wearing?" she said.

I laughed long and hard, longer and harder than the remark required. "That's the kind of thing I need from you," I said.

"You need a bottle of wine and a good cry," Jules said, and I could tell by the slightest tremor in her deep contralto voice that she was crying. I took a breath and let it out in a sigh.

"Later," I said. "I promise."

I wore a navy-blue suit, my father wore a navy-blue suit, and the boys wore navy jackets. Wasn't it Diana Vreeland who once said that pink was the navy blue of India? But wasn't it true, I said at the lunch afterward at the Duanes' beautiful, rather austere home on a hill street parallel to our own, wasn't it true, I said, as I wolfed down chicken salad and pound cake, that navy blue was the black of college towns?

Of course no one laughed, and Mrs. Best said, "Always joking, Ellen." They all remembered that moment, over the next few months.

At the funeral luncheon my father was not himself, not the man who had taught me to say things like that. He was not the wit that day, smelling of white wine and lemon cologne, the bereaved wit talking of how my mother would have loved the chamber music and the chapter from Corinthians and Isabel Duane's eulogy. Instead he stood by a table clutching a mug of coffee and listened as others came up to condole and reminisce.

His hands shook, and his face was gray. He looked more ill than my mother had, those months ago, when he had come out onto the porch and told me I had no heart. He did not recognize Dr. Cohn when she took his hand, and when she bent near to say something in his ear his eyes were as glazed and blank as those of those people you see whiling their lives away in a mental institution. It was as though his soul had flown, too.

She asked me to walk with her out to her car, Dr. Cohn, in her black wool coat and a hat with a brim turned back from her strong face. She looked exactly like one of the Orthodox women I had seen on the Upper West Side on Saturday mornings, herding gaggles of small children, girls in dresses, boys in jackets and yarmulkes, to temple. Glibly I asked, "Do you go to all your patients' funerals?"

"The ones I particularly like," she said.

She opened the front door of the car, slid inside, and gestured for me to join her. She looked straight out the windshield at the old snow, in ugly piles along the curbs and driveways, as though we were driving somewhere and she was concentrating on the next turnoff.

Finally she said flatly, "I don't know whether to say this or not. But I will. The pathologist found something wrong during the autopsy."

I made a sound, half snort, half laugh. I was a little drunk and very tired. "News flash, Doctor," I said. "I guessed that there was something wrong with my mother."

"Don't be flip, Ellen. I mean they found that the cause of death was an overdose of the morphine."

"The pump?"

"Someone's already looked at it. It's fine."

"The pills?"

"I don't know. I just know that the toxicology reports showed that she had enough morphine in her to be fatal. More than enough. A great deal."

"So? So what? She took morphine all the time. You know that. And Teresa will tell them that my mother was in agony, she was like an animal by the very end, wearing diapers, drooling, never knowing what day it was, never able to get up. Who cares how she died? She should have been put out of her misery weeks ago. If she had been a dog they would have."

"Ellen," Dr. Cohn said, "you should watch what you say."

"I don't care what anybody thinks of me."

"Don't you wonder who did it?"

"Did what?"

"Are you listening to me? Someone administered a fatal overdose of morphine to your mother."

"Did you tell my father?" I said.

"We had to tell the district attorney."

I snorted again, louder. "Oh, God, Mr. Best," I said. "Who cares? Did you tell my father?"

"I tried," Dr. Cohn said. "But he seems so vague. I didn't quite feel that he was completely present, if you know what I mean."

And she was right. He did well enough in class, I heard, but he seemed abstracted and fatigued otherwise. The president had offered him a sabbatical, but he had replied as he had when I offered to clean the closets: No. Absolutely not.

And I wondered whether, as he drove across the bridge over the Montgomery River to the gray stone building where he held court in that corner office, as he handed out reading lists and oversaw senior theses, perhaps even as he was offered dinner and a good dry martini by some assistant professor still looking for a life companion and knowing, at least, that a widower had not been opposed to marriage as a matter of course, I wondered whether all was obscured by a vision of his hand holding a spoon with a small seashell pattern on the handle, my mother's second-best dinner setting, carrying rice pudding from the bowl to her mouth. After the funeral, after Dr. Cohn told me about the morphine, even before I really understood that someone was going to be hell-bent on finding out how it came to be in my mother's raddled body, I began to think about the pudding.

I wondered about it as I packed up, the silver clean, the furniture back in its original position. I heard a whine, a hum, from the lower floors, and for just a moment I thought it was the wheelchair, moving from the living room to the kitchen. But it was only the furnace tuning up. I thought I heard a high cry from below, plaintive, tortured, alive. But it was some bird, knocking against the kitchen window at its own seductive reflection, falling in love with its own image in a case of mistaken identity. *Knock, knock. Knock, knock.* It went on and on as I filled my vanity bag with aspirin and Vaseline and my diaphragm and some tubes of lipstick. There was an empty plastic container that had once held morphine tablets and I dropped it into the trash as I had the one that had stood on the table in the den, that morning after, as my father sat and whispered to my dead mother, his dead wife, his voice so soft and intimate and finally broken that I had gone into the other room and put on Vivaldi, loud, so I could not hear him, before I made a pot of coffee in the kitchen.

Knock, knock, went the bird again, but the timbre was different this time, and I went down, my bag in hand. The train schedule was on the table in the hall. The 6:10, I thought. The 6:10 that I had last taken that day in September, after I drank the orange juice and smashed the glass and vowed to show I had a heart.

They were knocking at the door, two men in suits, their knocking an echo of the bird, a cardinal it was, smashing himself so determinedly against the window that there were now smears of some sort of mucus and a trace of blood. The two men stood on the doorstep and when I opened the door neither moved, but the older one, the one with the brown suit, said pleasantly, with a half-smile, "Miss Gulden." It was not a question.

Officer Patterson, and with him Officer Brown, in the brown suit. If I could raise my father from his torpor it would be by telling him that, by telling him that it was a cheap faux Dickensian trick, telling him how Officer Brown worked the knot of his tie back and forth just before he asked a question, as though someone had created him on the page determined to give him some defining characteristic. Officer Patterson said, "Nice house." Officer Brown said, "We'd like to ask you some questions." Officer Patterson refused coffee. Officer Brown asked if I could come downtown.

"What's that noise?" Officer Patterson said.

"A bird bashing his head into the kitchen window," I said, and they looked at one another.

My duffel was on the floor by the gateleg table. The train schedule was tucked beneath a blue-and-orange Chinese bowl. Everyone admired it, including Officer Brown. My mother had been jubilant about that always, because she had purchased the bowl from a grocery and kitchen supply store in Chinatown for $25, having bargained the proprietor down from $35 and demanded a bag of fortune cookies thrown in into the bargain. "A good housewife makes a happy home," one of the cookies had said, but it was I who got it, and wrinkled up my nose as I read it aloud.

As I walked out to their black sedan I could see my futon in the garage, ready to be thrown into Jeff's jeep later in the week and carted back to Jules's apartment. After we were gone, two other police officers came, with my father, and searched the house, and they found the empty pill vial in the basket, and another at the bottom of a trash bag in the garage, and the diaphragm, and the train schedule, and the duffel bag. It said in the papers later that I had been preparing to flee. "I was catching the six-ten, for Christsake," I said to Jeff in a diner over a club sandwich and a chocolate milk shake after he and Mrs. Forburg bailed me out. "I was going back to where I really live." Someone heard me say it, and that was in the paper, too.

Officer Brown asked me what my mother ate, what she drank, how she slept, how she looked, whether I liked her, whether I loved her, whether I was anxious to stop nursing her and get back to the city and a life of my own. He asked me about morphine dosages, administration, side effects, pills, and pumps. I knew all about it, and I told him so, and the stenographer took my words down, and the sun had set outside the windows of the municipal building and Mr. Best was waiting anxiously in his office and the 6:10 had just pulled out of the station when they arrested me and charged me with killing my mother.

"You've got to be kidding," I said, and that was in the paper, too.

That next morning, after I'd spent my night in jail, the hum of the electrical lines lulling me to sleep, after I'd appeared in court and moved carefully through the clot of reporters at the front entrance, after I'd climbed into Mrs. Forburg's old beige car and taken off with her to meet Jeff at the Greek diner two towns over, I told her that I couldn't wait to tell my father about Officer Brown in his brown suit, about the Grand Guignol of the court-room, so very Evelyn Waugh. And it was then that it occurred to me that he hadn't been there, not during the night, not in the morning. "He has an early class on Thursdays," I said.

"I could beat that man with a stick," Mrs. Forburg said.

I didn't see my father again for eight years, except for one afternoon down the long gray high-ceilinged corridor of the county courthouse, both of us yet again in navy blue, both of us knowing that the illusion of our inseparability, our fused identities, crumbling these many months since he had said I was heartless and I had set out to prove to him that I was not, that the illusion was now blown apart forever.

It was either him or me. For the last time, after they arrested me, I chose him.

It was the summer when I had just turned eight that I went to stay with my Gulden grandparents for two weeks and it rained without ceasing. It was that thick gray chilly rain that sometimes grips the northeast in August and sends the children of summer colonies and beach towns into sporadic fits of Monopoly, bowling, Old Maid, hide-and-seek in the closets and the basements of houses pungent with damp, sends them finally to driving their parents crazy, until their mothers let them play in the rain as one last desperate diversion.

My grandmother taught me War during those days, both of us with sweaters over our summer clothes; I remember the lamps, turned on to make a show of light against the gray outside, glinting off her wedding band and the buffed surfaces of her nails as she laid the cards down. Although I had long outgrown them, we played Chutes and Ladders and Candyland; although I played clumsily, we played Risk and Parcheesi.

My grandmother said my grandfather would teach me chess, but he never did. Even as the rain poured down outside he went about his normal round of seasonal activities at the camp, turning off the water to the cabins, caulking windows and floating empty plastic bottles in toilets, putting antifreeze in the pool lines. He came in for lunch and dinner, hung a yellow waterproof parka, streaming with water, on a peg near the back door, ate and then went back outside, ate, and then sat in the lamplight himself in the evening for an hour or two, reading books about the Civil War or watching baseball players in sunny cities flicker by on the television while my grandmother knitted, her needles, too, catching the light.

A bottle of beautiful amber-colored whiskey sat on the little table next to his chair, and a tumbler that always had an inch or so of amber in it. It did not make him garrulous, brilliant, or mean, the way it did my father. A deeply silent man, it merely made him more silent. I can remember the words my grandfather said to me one by one, like trees on a plain, there were so few of them.

When we ran out of things to do, my grandmother took out her scrapbooks—tooled leather covers held together with rawhide ties, thick, rough black paper covered with pictures held in place with little tan triangles, the pictures with the wavy edges and flat black-and-white vistas of my grandmother's girlhood. The picture I remember best was one of my father and his father standing side by side in front of the lake that was the southernmost perimeter of the camp.

Perhaps what first caught my attention was the date, which showed my father to be the same age in the photograph as I was at the time. But what I remembered afterward was how puny he was, a slight boy in a checkered shirt and dark shorts, his knees big knobs in the ungainly line of slightly bowed legs, his hands on his hips, his arms akimbo and shoulders squared as though he sought to take up more space in the frame than his body would normally dictate. His father was a big man, tall and square— *stalwart* is the word that comes to mind—with curling dark hair and a square jaw, with big arms and big hands, but he looks even bigger next to his son, some great dark evergreen next to a pale-green blade of grass. Both of them had fixed expressions on their faces, and I could almost imagine my grandmother telling them to smile, smile, smile, as my mother had always told me, and their expressionless faces only becoming more grim as they stood silently without complying. In her efforts to include all of my father in the picture, my grandmother had nipped off perhaps two inches of her husband's head.

My father had been like the boy in that picture in the two weeks after my mother died: diminished, overshadowed, frozen in some posture out of his customary place in the world. Perhaps his children contributed to that, for when they arrived home, the evening of the day on which she died, my brothers ignored him. Not in any mean way, but as though their connection to him had always been a secondary one, by means of the woman he had married and they had loved. If our family had been a wheel, a perfect round thing moving in perpetual motion down an easy road, she had been the hub and the route all at once. We were directionless, he as much as we three. He more, actually.

It was why, waking in a strange bed in a strange house the morning after I had been arrested and arraigned, I was the only one who was unsurprised that my father had not come to rescue me. He seemed so small now, so shrunken, that I could not imagine him capable of such a thing.

Besides, the others did not know what supporting me would require him to do, to admit, to confess. The rest of them had not watched him feed his wife rice pudding, the spoon sweeping through the air like a pigeon with a message, coming home. The rest of them had not heard her whisper "Help me." In a square and drab room with a single bed, a dresser, and no pictures on the walls I closed my eyes and saw him again, lifting, spooning, lifting again. The rest of them were wondering where the morphine had come from, but I believed I knew. My mother had made perfect order in her home in large part because her husband craved it, and then she had disordered it—the undusted tables, the wheelchair, the night terrors, the hospital bed, the smell of rank perspiration and chemicals. Perhaps he could not bear it. Perhaps he felt sorry for her.

Perhaps he even loved her. Perhaps she had asked of him, that last night when I heard them talking, what she had asked of me and he had had the courage and the love to do what I had not. For that possibility alone I believed he deserved my protection. At least that is how I think I felt when the woman I am today analyzes the one I was then.

"There's coffee, Ellen," said Mrs. Forburg, turning off the radio when I came out into the little kitchen in the same pants and sweater I'd slept in in the little cell in the Montgomery County jail.

In silence I sat at a small white table and looked down at its surface, drawing patterns with the side of my spoon. After a moment Mrs. Forburg sat opposite me.

"No school today?" I said.

"I took a personal day," she said.

"Personal, all right," I said.

"You can stay as long as you like."

"How much money did you pay to get me out?" I said.

"Ten thousand dollars. Ten percent of your bail. I get it all back unless you leave town."

"Skip town," I said.

"What?"

"That's what they always say in the movies. Skip town. Don't worry. I'm not going anywhere."

"That's why they say they arrested you, because you were getting ready to flee."

"Well, I guess that's one way of putting it. I was packing my duffel bag to go back to New York. Two guys showed up at the front door, told me they wanted to ask me some questions at the police station, and the next thing I knew I was under arrest."

"Ellen, you knew what the autopsy found. The doctor says she told you last week, after the funeral. Why didn't you do something?"

"Do what?"

"Get a lawyer. Talk to someone. Come to me. Didn't you understand what would happen?"

"I didn't do it," I said simply.

How many different ways were there to say it? When the investigators at police headquarters had asked me, sitting in a room the color of my palms on the same kind of molded plastic chairs my mother and I had sat on as we waited for one of the nurses to clear a room for chemotherapy, I said it over and over again. I didn't do it. Did I give her the pills? No. Did I know why the vial was empty? No. Did I love my mother? Did I hate my mother? Did I resent my mother? Did I want my mother dead?

"If you had seen my mother and you understood what she once had been, you would have wanted her dead, too," I said, enraged.

Did I kill her?

No.

But I could see the spoon go up and over, into her mouth and out again, her eyes glittering in the light from the lamp. I never said anything about the spoon. I never have, all these years.

That summer when I was eight my father drove me to his parents' house, a cabin on the grounds of the camp, screened from the kids and the counselors by a row of enormous pines my grandfather planted when my father was just a baby. "Georgie's trees," my grandmother called them. It was a long drive, three hours and then some, and we stopped at a restaurant in a town called Liberty and had club sandwiches and iced tea. The rain had already started, although they were saying on the radio that it would end the next day. But I didn't care. As we drove my father recited poetry in his changeable actor's voice, Shakespeare and John Donne and even Edna St. Vincent Millay:

> What lips my lips have kissed, and where, and why,
> I have forgotten, and what arms have lain
> Under my head till morning; but the rain
> Is full of ghosts tonight, that tap and sigh
> Upon the glass and listen for reply,

And in my heart there stirs a quiet pain
For unremembered lads that not again
Will turn to me at midnight with a cry.
Thus in the winter stands the lonely tree,
Nor knows what birds have vanished one by one,
Yet knows its boughs more silent than before:
I cannot say what loves have come and gone,
I only know that summer sang in me
A little while, that in me sings no more.

The words, the sentiments, which I did not understand, seemed to fill the car, the end to reverberate—"that in me sings no more"—and there was a long silence afterward that seemed longer because of the small intense sounds of the woods which surrounded us on either side—the high incessant trill of some bird, the long whirr of what I assumed were bugs. Then my father looked at me and shrugged.

"Even second-rate poetry is better than no poetry at all, Ellen," he said. I remember the sense of relief, almost a physical feeling, that I had waited for him to speak first, to tell me what to feel, that I had not told him immediately how beautiful I thought the poem was.

"You are an exceptional child, Little Nell," he said, when he looked over at my dazzled face.

Deeper and deeper into the woods we drove, the inside of the car dark because of the great old oaks and elms that arched their branches to touch one another across the narrow country roads. We went for miles without seeing a house, a car, anything more than wild-eyed rabbits and the fat and sluggish groundhogs that grazed on the sparse grass that grew along the roadsides. It was what the parents wanted for their children when they sent them to camp, this isolation, the sense that they were being set down in the real America. But it was difficult to imagine my father here, poring over Aesop's *Fables* by the light on his old desk, riding the school bus twelve miles to the nearest town and its stolid red-brick elementary school, leaving here with his bags packed for prep school, where the trees had been thinned and light poured in.

We were not far from the big wooden arch that marked the turnoff for the camp when the doe leapt in front of the car. For a moment I could see her face turned toward me, the muzzle soft-looking even from that distance, the eyes black and round, those enormous ears outstretched to know the road just an instant too late. The impact when we hit her was tremendous, and flecks of black and red spotted the windshield as my father veered sharply onto the shoulder and jammed on the brakes. Afterward, when I looked into the medicine cabinet mirror in my grandparents' cabin, I realized I had hit my head on the dashboard. There was an abrasion and a bump.

"Holy shit," he said.

The deer was on the verge across the road, making a scrabbling motion with her narrow pointed feet. But she could not stand or even push herself along, and she only turned her body slightly, this way and that, her neck arched so it looked as though her head would touch her long, beige-gray silky back.

My father got out of the car and went around to look at the front bumper. "Damn," he said, his face tight with rage, glancing across the road, then back at the car. "Damn."

The noise the deer made with her feet was like someone using a typewriter: *staccato, stop, staccato, stop.* For a moment she would rest and her arched neck would fall and I could see her face, her nostrils working in time with the ragged rise and fall of her sides.

My father got back in the car and put it into gear. "Don't say a word," he said. I was even afraid to turn in my seat to look as we drove away.

My grandparents were outside when we pulled in at their house, past the cabins, empty as old shoe boxes, past the paddock and the pool. Through the trees you could see a sliver of lake, just below the rise on which their house sat.

"I need a drink," my father said to his mother when he got out of the car, and he told her what had happened.

"Oh, George, what a terrible thing," she said as she held his arm, walking him toward the house.

"The animal?" my grandfather said in his guttural voice, which clotted around the consonants.

"It's done for," my father said.

"It's by the road," I said.

My grandfather went into the house and came out with a shotgun. He put it into the back of his old station wagon and pointed at me. "Show me," he said.

"Nature will take its course," my father said. But my grandfather started the car and reached across to open the door for me.

"For God's sake, I'll come," my father said, shrugging off his mother's arm. My grandmother's face looked like the doe's, eyes bright, mouth soft and trembling. I was already in the front seat and my father tried to pull me out by the arm, but I hung back next to my grandfather and shook my head.

"How many Goddamn deer do the townspeople shoot every fall?" he muttered.

When we got back to the place in the road, with its curly ribbon of black skid marks, the deer was still alive, still moving its legs fruitlessly. My grandfather pointed the gun at her head, and for a moment she arched away, turned to look, then lay still. His shoulder jerked back just a bit as he shot her. I cried all the way to the cabin, my face in my hands. My grandfather patted my shoulder and my father looked out the window.

"I need a drink and a new car," he said to my grandmother as the two of them went into the house.

That and the photograph of him and his father together, those were the two things I thought of most often as I slept in Mrs. Forburg's guest bedroom and drank coffee at her kitchen table. That afternoon Jeff came to the back door, cutting through the woods so he could avoid the local reporter and photographer who were sitting outside Mrs. Forburg's house. He tapped on the glass of the kitchen window and peered in, his eyes framed by the yellow café curtains.

"This is like a bad spy novel," I said.

"I have some calls to make in my room," said Mrs. Forburg.

Jeffrey and I sat and looked at one another across the kitchen table. "You look like hell," he said.

"I know, but what can I do? I've been wearing the same clothes for two days and I'm out of moisturizer."

"I have your duffel in the jeep. I'll bring it in if those guys outside leave."

"They'll get bored sooner or later."

"They're not going to get bored. Tomorrow there'll be ten of them, then twenty. This is what they call a headline grabber. That's why that asshole Best had you arrested in the first place—not because he can make a case, but because he can make page one for days and days, making speeches about mercy killing and justice for all. There are people in town saying this never would have happened if you hadn't written the essay for the contest. Between that and the doctor who keeps hooking people up to an IV drip and the nurse up in Canada who pulled the plug on all those people last month, this is a big story."

"It'll pass."

"Not soon, sweetheart. Not soon."

"What else are they saying in town?"

Jeff bent his head, and the glints of red in his hair made me see my mother for a second. "Some of them say that you were justified in what you did," he said.

"And the others?"

"That you weren't."

"Is there anyone who believes that I didn't do it?"

He shook his head.

"You?"

He looked up in surprise. "El, you have a lot of character failings, the most profound of which at this point seems to be the mistaken impression that people are sane and sensible. But you've never been dishonest in your entire life. To a fault, I should add."

"Brian?"

"Bri's really fucked up. He calls from school and just cries and cries. I don't think he cares what killed her, just that she's dead. That's what these fools messed up with this thing—our right to just deal with the fact that she's gone, instead of how she got that way. Cancer killed my mother. Our mother. That's what I say."

"When are you going back?" I said.

"I'm staying here until this is over."

"In the house?"

"I'm there as little as possible. Pop and I have some difficulty communicating."

I thought of my father, quiet and shrunken, in the house that Kate built, imagined his hand with the spoon in it going up and over, up and over, into her mouth and out.

"He really wants to see you, El," my brother said. "Every morning at breakfast he says, 'I must speak to your sister' and every night at dinner he says, 'Have you spoken with Ellen?' He says the two of you need to talk. He wants me to arrange a time here when you can be alone together. He says he understands if you won't come to the house."

"I need to not talk to him right now," I said. "And he needs to not talk to me."

Jeff squeezed my hand. "He won't take no for an answer."

"He'll have to," I said. "Tell him it's impossible."

"His lawyer told him he shouldn't see you until after the grand jury meets," Jeff said, "but he insists you have to talk."

"He has a lawyer?" I said.

"Yeah. And you need one. A good one."

"Maybe I'll call Jon for a referral," I said.

"Jon?"

"F. Lee Beltzer. Mr. Jurisprudence. My nominal boyfriend." At the funeral Jon had worn navy blue, too, but he had only taken my hand at the church after the service and had not come to the Duanes' afterward.

"Haven't you read the papers?" Jeff said.

I shook my head. "Shit," Jeffrey said, and he got up and looked in the refrigerator, closed it and then opened it to look again.

"Jon is your problem," he said. "After Mom died he told his old man that you'd been saying you wished she'd die. His old man heard about the autopsy and went to Best to get extra tests done. Jon nailed you."

"Jon?"

"Yeah."

"He gave me up?" I asked.

Jeff nodded.

"Pretty extreme way to end a relationship," I said.

"Cut that crap, Ellen. He screwed you, big time. He's scum and he always was scum and now you're going to pay for your shitty taste in men." Jeff took my hand again. "I know what happened," he said. "Don't you think I know what happened? There's only one person you'd ever do this for."

"I'm doing it for her," I said.

"Who?"

"Mama," I said. "I'm doing it for her. Jeffie, I can't talk with you about this any more. Not one more word. I just can't. Will you get me a lawyer?"

"What should I tell Pop?" he said.

"Tell him I understand," I said. "Tell him we'll talk sometime. I just don't know when."

"And if I run into Jon?"

I thought for a minute, my hands in my lap. I thought of Jon calling his mother in California, asking her how she could have just walked out one day and left him behind, left a two-year-old to grow up with a hole in his heart. I thought of him hearing her reply, "I just did." I thought of his hands on my lower back and my breasts, his mouth on my belly, of the datebook and the apartment he had probably already sublet, with a big double bed. My head hurt.

"Tell him to go to hell," I said.

"It's a deal," Jeff replied.

When my therapist asked me to keep a journal dissecting the events of that year, she wanted me to particularly deal with the emotions I experienced immediately after I was arrested, before the grand jury heard and decided my case, decided whether to indict me or not. For a while I thought about doing what I had always done for Mrs. Forburg when I wrote compositions or poetry in her class, spinning synthetic emotions out of the silky yarn of intelligence. I was more likely to scam my therapist than Mrs. Forburg, who was far sharper and harder than her often twinkly manner would suggest. She would send my poems back with the dismissive "Clever . . . but!" or the softer "Nice language, but where are you in here?"

It was difficult to tell my therapist, as I finally did, that I felt very little during the weeks after I was charged with my mother's death, although if I had known as much about psychiatry as I do today I would have realized that this was an eminently acceptable answer, easily classified as "lack of affect." At the time I assumed it was because I had lapsed, like an alcoholic or a mental patient who must be recommitted, that I had made a stab at being my mother's daughter and had now reverted convincingly to being my father's, my emotions pickled in a solution of cynicism and self-involvement. Sometimes I wondered whether all children had to choose in that fashion. I pictured my mother sitting watching a toddler, looking for the early signs: which would it be, his or hers? Like embroidered hand towels. I wondered if that was why there were three children, to break the tie. On numbers my mother had been the big winner, but perhaps not on sheer strength of devotion, at least not until the end.

It was difficult to explain how ordinary your life can be, even when extraordinary things are happening around you. Jeff was right; the number of reporters outside Mrs. Forburg's house grew in the next few days, then ebbed, then grew again when new reports surfaced that the prosecutor was asking for help from a famous pathologist in Florida, that my former boyfriend was expected to appear before the grand jury, that the school board was considering disciplinary action against Mrs. Forburg, who walked into the glare of television lights and a half dozen flashes every morning when she left for school.

"Let them fire me," she said, making coffee the morning this last appeared in the *Tribune*. "I can get my Social Security and maybe it'll teach my students something about doing the right thing."

"I still don't entirely understand why you're doing this," I said.

"A mind is a terrible thing to waste," she said.

"Seriously."

"Seriously, you needed help and I was in a position to provide it. There's no mystery in that."

"You're playing the Shirley Booth role in this movie."

"I always hated Shirley Booth," Mrs. Forburg said. And then she left and you could hear the noise, a hum and then a fusillade, lousy with fake intimacy: "Brenda, are you going to lose your job?" "Can you tell us how Ellen is doing?" "Have you talked about what she did?" Then the noise of the car turning over and scattering gravel as she pulled out of the driveway, and the questions died away.

That was the only peculiar thing about my life, that and the way people looked at me in the supermarket or at the mall, the sidelong glances and the stares. After the first two weeks the reporters outside drifted away, waiting for the next hearing, the easy drama of the courtroom. But the *Tribune* kept running the picture of me leaving the courthouse after my arraignment whenever Mr. Best would make a new announcement, and I had only to smile slightly when a little girl lifted her skirt over her head in a grand gesture in the produce aisle or I thought idly of something my mother had once said about mall rats, and someone was sure to narrow their eyes and peer at me. Yes . . . I'm not sure . . . yes, it is . . . that's her.

"Her mother," you could sometimes hear them whisper. The little girl would drop her dress and move closer to the stroller in which her baby brother slept, mouth open, chubby legs bowed on either side of a great diaper bulge.

In the Safeway an elderly woman pressed a little book of daily meditations with a rose on the cover into my hand. "God bless and keep you, dear," she said.

"You're better looking than your pictures," said the checkout girl.

And the telephone answering machine in Mrs. Forburg's dining room was full of messages. The *Tribune* reporter, Julie Heinlein, was tireless in her pursuit of me, scenting the sort of break that would take her away from Langhorne and on to somewhere bigger, better. Her voice wheedled and coaxed on the tape—an interview, an off-the-record conversation, a first-person account. Once she said, "I've been told that you, too, are a journalist." And I remembered Bill Tweedy's disgusted judgment one night over boilermakers in the Blarney Stone downstairs from the magazine offices: "A journalist is a reporter who worries too much about his clothes."

There were the nut cases, of course, offering to marry me or to hold me down and kill me painfully so that I would fully appreciate my sins. And there were the advocates. The Center for the Right to Die had taken up my cause and offered to provide me with a lawyer.

"It is time for every one of us to realize that family members know better what is right for the terminally ill than the courts, the police, or the medical personnel who would keep them alive at all costs," said a man who identified himself as the executive director.

"I didn't do it," I said to the machine.

"You have become a symbol to millions of people of how caring family members are victimized by a system that offers no hope to their loved ones," he continued. "You could be an important voice for the movement to allow people to die with dignity and, if necessary, with assistance."

"I didn't do it," I said again.

The next message was from a man who said that he knew a variety of sex acts that I would enjoy. I listened to the messages myself because I didn't want Mrs. Forburg to have to hear them, but afterward I felt sick, as though I had stomach flu. I lost weight during those weeks. I could not keep food down.

Every few days on the machine there was a voice I knew as well as my own, that in cadence and timbre was much like mine. "Ellen?" my father would say. "If you're there, would you kindly pick up?" In the silence I would hear his breathing, a little ragged, as though he'd been running. "Ellen?" There was never more of a message than that, my name and the demand that I respond, until one afternoon he began to speak.

"Ellen," he said quietly, "I would like to talk about what happened. I know it's difficult for you. But we cannot leave this unsaid." There was a long pause. The tape made a clicking sound as it moved around its eyelike spools. "I didn't know what they were doing at the police station," he continued. "I had no idea they would arrest you. I would have come. I didn't know. I wouldn't—" there was a choking sound, a sharp breath. "We should talk," he said. "We need to talk." And then there was the noise, so final, of the receiver being put down.

That was the last message I got from him.

Apart from that, the days were ordinary, almost tedious. I think now the only real manifestation I had of what was happening around me, in the newspapers, in offices at the courthouse and the municipal building, was a feeling not unlike the homesickness that always filled me for the first few days when I went to stay at my grandparents' house, and even, I was stunned to discover, during the first few months of my freshman year at college.

It was not really the home my mother had made that I yearned for as I wandered through Mrs. Forburg's rooms; I remembered how empty it had seemed after the hospital wagon came and the attendants efficiently, almost magically, took the body away. But I was sick in my soul for that greater meaning of home that we understand most purely when we are children, when it is a metaphor for all possible feelings of security, of safety, of what is predictable, gentle, and good in life.

During those weeks in Mrs. Forburg's house, much of my life was predictable. In fact it was much like the life I had lived those last few months tending my mother, and yet it felt so empty by comparison. There was no center to it, no point. It was an empty housewife's routine of sweeping floors, folding laundry, even watching soap operas. I cooked and cleaned and read; I simmered casseroles and made pies. But there was no one, nothing, around which all this activity revolved. It was simply the white noise of my life, the way to make the time go by least painfully. I was like a mother whose children have been killed in some horrible accident and yet who continues to put a pan of brownies on the table on a trivet every afternoon at three.

One night I went to put out a bag of garbage, to leave it at the end of the short drive off the graveled country road where the McNulty brothers would get it in the morning. They would throw it into the back of the truck they took to the dump, where they were as constant a sight, with their low foreheads and dirty watch caps, as the big oily-feathered birds who picked with sharp beaks at the orange sections spotted with coffee grounds, smeared with mayonnaise and lettuce.

I had put another bag there earlier, and by the light of the nearly full moon I could see a racoon with its pointed snout buried in one corner of the glistening green plastic. It whirled to greet me, baring its little yellowish teeth, nothing cute or cartoon-ish in its ratlike eyes and scrabbling hands, and then it ran across the road and into the dark. I saw that it had spread its booty around the mailbox post, an untidy heap of bones cleaned to gray whiteness like the moon, a tuna can, a small jar that had once held tartar sauce, a half lemon now reduced cleanly to a bowllike bit of yellow peel, two greasy paper towels like dying flowers.

I began to work off the twist tie of the bag I was holding so I could put all the things inside it, but as I stooped to pick up the first bone, my ankle went awry, slipping sideways, and I fell heavily into the grass and dirt and began to cry, long rattling gasps that held my chest down like a hand on my sternum. I sat and wept, my face lifted to the sky as though the moon might warm it. A chicken bone, the fragile ribs and cartilaginous center bow of a breast, was beneath the heel of my hand, and I picked it up and threw it with all my might, hearing no sound as it landed in the scrubby weeds on the other side of the road.

"Goddamnit," I cried, and I tried to get to my feet, but Mrs. Forburg was behind me, bending stiffly to put her hands on my shoulders.

"It's just the Goddamn mess," I said. "Look at it." I moved my hand in a wobbly arc and finally brought it up to my chest, feeling my breathing catch and slow, catch again.

"Go inside," she said. "I'll do this." And I did.

Sometimes I helped her with her homework, editing senior essays with a red pen, grading the true-and-false tests. True, they said, Shakespeare began a sonnet "Death Be Not Proud." True, they said, Mr. Darcy is a character in *A Tale of Two Cities*. True, they said, *Silas Marner* was written by a man named George Eliot.

It's funny, isn't it, what will make you break? Your lover moves to London and falls in love with a news reader for the BBC and you feel fine and then one day you raise your umbrella slightly to cross Fifty-seventh Street and stare into the Burberry shop and begin to sob. Or your baby dies at birth and five years later, in an antique store, a small battered silver rattle with teeth marks in one end engraved with the name Emily lies on a square of velvet, and the sobs escape from the genie's bottle somewhere deep in your gut where they've lain low until then.

Or the garbage bag breaks.

Wrong, wrong, wrong went my big red checks on the test papers, and then I got to *Silas Marner* and George Eliot and I pressed my hand to my face, trying to keep everything inside where it belonged. I walked, head down, to the one small bathroom in Mrs. Forburg's house.

"You can't keep it all bottled up," she said when I came back out.

"Sure I can," I said.

"Do you want tea?"

"No. What I really want is a drink, but that way lies disaster."

"Amen," said Mrs. Forburg, who went to Al-Anon meetings twice a week in the basement of the Lutheran church, as she put a bowl of peanuts on the table. "Don't get grease on my papers."

"You guys always do that," I said, struggling with a smile. "Even at college, you always call them 'my papers.' Why are you so fierce about the possessive?"

"I never thought about that before," Mrs. Forburg said, eating a handful of nuts. "Maybe it's because they're the only tangible part of teaching. Except for you guys, of course, the finished product, but even that's ephemeral. You watch the students work in class and you know that what you're doing is taking hold, but there's nothing really to show for it except this." She held up a paper covered with red ink. "Bad example, but you understand my point. You look at the papers and you can see what sticks and what doesn't. It's one visible manifestation of how well you're doing what you do. That, and occasionally you'll get a letter from one of them that lets you know you did a good job."

"I should have sent you a letter like that. I was full of what you taught me. I mean, I lived on what I'd learned from you through four years of English lit."

"Thank you, my dear. That's what you always hope will happen, but it doesn't really give you much to hold on to. I suppose in a way it's like having children. No one really knows how good a job you've done unless, paradoxically, you've done a bad one and a child goes wrong. Otherwise, you've spent years on this work with precious little credit."

I don't know what I would have done without Mrs. Forburg during all those weeks. It was like living with a softer, more gentle version of my father, ever anxious to discuss the link between literature and life but not judgmental about opinions that diverged from her own. In the evening we had dinner together, watched the evening news, and talked for an hour or two afterward at the table in the kitchen, with the blinds always shut tight. When she went out to her meetings I watched television sitcoms and read mystery novels and talked to Jules on the phone.

"People aren't supposed to ask about AA things, are they?" I asked one night after Mrs. Forburg had come home from her meeting.

"I don't know about people," she said. "You can certainly ask me about Al-Anon."

"Why do you go?"

"Because it helps me to understand why I do some of the things I do," she said.

"Sorry, I put that badly. You usually go to Al-Anon if you have a family member who is an alcoholic. Who's the family member?" I raised my arms, palms open, as though to indicate the empty house, empty of photographs or mementos, too, so different from my mother's house. "Sorry," I said, "that was a nasty way of putting it."

"Have you noticed you apologize a lot these days?" Mrs. Forburg said.

"Is that a way of evading my question?"

"No, it's something you might want to think about. The answer is that my ex-husband was an alcoholic. My father was an alcoholic. And my mother was an alcoholic. And I was, in the vocabulary of the addiction, the enabler who made it possible for all of them to go on drinking. I took care of my mother when she was drunk and then when she was dying, and I adored my father and made excuses for why he did what he did."

"And your husband?"

"Oh, he was my father all over again—charming, smart, and crippled. You can find my story in any handbook on alcoholism. But knowing that you're typical doesn't go a long way toward making you feel better in your day-to-day life."

"How long have you been divorced?" I asked. I could not remember Mrs. Forburg ever being married.

"Twelve years," she said.

"It takes you that long to get over it?"

"That's a naïve comment from someone as intelligent as you are. It takes your entire life to get over some of the people you've loved, and some you never get over."

"You always do that. The intelligence thing. It's as though if you're smart, you will understand yourself."

"You're right. That's naïve of me. Particularly of me."

"Is your father still alive?"

"He died three years ago. But if my head counts for anything, he'll live forever."

I understood that. I thought of my father all the time during those weeks. When I did not think of him, I dreamed of him. People were chasing me in those long, attenuated, slow-motion chases that are so common in dreams and, perhaps, more than we ever understand, in life. Sometimes my father would be one of them, sometimes he would be a bystander, sometimes he would try to help me but let go of my hand as I went by, our fingers slipping past one another like fish swimming parallel for a moment, then off in opposite directions.

When I was twelve or thirteen, I remember, I went downstairs for a glass of milk and found him and my mother sitting at the table, the round oak table, beneath the sampler of our family tree: George and Kate in cross-stitch below a stylized line of grass and flowers, and then the three of us in the branches, full names, careful script in straight stitch.

My father had had a big balloon glass of brandy in front of him. I could smell it, sharp but with that lingering sweetness. He was wearing an Irish fisherman's cardigan, bulky with cables, and his sports coat hung on the back of the chair. He was leaning back on the back legs, which we were never allowed to do because my mother said it was bad for the chairs.

"Ellen, an opinion," he said, letting down the chair with a clunk and leaning forward to cup his brandy in his hands. "Did you see the story in today's *Tribune* about the apartment complex they are proposing to build down from the college?"

"No," I think I said. Was I thirteen then, or fourteen? Did most girls my age read the paper?

"Here," he said, handing me a section of newspaper that had been on the floor below the table. "Background." His words were very crisp, in the way they were when he had had a good deal to drink.

The story said that the state was proposing to build a complex of twenty-four apartments for low-income residents, on a wooded site directly behind the quarry.

I looked up.

"Your mother," my father said, "finds this perfectly acceptable."

"That is not what I said, Gen," my mother had said.

"Perfectly acceptable. Here you have a lovely wooded area which will be raped for the sake of building some crackerboxes for people who, within weeks, will have left old cars on the lawns and written their names all over the walls. Your mother does not find this troubling."

"That's not what I said, Gen."

"Well, what was it you did say?"

"I said that everybody has to live somewhere."

"There you have it, Ellen. Words to live by: everybody has to live somewhere."

"I'm going to bed," I said.

"So am I," said my mother.

"No one wants to engage in civilized debate in this household," my father said.

Do I remember this correctly or do I remember it now as I wish it had been? When I remembered those occasions in those weeks, I remembered myself aligned with my mother against my father. Can any of that be true? Or was it just the trick of the light, that when she was alive shone on him alone and now shone only on the place where she had once been, nothing but Jesus rays and dust motes and a circle of silver on the ground? All my stories have alternate endings now, like "The Lady or the Tiger." There is the ending where I am brittle and clever and he looks at me over the rim of his half glasses, the blue of his eyes bisected by tortoiseshell, and his mouth curves just a little at the corner and I know that I have done the right thing. And there is the other ending. My mother's ending.

"There you are," he said, "words to live by— everybody has to live somewhere."

"I'm going to bed," said my mother.

"And you, Ellen?" he said.

"I'll stay down here for a while," I said. "Do you want another brandy?"

One night I had a dream that I was driving our car, sitting on a telephone book so that I was high enough to see over the dashboard, and that I hit the deer and he said, "Very careless, Ellen," but you could tell by his smile that he was not really angry. And my grandfather got the gun and we went back but the deer was gone and in its place was a woman in a nightgown, her face turned away. "Who's that?" my grandfather said, but neither my father nor I recognized her.

I liked my lawyer. Not my first lawyer, the one who stood beside me at my arraignment, when the edges of my fingers were still black with the ink the police used to fingerprint me. Not the lawyer whose name, as nondescript as his clothes and his observations, was Smith.

But the lawyer who took over my case, who was paid for by Jeffrey with money that I only realized afterward, when the need for lawyers had long passed, was equal parts the money left Jeff by our Gulden grandparents and contributions from a handful of families in Langhorne who had been friends of ours and who believed that I should not be prosecuted. Most of them, I think, believed that I had killed my mother, but they believed I had done it out of kindness. Jeff told me that Mrs. Duane would only repeat, "If you had seen her pushing that wheelchair . . ." as she wrote him a substantial check on the bookstore account.

The money was not enough, I knew that. Jonathan had once told me he could expect to bill out at $300 an hour if he made partner in the firm he most coveted, the one with the atrium full of ficus trees and the private dining room with the nouvelle American chef. And I knew that Robert Greenstein would spend hours on this case even before it came to trial. His office had no atrium, no chef. He ate chicken salad from paper bags on the green blotter of his desktop; I ate with him on a few occasions.

But he was still a respected criminal trial lawyer, and the $25,000 my brother gave him was not enough. I told Jeff we should pay him in food, bring in the lasagna in disposable foil trays, the crockpot soups, the pineapple upsidedown cakes and the brownies that still littered the counters in my mother's house and filled the freezer so that it was impossible to open it, Jeff had told me, without having some funeral meats fall at your feet. Let him eat cake, I said.

"You'll give me the rest when you sell your story to television," Bob Greenstein said, "like that girl upstate who had her father killed because she didn't like her curfew and he didn't like her nose ring."

"Fat chance," I said, my mouth full of chicken salad.

That was one of the things I liked about him, that there was none of the hush, the reverence, that accompanied conversation with most people on the subject of my mother's death, no matter how they thought it might have happened. Even the reporters would talk in funeral home tones, what passes for understanding when people talk about death. "I know this is probably a difficult time, but if you could give me a half hour," they would say on the messages on Mrs. Forburg's home machine. "We do hair and makeup," said the assistant to a producer at a television station. "In case that's a concern."

But Bob never dropped his voice, never leaned toward me with concerned brown eyes beneath lowered brows. He was in many ways an unattractive man, short and squat, with only a fringe of hair, a tonsure that looked as though it had been drawn in with an eyebrow pencil. His shirt fronts stretched tight and dully white across his paunch, and his office smelled of cigar smoke, although for some reason he never smoked in front of me. His desk was a mahogany reproduction piece, perhaps of something at Monticello or Mount Vernon, and its big surface was scratched, the finish worn off here and there by a cigar that had been allowed to burn low, taking the veneer with it. One wall was lined with file cabinets, with files piled untidily atop them, and behind him was a breakfront with photographs of a boy and girl, stiff school portraits with fake rustic backgrounds.

"Wife?" I said when I first sat in the chair across from him.

"Left," he said.

I enjoyed communicating with someone like that, without explanation or recriminations, without psychologizing or pontificating, just clean and pure, almost like math: Wife. Left. I was a client to Bob Greenstein, a case, a problem, a fact pattern, a task to be mastered. I liked that, too. It was a great relief to be with a person who did not want to know my soul, my deepest secrets. Quite the contrary.

Jeff would drive me in the jeep up the interstate to a small city that rose just beyond the highway the way all the others did, the shabby houses beneath the overpass ranged around the ramps, and then the center of town, and then just beyond it the homes of those with money and position. In the years to come, when I traveled more, I would realize that every American town was so constructed, that only New York was different, the rich and the poor hopscotching across the horizon, Park Avenue one way in the eighties and another in the hundred and twenties, Riverdale and the South Bronx only a long, long short walk away from one another.

I don't know where Bob lived, although I had his home phone number in case, although I was never entirely sure what in case was in this case, whether the police might come in the middle of the night or the judge revoke my bail without cause. I imagined him in a bare apartment somewhere, his wife living with the children in one of the Tudor houses just beyond the center of town, so like the ones in Langhorne. Although for all I knew he had a splendid contemporary on a swath of open land ten miles away, with a Jacuzzi that provided a view of the woods and lots of action in the evenings.

I didn't need to know much about him, nor him about me, except for the story. I told him of how the police had brought me to the station for questioning a week after my mother's funeral, of how they arrested me after talking to me for four hours.

"And you talked to them?" he said.

I shrugged.

"Never asked for counsel?" he said. "Answered all their questions? Cooperated fully?"

I nodded.

"You went to Harvard?"

"I didn't go to the law school," I said. "My boyfriend did."

"Yeah, your boyfriend. Some boyfriend. You watch television, Ellen?"

"Not much. Old movies, mainly."

"Don't talk to the police. The police are not your friends. If your cat is up a tree, then you want to be nice to police officers. If you are under suspicion in a murder case, you do not. They are on the other side. They are not interested in the search for truth. They are interested in the search for you."

That's when you could see what Bob Greenstein would be, when he made a speech like that. He came on like a nightlight, a faint and steady glow of something not quite conviction, something closer to what carny salesmen used to do when they sold patent medicines and Bibles.

"You're cynical," I said quietly.

"I'm realistic," he said, shaking his head. He kept shaking it as he looked through a pile of papers on his desk. He lifted the blurred Xerox of a newspaper piece, and when I saw the headline and picture I winced.

"Yeah," he said at the gesture. "I bet you are very sorry you ever wrote this essay, or at least that you won with it."

"I'm not sorry I wrote it. I'm only sorry it's not better."

" 'A fifteen-year-old dog lies on a metal examining table,' " he began to read. " 'His breathing is ragged. Behind him a veterinarian fills a needle with clear fluid to do what needs to be done—put the animal out of his misery.' "

He stopped and peered up. "Where'd you see them put the dog to sleep?" he said.

"I never did. I made it up."

"Age of the dog and everything?"

"And everything," I said.

He sighed. "Blah blah blah blah," he said, a stubby finger running down the article. "Blah, blah, blah, here, 'It seems outrageous that those humans suffering just as much as animals, even those who say that they are tired of life and want to end it, are kept alive by extraordinary means. What are feeding tubes and respirators but playing God on the part of men? What is keeping people alive when they would be better off dead than extreme cruelty?' Blah blah blah, 'participate in decisions about our own deaths,' blah blah, 'truly, mercy killing is an apt name.' Yow."

He looked at me again.

"What can I say?" I asked, shrugging. "I was seventeen years old and I knew nothing about the subject. It's glib, it's self-righteous, and it's badly written."

"You wrote it?"

"Yes."

"Did your mother ever read it?"

"Yes."

"Did she disagree with your conclusions?"

"We didn't discuss it." Actually, I think she said, when I was mailing it in, "It's a horrible subject." Or perhaps that is only my reconstructed memory.

"Your father?"

"There's a grammatical mistake near the end. A 'that' where a 'which' should be. He was livid. We didn't discuss the content."

"I'm curious about your father. He's been the mystery man in this case. Do you talk to him."

"No," I said.

"Why not?"

Again I shrugged.

"Why didn't he bail you out?"

"Ask him."

"He's been asked. He says he didn't know they were holding you until the next morning, by which time you'd already been released by your English teacher. Is that possible?"

"Yes."

"He was sleeping when your mother died?"

"Yes."

"He was not alone with her the night before?"

I paused. I did not know what my father had told the police. As though he read my mind, Bob added, "That's what he says."

"Right," I said.

"But you were with her. She was in a completely helpless state. And when she died you didn't call him, you just sat with her until morning."

"Yes."

"Why?"

"I didn't want to let go of her hand," I said, and he nodded. "Good," he said. It was the right answer. It was true as well. I felt as though I'd won an office pool, some sort of lottery. Correct and accurate.

"What was the last thing she said to you?" he asked, but I could not remember. I could only remember the endless silence of that night, rubbed raw with the sounds of breathing.

We went over everything I had gone over with the police, the morphine pump, the settings, the mostly full vial of pills. And all the time I saw the spoon with the rice pudding going in her mouth and out again, my mother's eyes glittering like topaz: I saw her mouth work until the food went down, saw the death's-head on the pillow as we breathed in tandem. Bob took notes on some sheets of paper. Then he leaned back, rocking slightly in an old wooden desk chair with a pillow placed at the small of his back.

"Here's the problem with what's appeared in the papers so far," he said. "And I say that because I'm getting a whole lot more on this case from the *Tribune* than I am from Ed Best, who is playing this very close to the vest. Maybe that's because he only did it in the first place to get himself in the papers so he can be attorney general or run for Congress. His wife, by the way, says you were cracking jokes at the funeral. Anyhow, you put it all together, and people will see this one of two ways. Best case scenario is that you did give your mother the morphine, but that you had justification for doing so, that it was the right, even the moral thing to do."

"Uh-huh," I said.

"The other is what will be the prosecutor's case, and that is that you are a very tough, very hard young woman who got tired of being tied to this dying mother and gave her the morphine so you could go on about your business."

"Well, that's the view of me that conforms more closely to reality."

"Now, you see, that's the sort of thing that you say that is counterproductive in this context. It's very Upper East Side, but it's like telling the police that anyone in their right mind would have killed your mother if they had a chance—"

"That's not what I said."

"All right."

I folded my hands and looked down at them, the veins seeming bigger, bluer, knottier than they had before. "I know people like to make up little stories about life," I said, "that they like things to have a certain shape. Daughters who adore their mothers and would lay down their lives for them. Daughters who hate their mothers and kill them. Noble gestures, grand passions. The right thing. The wrong thing. Made for each other, happily ever after."

I looked Bob Greenstein straight in the eye and continued, "Everyone makes up their little stories and then they wonder why their own lives aren't like that. It makes life so much simpler if they can get rid of all the loose ends. Ellen is such an angel, loved her mother so much she couldn't bear to see her suffer. Or, Ellen is such a witch that she walked over her mother in spikes to get what she wanted. I can't be responsible for other people's little stories. I have enough trouble making sense of my own."

"That's very poetic, but here's my trouble, and I'll lay it right out for you. I need some little story to go into court with, because experience tells me that if I don't have one you are in big trouble."

"I'm already in big trouble," I said.

"A trial and a possible jail term will be bigger trouble. Much bigger. You have no idea."

"I'll tell the grand jury that I didn't do it and they won't indict me," I said, almost believing it.

"Very bad idea for you to appear. Very bad. I don't envision having you testify."

"I'm testifying," I said. "I need to testify. I insist. Absolutely."

Bob Greenstein leaned back and sighed. "Oh, what a prize I got with you, kid," he said.

Being in therapy always reminded me of being in Bob Greenstein's office, of watching someone try to make my little story into a coherent whole. Sometimes I wished my therapist would just lean forward, her hand splayed over her notebook, and say with feeling, "Oh, what a prize I got with you, kid." Sometimes now at work I think it myself. What a prize.

Easter did come early that year, before the gray sticks of the azalea branches had begun to soften with a pale-green haze, before the crocuses and snowdrops were anything more than sharp points lifting improbably from soil still hard. The little girls would be disappointed, their flowered dresses hidden at church beneath their worn winter coats, their white straw hats incongruous above the wool collars, their white patent shoes incongruous beneath. Mrs. Forburg went to visit a cousin in Philadelphia. Brian came home for the weekend, but he didn't call and he didn't come to see me. Jeff went to stay with a girl he knew from school.

Bob Greenstein had told me to stay close to Mrs. Forburg's house, to keep a low profile in Langhorne, to live like a nun. But I felt so lonely that weekend, after I'd waxed Mrs. Forburg's linoleum and washed her curtains, that I ignored all his advice and went out on Good Friday. I drove alone to Sammy's in Mrs. Forburg's beige Chevy sedan, drove through the thick rich blackness of the cold night until the bar sign sprang from the darkness of a corner just shy of the center of town, its neon profile of a corpulent gentleman in a red stock tie bright against the starless sky. There were few cars parked outside. I'd combed my hair but I was damned if I was going to put on lipstick just so the auto mechanics and retail clerks of Langhorne wouldn't talk about how I'd lost my looks.

"Where is everybody?" I asked the bartender, a guy named Mark who had graduated from high school four years before I did, one of those guy who always wore a baseball cap in a vain effort to disguise premature baldness.

He shrugged and brought me a beer. "Easter's one of those vacations kids don't come home for. Too short, I guess."

"So where are all the Langhorne kids?"

"There's a dance there tonight. The place has been dead since the lunch crowd left." All but one of the tables were empty, the red glass globes burning steadily in their centers. Against the wall four men somewhere between senior year and middle age were hunched forward over their candle, their chins red in its reflected glow, reminding me of the game we once played with buttercups, looking for the yellow to tell us who liked butter. One man met my eyes across the room and let his drop conspicuously. I turned around.

"You haven't been in in a while," Mark said, putting a bowl of Goldfish crackers in front of me.

"Christmas holidays, I think," I said.

"You still at Mrs. Forburg's?" he said.

"You'd read it in the paper if I wasn't."

"All I read's sports," he said.

"Bull," I said. "Even if that's true, you'd hear it in here twenty minutes after I pulled out of the driveway."

"She's a nice lady," he said.

"Nobody could agree more," I said.

"Yeah, well, if you think she's so nice, why'd you go and get her in trouble? They've got a committee investigating her, some parents have transferred kids out of her classes, the other teachers are giving her a hard time."

"Who says?" It took me a moment to remember that Mark's mother was one of those large and faceless women in hairnets who worked the steam table in the cafeteria. One of the nice ones, too, the ones who gave double mashed potatoes and big slabs of cake.

"That guy Murphy on the school board, who's hated her since she stood up for the kids on the newspaper when they wrote that poem making fun of the superintendent? He's been telling people she's a dyke, that the both of you are dykes. Didn't she say anything?"

"Maybe she doesn't know."

"She knows," he said.

"She says she doesn't care."

"She cares,' he said, wiping off the bar.

Another man slipped onto the stool next to mine. He was short and stocky, broad through the shoulders and torso, with the kind of build that would have guaranteed him a berth on the wrestling team in high school. Familiar strangers, I'd always called them, the dozens of people a year or so older or younger than I whose faces I knew from the halls of the high school but whose names I could rarely immediately place, so that my mother had become accustomed, during college and afterward, to those times when I would come back from shopping and blurt out "Lauren McNulty" or "Jim Bettman" at the dinner table.

This one ordered a shot and a beer, looked down one end of the bar and up the other, taking pains not to meet my eyes. He raised a glass to the four men in the corner, but they were of no help to me: "Hey" is all one of them called across the room. I thought he was older than I was, a year or two, and the longish hair meant he was a townie, probably a working man; all the college boys wore their hair short now. He kept his shoulders high so his head sank down between them, almost disappearing in the blanket plaid of his coat, like a turtle or an old man.

"Hi, Ellen," he finally said, throwing back his longish hair with a peculiar twist of his head, and I thought about how much easier this would be in the city, where everyone wanted to establish their bona fides: perhaps you don't remember? we met at the Lincoln Center party for the anniversary of the magazine. I was with a friend of mine who's at Jensen, Jensen and Bates, I think you knew his fiancée from college. The litany was endless—tangential relationships, friends of friends, restaurant near-misses—"I was just at Le Besoin last Tuesday!"

But not in Langhorne. "How are you?" he asked, and then he ducked his head and asked Mark for another shot of Wild Turkey. That Wild Turkey was the prettiest color in the muted bar light, the amber-brown of beautiful eyes. "I'll have one of those, too, Mark," I said, but when I put more money on the bar the man picked the bills up, folded them in half, and put them beneath my beer mug. "Chris," I thought suddenly, and it was all I could do not to say it aloud. "Chris Somebody." He lifted his glass of Wild Turkey and sipped for a second, then threw it down.

"Ah," he said, a short burst of breath, and then grinned, still looking straight ahead, so that I could see the grin only in his eyes reflected in the mirror over the bar. The bottom part of his face, his mouth and chin, was blocked out by the wall of bottles, of Stoli and Bushmills and Courvoisier, another pretty color, darker than the Wild Turkey. Even the top of his head, his hair, was cut off because the mirror over the bar at Sammy's was edged with college pennants, Langhorne hanging cheek by jowl with Michigan, Stanford, Yale, Penn, to show how important it really was. The little college that could, the last president had called it sometimes, and when he did my father had always rolled his eyes extravagantly. I lifted my own shot glass, and, closing my eyes, drank it off. A shiver shook me, the kind my mother used to tell me meant someone walking over your grave. When I opened my eyes Chris Somebody was looking at me in the mirror, and he winked, an insouciant gesture so obviously foreign—he did it too slowly, for one thing—that for some reason it made me feel warm, and my eyes filled. Or maybe it was just the Wild Turkey.

"You don't remember me, do you?" he said, talking to my reflection in the mirror, as though secondhand was safe enough.

"Yeah, I do," I said, feeling the Wild Turkey moving to my stomach, my groin, my joints. "Chris."

"Chris Mortensen," he said. "I was one of the guys who put the lights on the trees this year."

I couldn't remember even seeing the guys putting the lights on the trees. "Were you one of the guys who put in the poinsettias that year they all died?"

We were still talking in the mirror. Mark had moved down the bar and was arguing with two town kids who had produced fake ID. Only the stupidest or most naïve tried to get a drink in Langhorne, where everybody knew your high school class. Most of them went two or three towns away to drink, or had someone go into the state store and buy them a big bottle of sangria to drink sitting in the car or wrapped in blankets beneath the bridge. Jon had always stolen vodka from his father, poured it in a jar and then added water to what was left in the bottle.

When I asked about the poinsettias Chris ducked his head again, like I'd caught him in something.

"Long before my time," he said. "But my cousin was on that crew. He said he knew they'd die but he just put them in anyhow."

"The provost's wife wouldn't talk to my mother for years after that. She knew they'd die, too. My mother, not the provost's wife."

Chris looked down at his empty shot glass, then raised it so Mark could see. The bartender nodded down the length of the bar. "I'm not serving you no matter what, so you might as well go home or drive over to Montgomery Heights," he said, and swearing under their breath, the kids left.

"You want another?" Chris said.

"Sure," I said.

It went down easier for both of us the second time, and the beer felt sharp and tingly on my tongue right afterward, like needles on velvet. "That stuff is the prettiest color," I said.

"Yeah, huh?" he said. His hands were laid flat on the bar, as though he was bracing himself. They were like the rest of him, compact, thick. Across the back of one was an enormous scar, raised and pink, a bright ugly worm of a thing. I put out an index finger and touched it lightly, then looked at him in the mirror. He looked down.

"It was a real stupid thing," he said. "I was cutting Christmas trees out at one of the farms for that big lot downtown, the one in the back of the market parking lot?" Everything he said was a question, as though it was up to me to correct him, to insist that there was no farm, no market, no lot. "The chain saw just slipped and *zipp, whoa,* there it was." This he seemed surer about, but not as sure as I, seeing the blood, the white bone, smelling the sweet smell of gore and the medicinal tang of the emergency room, the little plastic bags sealed with the sutures inside, a made-up memory more real than a true one.

I shivered again. "Jesus," I said.

The men at the table were arguing about the upcoming baseball season and a skinny woman at the end of the bar was trying to talk Mark into selling her a six-pack. She had bad skin and her clothes hung loose on her, a pink sweater and jeans. "He'll kill me," she kept saying while Mark wiped the bar without looking at her and shook his head. Finally she left, the open door letting in fresh cold air, sweeping away the smoke and the warm stuffiness for a minute. I was beginning to feel very drunk, so drunk that when I looked toward the door and saw Jon come in, the collar of his down jacket pulled high around his neck, I thought I was imagining him, until I saw him stiffen at the sight of me. You could tell by the way his eyes moved, just for a minute, that he thought about turning around and going out again. But when we looked at one another I knew he'd never let himself do it.

"Ellen," he said as he walked down the length of the bar and took a table near the back.

"Jonathan," I said.

I looked at Chris in the mirror. He looked sad.

"Want another?" he said.

"Sure do," I said. That one I sipped, but it didn't really make much difference.

"Your boyfriend from high school, am I right?" Chris said.

I nodded.

"I sort of remember you from high school," he said, "but you were pretty much younger?" Again the question mark.

"High school wasn't exactly the high point of my life," I said, probing with my tongue to see whether I could still feel my gums.

"I liked high school," Chris said, running one finger over the scar on the back of his hand. "It was the closest to being an adult without any of the bad things about being an adult, like rent and taxes and just responsibilities, if you know what I mean."

"That's how I felt about college," I said.

"Oh, well, college," he said, shrugging.

I had to go to the bathroom so badly that it was like a pain in my midsection, but I'd have to pass Jonathan's table to get to it. Finally I slipped off the stool. The light in the bathroom hurt my eyes, and I leaned into the mirror over the sink after I'd washed my hands and looked hard at my own reflection. "Oh, Ellen," I said out loud.

As I went back to the bar, Jonathan called my name again, this time with urgency, but I just waved him off over my shoulder.

"You want to get something to eat?" Chris said.

"Here?"

"Somewhere else?"

When we went out into the night it was so black we could scarcely see each other, which was just as well. In the cab of his truck he tuned in the radio before we drove away and the little yellow-green backlights from the tuning bands lit up his scar so it looked lavender, like a ribbon.

"I'm not really hungry," I said.

"No? Me neither."

I don't remember much about the ride, except the cold, how my fingertips ached, how our breath came puffing out white in the closed cab even though the heat was on, making my toes burn. I sang along to the radio, loud. It was as if I was alone when I did it.

I remember a trailer, a double length made over to look like a ranch house, with shutters and even a little porchlike thing appended to the front, and Chris saying that his father was gone— "Good riddance and sayonara and all that," he said, but there was nothing blithe in his voice, I do remember that—and his mother had moved to California and left it all to him. I think he said that proudly and then tentatively, still with the questions in his voice. He gave me a drink, and then another, vodka this time, with no color to it at all, clear as ice.

The only thing I remember really clearly is the quiet in the trailer, as though nobody lived there, the quiet outside deep in the pinewoods, and my own voice as he got on top of me in the bedroom where the double bed filled nearly every inch of space, so the bureau served as kind of footboard. I turned my head away from his face as it came closer, closer, and on the edge of the bed I could see his hand, the one with the scar, and at some point I said, "I just want to feel something." I thought I was thinking it, but it came out in words, and in that way they do when you're drunk, the words vibrated in my head. I heard them as though from far away, and they seemed to hang in the air like mobiles, each one turning slowly over the bed. "I just want to feel something," I said again, and I did feel something, but it was happening far away, down nearer to the foot of the bed, where the bureau was.

It was just before dawn when I woke up. The pain was starting behind my eyes, and my tongue was fuzzed. I lay for a moment and tried to remember where I was. The windows in the trailer were squat and narrow, so that only a sliver of sky, still dark but beginning to lift just a little, was visible between the trees. The room smelled of sex, used sheets, and space heaters. I got up and went to the bathroom, drank two glasses of water and stared at myself in the mirror. Then I put on my old underpants, the ones with the run in the back, and my cords and my sweater. My bra was in the living room. I put it in my purse, thought for a moment, then picked up the keys Chris had laid on a small table by the door, the kind of little table that Langhorne High boys sometimes made in shop class, with bright brown stain and a high gloss coat of polyurethane. There were two framed photographs on the table, a portrait of Chris in a tie and plaid shirt that had to be his high school graduation picture, and a hand-tinted old-fashioned head and shoulders of a girl who had his eyes and mouth.

I went out to the truck and started the engine, but it was sluggish because of the cold. Twice I had to pump the gas pedal to stop it from idling low and then dying. The second time I heard a knocking noise and jumped when I saw a face on the other side of the steamed glass. Chris was wearing only his pants, and the hair on his chest sprang up from the goose bumps.

"Where you going?" he said. "It's five o'clock."

"I have to go back," I said. "I shouldn't have fallen asleep."

"Well, hey," he said, moving from one foot to another on the cold ground. "I mean, hey, who wouldn't?"

I gunned the engine.

"You want to go to the movies tonight?" he said.

"No," I said.

"Dinner maybe?" The pain behind my eyes was getting worse.

"Look," I said, "my life is strange now and I don't have the energy or the patience to turn a passing conversation in a bar into some big enormous deal. Because it's not." You could see him flinch, almost as though I'd hit him, and I knew that that was exactly what he'd done, that in between that first shot of Wild Turkey and the moment when he'd pulled my sweater over my head he'd probably spun himself some homey fantasies about dinner, conversation, confidences. It had to be lonely, nights out here alone in the trailer, the paneled walls of the tiny bedroom with no pictures. It was deep dark out here, like the inside of a closet when you were playing hide-and-seek and the others had stopped looking for you. Later, when I thought about it, I imagined he mainly wanted the sex for the sake of the company.

"My truck?" he said.

"I have to go back to Sammy's and get my car. I'll leave the truck there with the keys under the mat." It never occurred to me to wonder how he would get there himself, and he didn't fight with me about it. I rolled up the window and pulled out of the narrow opening in the trees that led away from the trailer. In the rearview mirror I could see him standing, hands in pockets, still dancing from one foot to the other.

In a place like Langhorne I would have known if he had told anyone about that night, but I never heard anything, not from Jeff, not from Mrs. Forburg or my lawyer, not secondhand through Mark or Jon or those faceless men who watched in silence as I staggered out of the bar. Chris Mortensen acted like a nice guy that night, and I suspect he probably was. Which made me something much worse than I'd even felt that day, driving his truck through the gathering morning between black rows of pines, leaving him to stare at the four walls of his bedroom.

Let me be honest," said Jules, who had left the magazine to be an articles editor at one of the fashion journals. "The utter degradation you're describing so vividly is all in a night's work for your average New York career woman."

"I know," I said. "It just feels different here."

"Different how? Because everyone knows everyone else's business? Because everyone is interested in yours?" Jules had quit in large part because James had demanded she write a first-person memoir of our friendship. She had called him a fucking slug and emptied her desk before Bill Tweedy had heard of the assignment and killed it. "You ARE a fucking slug," someone told Jules he'd said to James, who replied that a real journalist—bad choice of words, but James had never understood the boss—used his life to enrich his work. "So does a black widow spider," Bill had said.

"I feel like my mother's watching me, judging me, like she sees everything I'm doing," I said.

"Oh, honey," said Jules, "I've always felt that way about my mother."

"But now I feel like she has the right."

"Oh, honey," Jules said.

By the beginning of April the grand jury had heard a dozen witnesses. Jonathan had been in town Easter weekend for his appearance. When I told Jeff I had seen him in Sammy's that night, he said that he imagined Jon wanted to talk to me.

"Did you throw a drink in his face?" he said.

"The thought never crossed my mind."

"Before I die I'm going to break his nose," Jeff said.

"You have my permission," I said.

Jeff took me to the cemetery several weeks after Easter. He waited in the car while I wandered between the rows of stones like a tourist, reading all the familiar names, the names in the Langhorne phone book, on the high school class rosters, on the war memorial in the middle of the town square, on the brass plaques to one side of the doors of the lawyers' offices and doctors' suites, in the engagement and wedding announcements in the *Tribune*. James, Benson, Warren, even Best, Mr. Best's mother, aged eighty-nine. They always said that he had been unusually devoted to her. Perhaps that was my bad luck. Or perhaps it was all the imagined slights over the years, the way I had always looked half amused at his wife's dithering, the skating and swimming at the lake from which I had excluded his children, the puerile graduation speech criticizing the town fathers for their insularity. "Holden Caulfield couldn't have said it better himself," said my father, who was as contemptuous of Salinger as I'd been of the soft and pudgy Best children, improbably named Allegra and Herbert after some long-dead relatives. KATHRYN, said Mr. Best's mother's stone. Again my bad luck. Or perhaps he merely thought he was serving justice, or pouring the concrete footing of a midlife shift to politics. Perhaps there was nothing personal in it for him at all.

My mother's stone was already in place, a small gray rectangle of granite. KATHERINE B. GULDEN, it said. 1945-1991. I knelt and put my hands against it. I looked back and saw Jeff's head turned away, the sunlight making a bright stripe in his auburn hair. Faintly I could hear a guitar riff from the jeep's tape player.

From the pocket of my jacket I took a trowel and began to dig two shallow troughs. The ground was cold and friable, with limp stringy remnants of yellow grass just below the surface. The deeper I dug the warmer it became, and I imagined that six feet under it was warm as toast. Warm as toast, I said, to soothe myself. Warm as toast. I looked at the stone and imagined the line beneath the dates: HER LAST MEAL WAS RICE PUDDING.

The stripe in Jeff's hair was just the color of her own, a warm red-gold, as though the sun was always shining on it. The dirt beneath my nails was a shade darker than her eyes. The Wild Turkey had been just a little lighter.

I had gone to a farmers' market to buy seeds and cold frames for Mrs. Forburg's house, to plant her a perennial border and a vegetable garden. Moving toward the big stall where an Amish woman with silver-blond hair and almost colorless blue eyes had always sold bulbs, I saw a woman with red-gold hair wearing a navy peacoat. Her back was turned to me; she was picking over bulbs, leaning forward to look at the small photographs of flowers that were spiked above each bin, leaning in to ask the woman, in her white bonnet with a virginal frill framing her long oval face, some question about a small knotty tuber on the palm of her outstretched hand.

So foolish, I thought to myself as I edged around people carrying hanging plants and flats of flowers, brushing by women with big pots of garish red tulips like rapacious mouths swaying on their pale green stalks. So stupid, as she moved away from the bulb stall, still with her back to me, and on to a circular wire display of Burpee's seeds, looking at the Big Boys and Better Girls. She went over to a corner of the big warehouse building where peat and fertilizer were stacked in fifty-pound sacks, and out a side door into a blue car with some unreadable college sticker on the back windshield. I think she flashed a glance at me in her rearview mirror, and then she was gone, her hair still curving just above the navy collar of her coat.

Years after, I remember, I read a monograph on grieving that studied bereaved children and found that many thought their mothers had moved away, gone to a new house, a new life, new children. "We are all children," I said aloud as I read it, feeling foolish, foolish and correct, too.

The troughs were finished and I took from my pocket the assortment of bulbs I had gone back and bought after the car had driven away, twenty-four in all: a dozen tiny grape hyacinths and a dozen dwarf tulips, small sturdy things less than a foot tall that would have ruffly pale-pink petals like improbable little birds. I dropped them randomly into the holes and patted them softly into place, planting them out of season.

"You're not allowed to do that," said a man walking by in gray work clothes and a checked wool jacket stiff with dirt.

"So arrest me," I said, picking the soil up in small handfuls and letting it drop onto the bulbs until they finally disappeared. When the holes were filled, I put some mats of dead grass on top to keep the bulbs warm until the earth thawed, and wiped my hands on my pants.

Jeff took me out to a diner on the highway afterward. We ate burgers with cooked onions and greasy fries and chocolate shakes and he talked about the handball game he had once a week with Mr. Duane and how difficult it was to tread the fine line between giving the older man a good game and not going all out and trouncing him. "Plus," Jeff said, his mouth full, "aside from the question of leaving him with a shred of dignity, there's the very real possibility that if I run him around enough he will keel over with a coronary. Pop's in much better condition than Mr. Duane and he starts to get windy on me pretty early on when we play tennis these days."

"How is he?" I asked.

"Ah, you know Dean Duane. One story about the glory days of the bull market after another. When giants walked the hallways of

Dean Witter Reynolds and the corporate raiders were in the full flower of their manhood."

"I meant Papa," I said.

"He's the same," Jeff said. "Maybe a little better. I think he really misses the both of you. It's like he had these two great things going and now they're both gone. He's stopped asking me to talk you into seeing him."

"Do you guys talk about me?"

"Never," said Jeff.

"Mama?"

"Nope. Nor will he discuss Edith Wharton or Jane Austen with me, or the shortcomings of the modern English major. It doesn't leave us with a whole lot to talk about over our TV dinners."

"Not really TV dinners?" I said.

"Nah, I just wanted to make your skin crawl. Actually, it's a lot of pizza and takeout. Have you ever had the Chinese food from the place in the mini-mall just past the Safeway?"

"I don't think so," I said.

"Unfuckingbelievable, El. It is the worst stuff you've ever tasted in your life, but if you pick it up late all the guys who work there are sitting around eating bowls of what looks and smells like Chinatown food, great fish and vegetables and sauce. So one night I point to this guy's bowl and I say, 'Gimme that' and they all start talking to one another in Cantonese dialect or something, and when I get the stuff home, it's moo-shu pork and fried rice. It's Caucasian discrimination, like they think real Chinese food is too rich for our blood."

"Did Papa get a laugh out of that?"

"I didn't tell him. He doesn't really resonate to that kind of thing, if you get my drift."

"You just don't try with him," I said.

"And the feeling is mutual, dear, unless you've forgotten."

"You could have felt the same way about me."

"I did. But there's more to you than meets the eye. Besides, you know many attractive women who can be introduced to me.

Speaking of which, I saw Teresa the other day on Maple Lane. She was visiting Bobby Jackson's dad, who has lung cancer."

"Wow," I said. "For us, Mama was her only case. But for her, it's one of so many."

"Yeah, but she has a special spot in her heart for you still, I think. She told me to tell you that she's not seeing the guy anymore, and to ask you why the gorilla crossed the road."

"Because he thought he was a chicken."

"*Whooa,*" Jeff said, "you are good. Very good."

"That means the lady with the kids and the breast cancer has breast cancer again." I shook my head. "It never ends."

"She said just the opposite. She said to tell you she thinks of you often and it will all be over soon."

"I know. She called me that night after she saw you. She sounds good, although she says she has two patients now who are fading fast."

"Are you going to go see her?"

"Maybe," I said. What I didn't say was that when I had asked Teresa whether I might take her to dinner to thank her for everything she'd done, she replied quietly, "The hospital has asked me not to see you until after all this is settled."

"*Et tu,* Teresa," I said.

"That is not fair, Ellen," she said evenly. "I want very much to see and talk with you and I am very concerned about you. But it is important to other people that, for now, I keep this job."

"I'm sorry," I said.

"We will talk after," she said. "For a long time."

I made no social feints, no more trips to Sammy's. I knew why Jeff chose a restaurant fifteen miles from home and then chose a booth with no other diners seated around it. My voice had automatically taken on a quieter timbre, the better to avoid being overheard. There were fewer messages on the machine, but the assisted suicide and euthanasia zealots still pursued me, and a psychic from Missouri called twice to say that she had talked to my mother, who was very happy and forgave me.

The huge bruise shaped like an open mouth on my left breast had turned from blue-purple to yellow-green, then disappeared, but I had never been able to reconstruct precisely how it had come to be there. Sometimes I would be reading or watching television, *How Green Was My Valley* one night, *I'll Cry Tomorrow* the next, and a momentary tableau would be there before me, a tangle of limbs, frantic movements, loud cries, and I would put my head in my hands.

"Do you remember a Chris Mortensen?" I asked Mrs. Forburg one night when she was correcting essays on *Pride and Prejudice*.

She nodded. "Nice boy," she said. "His father used to bounce him and his mother around a good bit and his mother was an alcoholic, and not a recovering one either, but somehow he turned out very sweet, the kind of boy who'd help you get your car out if it got stuck in the snow in the parking lot. I'm surprised you know him."

"I met him in passing one night."

"He comes to Al-Anon sometimes. I think he goes to meetings himself, too, although I can't say for sure."

"AA, you mean?"

She nodded again. "Whether he inherited it from Mom or started in because of Dad, I'm pretty sure he had a problem. Although maybe he's working on it now."

"Oh, Christ," I said.

"Things are tough all over," she said. She passed me a sheet of looseleaf with a single sentence on it. "The girl named Elizabeth in the story is a snotty bitch!" it said. "What should I reply?" she asked with a small smile. "It's true," I said. "But reductive," she said. "Write that," I said, " 'true, but reductive.' That'll knock him for a loop."

"Why do you assume it's a boy?"

"The bitch part. I don't know. The snotty stuff. It sounds like the cute girl with the locker next to his is ignoring him so he projected onto Jane Austen. Write: Please see me after class and we can compare and contrast the courting rituals of nineteenth-century England with your difficulty getting dates."

"True but reductive," Mrs. Forburg said.

"Are you going to lose your job because people think you're harboring a lesbian murderer for carnal purposes?"

Mrs. Forburg started to laugh. She was wearing a bright red sweater, and her face above it, red-cheeked and shiny, made her look when she laughed like the bride of Santa Claus. She even shook when she laughed, like a bowl full of jelly, although I would never tell her so because she was more sensitive than she pretended about her weight.

"I'm serious."

"I know, it just sounded so much like a cheap television tabloid show. Ellen, I'm sixty-three years old. I've been teaching for thirty-two years and I've been at Langhorne for twenty. I've been asked a hundred times why I don't get a job at the college and I've always had the same answer—"

"That George Gulden wouldn't hire you."

"That may be true. I suspect your father would think I'd irreparably sullied myself by teaching slow fifteen-year-olds. But I like teaching slow fifteen-year-olds. They need me more than the A.P. kids do, who think they've invented the sexual undercurrents in violence when they read *Macbeth* or start writing poetry without capitals, and, in most cases, without meaning, after they've read cummings."

"You've just described Ellen Gulden, class of eighty-five."

"Yes, I have, and if that was all I remembered about Ellen Gulden, class of eighty-five, she wouldn't be here."

"The girl named Ellen in the story is a snotty bitch."

"True, but reductive. I remember meeting your parents at an open school night when you were a sophomore, that year you were taking senior A.P. English and we were trying to figure out how to keep you occupied for the next two years. And I suddenly understood the pressure you must be under, trying to emulate this extraordinarily cerebral and remote man on the one hand

and this extraordinarily warm and nurturing woman on the other."

"It never occurred to me to emulate her."

"Then what have you been doing for the last six months?"

"I haven't a clue."

"Oh, that answer is really beneath you. You know exactly what you've been doing. You've been doing the right thing at enormous personal cost. And now at the end to somehow be blamed for it—it's a Goddamn outrage and I'll tell anyone who asks me. They say that no girl becomes a woman until her mother dies, but all this is ridiculous."

"In my case it should be father."

"Well, father then. Your father's dead to you, isn't he? You never see him. You never talk to him. Wasn't your image of your father always just . . ." she looked up, narrowing her eyes, as though she was searching for the word on the wall of the living room that held a print of Andrew Wyeth's *Christina's World*, the attentuated arms and yearning posture always reminding me of how my mother had looked that day when we'd had our picnic above the college. "Wasn't your image of your father always just refracted through your mother's belief in what he was? Wasn't he really just her creation?"

"He has a very strong personality," I said.

"Does he? He has very broad mannerisms, I'll agree, but that doesn't necessarily mean a strong personality."

"I feel like I'm in analysis," I said.

"Self-analysis," Mrs. Forburg said.

"You still didn't answer my question about your job."

"Sure I did. I said the best part of my job is dealing with the kids who need me most. And I'm eligible for Social Security. And if some of the parents of this town are dumb enough to boot me because a twerp like Ed Murphy wants to see empathy as a sexual perversion, they don't deserve me. And you've avoided my observations about your family."

"My father is not dead. He's in my head all the time. He's a running commentary, that voice of his, like subtitles."

"And your mother?"

"Her, too, but no commentary. Just a presence. Like God. There's not a whole lot of room for me in there."

"Oh, honey," said Mrs. Forburg, and she sounded just like Jules. "That *is* you."

The Montgomery County Courthouse was past its prime. It sat just beyond the green, up a small hill, behind a narrow swath of parkland planted with flowering fruit trees where people often ate their lunches in the warmer months. The library stood across upper Main Street from it, an old red-brick mansion with big square rooms that made for a rabbit warren of reference books, old texts, current bestsellers, and heavily used children's classics. The courthouse was white-gray, with columns along its front, a heavy urnlike light fixture suspended from chains above its ornamented doors, and at the cornice line, just below the front roof, a quote from Shakespeare, BE JUST, AND FEAR NOT.

The courthouse had been built at the turn of the century, and looked not unlike the building in which the Langhorne English department was housed; the same architect had designed them both. The smaller houses around it had been transmogrified into law offices and title companies. But all the time we'd lived in Langhorne there had been constant complaints about the old courthouse, that the courtrooms were difficult to heat and air-condition, that the judge's chambers were not large enough. Most of all there were complaints that the old courthouse was too great a distance from the offices of the prosecutor and the police, built some years before in one of the commercial developments that had insinuated themselves amid the corn and bean fields and stretches of undevelopable stony land far from Langhorne proper.

The courthouse looked like the sort of courthouse habitually used in movies, and there had been a huge uproar when I was in junior high school and a television production company had come to town to film a pivotal scene in a true-crime drama on the shallow steps that led up to its columns and front door. The *Tribune* had run stories on page one about the movie, about the leading actor, about the use of Langhorne locals as extras. It had been one of the biggest stories I could remember, but not bigger than my own.

But still there were complaints about the old building, although those who had lived in Langhorne all their lives held out against change, even when Ed Best was elected district attorney and made the construction of a new, more modern facility the linchpin of his campaign, along with more DWI crackdowns. His chief opponent was the assignment judge, a forty-year veteran of the bench named James P. Hallorhan who lived two blocks from the courthouse and had the biggest office in the building, a corner one with mahogany paneling and a small ornamental fireplace.

After he died his fight was carried on by his widow, a deceptively fragile-looking woman named Alice who took her exercise each day by walking to the courthouse, roving the halls greeting old acquaintances, some of them judges in the middle of hearing a case, and then walking home. But Ed Best, dim as he sometimes seemed, dreamed up a way to get Alice Hallorhan on his side, and that was how the county came to break ground, the year before my mother died, for the James P. Hallorhan County Justice Building on a cul de sac off the highway, a cube of glass and stone that would hold prosecutors, police, and all court functions.

It was only half done, having run into all manner of construction troubles, from the ventilation to the substructure, and so on the day I testified before the grand jury charged with deciding whether I had killed my mother, I did it in the old courthouse, which was as easy and familiar as almost any building in Langhorne to me. In tenth grade we had had a kind of rudimentary moot court competition on the death penalty, and I had been the judge. I had sentenced the defendant to life without parole after usurping the privilege of the Supreme Court from the bench and ruling the death penalty unconstitutional. I liked the view from up there. I liked the power.

Thank God no one had remembered, or, remembering, told the newspaper and television people. The day I testified before the grand jury the *Tribune* ran a profile of me which began on page one and was spread over a full page inside. They used my high school graduation picture, a photograph taken in the statehouse the day I won the essay contest in which I held my certificate to my chest in much the same manner I had held the ID board when my mug shots were taken, and, of course, the picture taken as I left the courthouse after I'd been bailed out. GOLDEN GIRL, said the headline, and below it in smaller type A LIFE OF STELLAR ACCOMPLISHMENT ENDS IN A MURDER CHARGE.

"Ends?" I said to Jeff that morning on the phone. "Ends? I'm not dead. I'm not even indicted yet."

"Count your blessings," he said. "There's not a single Angel of Death reference in the whole thing."

The truth was that it wasn't a bad piece. It was accurate as far as that went, except that it said that my mother's parents had emigrated from Germany and that my father's had operated a resort in the mountains, an error that made me conjure up my grandfather Gulden in a sun visor and plaid Bermudas instead of overalls. It quoted from the same sections of my mercy killing essay that Bob Greenstein had picked out in his office, and from my graduation speech: "Authority must earn the right to lead, and we owe ourselves the right to refuse to follow if they do not." "Oh, shit," I said, but even though I could remember standing at the podium on the lawn of Langhorne High School pontificating in a high voice, more frightened than I would ever have admitted, my mother's eyes hidden by her sunglasses, my father's eyebrows raised so slightly only someone who knew him as well as I did could have seen it, I could not remember speaking those words. But they sounded like me.

They'd talked to Jonathan's father, who said that he was confident that the jury would understand what I'd done and take into account how worn down I'd been by caring for my mother— "insanity defense" I said aloud—and to several of the Minnies, who talked of how tired I'd looked the day we decorated the tree. They'd talked to Halley McPherson, who showed them the crib with tears in her eyes and recounted my words "It'll all be over soon" when she visited before my mother's death. They talked to several anonymous nurses at the hospital, who said that I seemed unusually well-versed in medical techniques. They talked to high school classmates who did not like me, and high school classmates who said they liked me but could understand if others did not. There was a sophomoric poem I had submitted to the literary magazine, which had held up publication for several weeks while it was decided at the highest levels whether the word "fuck" could be rendered as F*** or whether the poem would have to be removed. "We all knew Ellen would have made a fuss about that," said my P.E. teacher Mrs. Schultz, who for some reason had been on the faculty board of the student publications.

God, it was a bad poem. And the *Tribune* rendered it as (expletive deleted).

Julie Heinlein, she of the soft-voiced phone messages, had written the story in a workmanlike fashion. But she had not talked to Jeff or my father, to Jules or Teresa, to Mrs. Forburg or Ed Best. When I read the profile all I could think of was what I had told

Bob Greenstein about people wanting their little stories neat, tied up with a ribbon. The newspaper article was accurate, as far as it went; it just wasn't exactly true, from the air of lugubriousness that seemed to hang over recollections of our family life to its rendering of me as a woman of steel, with neither qualms nor conscience.

"She didn't do it," said Bob Greenstein, in the third paragraph of the story. "That's all you need to know."

"I've known Ellen since she was reading the Nancy Drew mysteries," said Isabel Duane, if Julie Heinlein's description was to be believed, with some asperity, "and it has never for a minute occurred to me that she would have hurt Kate in any way. She loved her so much. If you could have seen her pushing her wheelchair when they came in here—nobody who saw them could believe it."

It was a lovely thing for Mrs. Duane to do, except that I'd always hated the Nancy Drew books.

Bob was furious about it when he came to pick me up that morning in the low-slung red sports car that he drove, I was convinced, only to prove he was capable of getting out of it. "Why do you think it's in there this morning?" he said. "Best leaked them the date of your appearance. It's bad enough you insist on doing this, without a whole mess of reporters and photographers there when you do it."

"But I thought the grand jury proceedings were all secret," I said.

"In theory they are, my friend, but in practice I would not put it past that shit to up his public profile with a well-placed word to someone from the *Tribune* at the Kiwanis." He shot a glance at me sideways. "Do us both a favor," he said. "Don't smile this time."

"Don't worry," I said.

When we got to the courthouse—BE JUST, AND FEAR NOT, I read aloud, and Bob just sighed—he swung around to a back entrance and tapped on a steel door, tried the knob, tapped again. A guard opened the door a crack, spoke to him, looked from him to me, and shook his head.

"We've got to go in the front," Bob said. "Don't answer any questions."

As we came up the steps I shivered. I was wearing the blue suit I'd worn for the funeral; Jeff had brought it from the house. My hair hung long and loose around my face, and for the first time since Thanksgiving I was wearing makeup.

The reporters were in the lobby, in the circular rotunda with its mosaic floor laid in the pattern of an enormous bronze and gold sun. One of them, a radio reporter with a tape recorder tucked under his arm, saw us first, and a kind of muted cry went up, and then like some grotesque animal they all moved together, cameras, notebooks, pens, and microphones held high like weapons. I could not pick out one question from another: Why have you decided to testify? What are your plans? What do you want them to know about what happened?

We pushed through but they moved with us to a bank of elevators at the back of the building, the elevators Bob had hoped to catch in the basement instead of on the lobby floor when he knocked at the door outside. Some of the questions were for him: Why did you decide to have her testify? Will she testify at the trial? I looked down at the toes of my pumps, which my mother had bought for me. We'd worn the same size shoes. I thought there was a little mud around the edge of the soles from the last time I'd worn them.

Bob guided me into the elevator and then stood in the doorway so no one else could get in. He held the door and leaned forward, his square bulk blocking me from their sight. "You tell Ed Best he could lose his license for a stunt like this," he hissed, and there was an infinitesimal moment of complete silence, and in it I heard the voice of someone, faintly, as though from far away, asking plaintively, "Well, who is it?" And the doors closed.

"That was smart," I said, "the way you did that."

"Yeah? Tell me why it was smart."

"Because now instead of focusing on me testifying, they'll focus on you threatening Ed Best," I said.

"You're smart, too," he said. "Just remember that smart helped get you into this mess and smart isn't going to get you out. You've reached the limits of smart."

"I know," I said.

I remembered from the day of the moot court competition in high school that the courtrooms had long narrow windows and burnished paneling like fine furniture around the bench, the jury box, along the walls. The courtroom ceilings had been high, and the symmetry of justice had been written in the seating arrangements, the judge above it all, the jury to one side, looking on, passing judgment.

The grand-jury room was nothing at all like that. It was less than half the size of one of those courtrooms, with two small windows along one wall that let in so little light that someone had put on the overhead fixture, a rectangular fluorescent light that flickered every now and then. Bob had told me that there were twenty-three jurors, but he had not told me that we would all sit in such close quarters that I only recognized the prosecutor, an assistant in Mr. Best's office, because he was the one wearing the suit and tie. The others were in less formal dress, ranged on hard chairs in a loose semicircle around a small table. In the beginning I tried not to look at them, as though eye contact would put them on the spot. I was sworn and I found something soothing about it, as though I had said a prayer for my own soul. I intended to tell the truth, although perhaps not all of it, depending on the questions.

But as the prosecutor began to ask me how I came to nurse my mother and how she had deteriorated and who had been alone with her the last day of her life I began to look, not at him, a man perhaps ten years older than I with a shaggy haircut and a shirt collar at least a half-size too small, as though he was finding it difficult to move past the person he'd been at twenty-five. I began to look at the people ranged around me.

Part of it was that I wanted them to understand what had happened, but part was simply curiosity. It was difficult for me to believe that there were nearly two dozen people in Montgomery County I didn't know by name, hadn't been served by at the five-and-ten or the luncheonette, hadn't seen in the parking lot of the supermarket with one of my classmates in the car.

The truth was that several of them looked familiar, not familiar enough to put a name to but familiar enough to know that I'd looked across the pumps at the gas station, perhaps, and seen him pumping gas into his truck, or walked by the beauty parlor that stood across the street from Sammy's and seen her under the dryer, bought tomatoes at a roadside stand from this one or seen that one shoveling a walk in front of some house across town from my own.

But there was one woman I thought I knew from the moment I first looked at her, although the longer I stayed in that room— and it was a long time, almost two hours, if you counted those times when I was sent out and invited back in again, the prosecutor with his lips pressed together over slightly protruding teeth— the more I realized I didn't know her so much as apprehend her, perhaps understand her. She was in that middle ground between aging and elderly, a thin woman with silver hair worn handsomely in a short bob swept to one side, eschewing the fuzzy permanents of her kind. She wore a medium-blue knit suit with a skirt that just covered her knees, and she held her hands clasped in her lap, narrow white hands dappled with the dark spots of age. From time to time she turned the two rings atop each other on her left hand. I could imagine her living in one of the pretty small houses just to the south of ours, the widow of a middle manager or even a Langhorne administrator.

But it was her posture that made me tell everything, after a while, to her and her alone, the face in the audience an actor chooses to emote to. She sat very straight but she seemed to yearn forward just a little bit, her shoulders ahead of her hips, and she looked into my face with a searching look in her blue eyes, as though she was waiting for me to solve the puzzle she'd been working slowly these many weeks, to tell her what really happened.

"Miss Gulden," said the prosecutor, whose name was Peters, "I'd like you to read something." He handed me a copy of the essay I'd written for the essay contest—the original copy, it appeared, for it was stamped with a date six years before and the *e* in the words was slightly lifted, something my electric typewriter had always done after I'd knocked it off my desk one day.

"You wrote this?" he said after I'd read it aloud.

"I did," I said.

"And won first prize in the annual state Young Writers' Competition?"

"Yes."

"Do you still agree with the sentiments in that essay?"

"Yes," I said, "as far as they go."

"What do you mean by 'as far as they go'?"

"I still believe that people are kept alive long past the time when life is of any use to them. But when I wrote that essay, I knew nothing about the subject firsthand."

They were all looking at me now, except for a young man, almost a boy, really, who was staring conspicuously out one of the windows.

"And now you do."

"Yes."

"From your mother's illness and death."

"Yes."

"Did your mother agree with the sentiments expressed here?"

"We never discussed it," I said.

"Not when you won the contest?" he asked.

"No."

"Not when you were caring for her, doing the things you've described, watching her deteriorate, in your opinion."

"No."

"Miss Gulden," he said, tapping the palm of his hand with a

pencil in a gesture so reminiscent of a movie gesture that I almost smiled, except that I heard Bob Greenstein's voice saying, "Don't smile, don't smile."

"Miss Gulden," he said, "did you believe that your mother's life in her final days was worth living?"

"That's not how I would put it."

"In your words?"

"I think my mother had lost her dignity, her place, all the things that made her life happy. She was wearing diapers. She was sleeping almost constantly. And for a woman like her, who'd always been so capable, so full of life, so lively—it was a terrible thing. It was terrible for her and it was terrible for me."

"Miss Gulden, did you tell police officers Brown and Patterson that if they had seen your mother they would have thought she was better off dead?"

"Yes."

"Did you tell Jonathan Beltzer that if you were a good daughter you would put a pillow over her face and suffocate her?"

"I don't remember if those were my exact words. I said something like that."

"Had you been drinking?"

"No."

"Did you know what constituted an overdose of your mother's morphine tablets?"

"Yes."

"Did you know that if you crushed or broke those tablets they would become even more toxic than they already were?"

"Yes."

The woman in the blue suit was leaning toward me, as though she wanted to say something, to ask me her own questions, perhaps to stop me.

"Do you recall what your mother's last meal was?"

It was the first time I had stopped during my testimony. I frowned and looked down at my hands in my lap and saw again his hand, elegant, graceful, with the silver spoon held in its fingers, up, down, and over, up, down, and over.

"I don't remember."

"No idea?"

"I hadn't had any sleep for several days. It was probably one of several things, either some cream soup, some applesauce, some pudding, maybe some yogurt. She couldn't eat anything that wasn't the consistency of baby food."

"You would have fed her."

"Sometimes she fed herself. It didn't go very well. I had to change the top sheet."

"Did that annoy you?"

"I was well past being annoyed, Mr. Peters."

That was a mistake. "How far past, Miss Gulden?" he asked. It was a rhetorical question.

"At the risk of repeating myself," he continued, "I want to go back. You believe that there are times when someone's quality of life is so compromised that death, whether natural or assisted, would be preferable."

"Yes," I said.

"You believe that your mother's quality of life was horribly impaired at the end of her life?"

"Yes."

"And did you give her a fatal overdose of morphine?"

"No."

"Given what else you've said, I've got to ask—why not?"

"Why not what?"

"If you believe in what you wrote and you believe in what you've said, it would be logical for you to have given your mother an overdose. You even told the police that that's what they would have done."

"Let me try to explain," I began, trying not to let my voice rise or harden, and I looked right at the woman in the blue suit, who was sitting perfectly still. "Maybe it's the difference between say-ing you're for capital punishment and being willing to sit there and pull the switch on the electric chair. In theory, I meant these things. But when it's real, when it's a real person—it's different. I was so busy keeping her clean and making her food and making sure she had her medicine, I never stopped to think about anything bigger than how we were going to get through the next hour. Maybe it was like having a baby in that respect. Everyone talks about how wonderful it is, how fulfilling, but I've always thought it seems like one little piece of drudgery after another, a feeding, a changing, a bath, and maybe it's only afterward that it seems wonderful. I didn't have time to think about anything more than all those little things, taking care of my mother. It's so much easier to know just how you feel about things, what you believe, when you're writing it on paper than when you really have to do anything about it or live with it."

"Could you have done it if you wanted, Miss Gulden?" he said.

"Yes. But I didn't."

He was finished with me, but she wasn't, I'm sure. They sent me out into the hallway where Bob sat, looking through some files. He looked at me over the half-moons of his reading glasses but neither of us spoke as I stood outside the door that said GRAND JURY in faded gold stenciling. It was a thick wood door, some narrow-grained wood, and no sound came from the other side. After a few minutes I heard noises from the end of the corridor, and looking down it I saw my father come around the bend and stop. He lifted his hand and waved, and it was when I saw him that I remembered how I had looked at them both that last night.

"Go take a rest, Ellen," I said to Bob Greenstein, and I started to shake.

"What?" he said, still looking down the hall.

"You asked me about her last words. She said 'Go take a rest, Ellen.' She wanted to be alone with him."

"Your father?" he said.

"Yes."

"Did they ask you about that inside?"

"No." I wrapped my arms around myself, and he put an arm around my shoulder.

"She sent me away," I said.

"He blew you a kiss," Bob said.

"What?"

"Your father," he said. "He just blew you a kiss."

"He waved."

"Looked like a kiss to me," Bob said.

The door opened. "Ms. Gulden," the prosecutor said. His hair was ruffled, as though he had been running his hand through it, and as I followed him back into the grand-jury room and sat down he turned his back on me.

"Miss Gulden, I have one last question. Did you love your mother?"

It was not what I had expected. When I had looked at her and she had looked back at me, the woman in the blue suit, with a question in her eyes, I had thought that question was the one which would most require me to lie. I had waited the two hours, in this wooden chair with curving arms, to be asked whether I had any idea who had done it. But to this question I could tell the truth if only I knew how to do it. "Jesus, kid," I could almost hear Bob saying, "the answer is yes. Simple. Elegant. Yes. Nobody needs poetry here."

But she was looking at me so fixedly, almost as if she'd asked the question herself. Bob had told me that any of them could tell the prosecutor they wanted a question asked, and that he was obliged to ask it unless he could dissuade them, that in theory he was there only as the jurors' agent. I looked at her and I was sure that the prosecutor had not wanted to ask the question, that it was she who had made him ask it.

"The easy answer is yes. But it's too easy just to say that when you're talking about your mother. It's so much more than love— it's, it's everything, isn't it?" as though somehow they would all nod. "When someone asks you where you come from, the answer is your mother." My hands were crossed on my chest now, and the woman in the blue suit turned her rings. "When your mother's gone, you've lost your past. It's so much more than love. Even when there's no love, it's so much more than anything else in your life. I did love my mother, but I didn't know how much until she was gone."

"Did you kill her?" the prosecutor asked.

"No I did not," I said. "I couldn't do it."

I guess, if the movies are to be believed, that when a jury is ready to tell you what they've decided you've done, or didn't do, you get to your feet in front of them and they tell you plainly, publicly, with the kind of ceremony that, in most of our lives, is reserved for confirmations or weddings. In the old days they executed you that way, too, but no more.

I was on my way home from the Safeway, from buying cubed meat, carrots, and tiny onions for a stew, from buying yeast and wheat flour for bread and shortening and pureed pumpkin for pie, when I turned on an all-news radio station and discovered that the grand jury had decided not to indict Ellen M. Gulden for the death of Katherine B. Gulden. Frozen in stone still, both of them were: the Harvard honors graduate, the wife of the chairman of the Langhorne English department. We had been distilled to our component parts long ago, Mama and me. Like the last veteran of some old war, I felt as if I was the only one left who knew us as we used to be, as we really were.

It was a chilly day but there was a little bit of warmth rising from the ground, so that you could imagine, if you took a good long sniff, that from this soil in the foreseeable future would come lilacs, then hollyhocks and roses. The Belknaps' perennial border would soon begin to come back from the dead. The grape hyacinths, those baby fingers of purple panicles, so small you had to search for them amid the grass, would unfurl slowly from the ground around my mother's headstone this time next year. The tulips would follow. Long after people had ceased to talk about me at parties and in the aisles between the Duanes' oak bookshelves, the hyacinths and tulips would revive, thrive, yellow, die, sleep, revive again. And she would never, ever see them. Even the flowers went on without you, so fierce was death.

"No bill" was what they said on the radio, "no cause." No case, no trial. No nothing. No nothing. I felt nothing as I drove over the curving back road that led to Mrs. Forburg's house, or perhaps what I felt was that odd sense you have when you are barreling down a street and you discover it is a cul de sac, a dead end.

I came around the S-curve and before me one of the small valleys surrounding Langhorne was spread, a patchwork of different greens, deciduous and evergreen, in the afternoon light. At the bottom of the hill was the house that had bailed me out two months before, and in front of it and across the road, too, I could see a coven of cars and a van with a satellite dish. I made a U-turn and drove down the road behind, parked on the shoulder and hiked through the woods, laden with grocery bags. They saw me, some of them, as I emerged from the line of trees and sprinted to the back door; I could hear someone shout and then the others begin to move, like a battalion on the battlefield. But I was in before they had time to shoot me.

The red light on the answering machine glowed in the dimness of the closed house, with its blinds drawn tight for so many days. "Ms. Gulden, this is Nancy Barrett at CBS. This—" and with a push of a button it was gone. Gone was the *Time* magazine reporter with the name that sounded as though it had come off a headstone in Boston's oldest cemetery, the *Times* reporter, who sounded as if she had a cold, and Julie Heinlein, her voice weary: "If by any chance you want to talk to anyone it could be completely on your terms." With the push of a button I made them all disappear.

Jeff sounded jubilant. "Don't go anywhere," he said. "We're coming to get you."

I could hear the reporters outside, one of them taking a coffee order for the others, prepared to drive all the way downtown to the luncheonette. "Regular or light?" he said. "Betts—I asked you a question. Regular or light? And a roll? What the hell do you think this is, a restaurant?" Two of the men were talking about their children, about how much trouble they were causing now that they'd learned to walk. "Wait until they're fifteen," someone else said.

I browned the meat. I rolled the crust. I kneaded bread dough and put it aside to rise in a bowl that Mrs. Forburg said had belonged to her mother. The phone rang, the machine picked up, and I heard her voice, "Ellen, if you're there—"

I picked up the receiver, leaving flour on the mouthpiece, the dial. "I'm here," I said.

She must have been in the pay phone just outside the gym. I could hear a babble behind her, dozens of voices in a fractious harmony, a shout or mock-scream punctuating it all. "Hello?" I said.

"It's noisy here," Mrs. Forburg said. Then there was silence again and I could tell by her breathing that she was crying.

"I'm making your dinner," I said.

"You just leave it there for me on the stove," she said, "and you pack your bags and you get as far away from there as fast as you can for as long as you can."

"They must have believed me," I said.

"They damn well should have," she said.

"Yo, Michael," someone shouted in the background, then said, "Oh, sorry, Mrs. F."

"You'll get your money back on the bail," I said.

"Lord, Ellen," Mrs. Forburg said, "you think of the most irrelevant things. Is Jeff taking you to the city?"

"I think so."

"When you get settled you call and give me your address and I'll come and visit."

"I'll miss you. Thank you." And after a time from the other end there was the echo, "I'll miss you. Thank you." When we hung up, the phone rang again immediately, a reporter from the Associated Press, but the machine just took the message while I sat down at the kitchen table and wrote out instructions on how to finish making the bread and when to take the stew out of the oven. Then it rang again and I heard a soft and slightly accented voice: "Ellen, this is Teresa Guerrero calling." There was a pause as though she knew I was listening. I don't know why it was only when I heard Teresa's voice that something inside me broke just a little, and I began to cry.

"Hello, Ms. Guerrero," I said.

"I am happy today, Ms. Gulden," she replied evenly. "And many of my patients will be, too, fellow sufferers who followed this with personal interest."

"How is the woman with the breast cancer and the kids?" I asked.

"Not so good."

"Teresa, I just want you to know something," I said. "I didn't do it."

"It is not important."

"It's important to me. It's important to me that you believe it. Especially you."

"I always have. But it was never important. You have many more important things to do. So much work. So much work. I pity you, friend."

"I have no job."

"Ah, Ellen," Teresa said, "you know quite well that is not the work I mean."

"Will you come and see me in the city?"

Teresa sighed. "Only for you would I go there. Only for you."

When Jeff came to the back door, his face pink with pleasure and the exertion of sprinting across the yard, my duffel bag was already packed.

"The last time I tried to do this, the cops came," I said.

"So we won't take any chances," Jeff said, and he grabbed my hand and together we ran across the backyard to his jeep, parked next to Mrs. Forburg's car, and jumped into our seats. The reporters were eating in front, eating and having their afternoon coffee, too, and they never even saw us sneak away, hand in hand, like Hansel and Gretel.

"Haul ass," I said quietly.

"Not yet," Jeff said, and he headed downtown, toward the town square and Main Street, the courthouse rising above it all. I thought of the woman in the blue suit, of how she'd seemed to lean just a little forward. "They must have believed me," I said as Jeff tried to tune in the all-news station.

The next day the papers said that maybe they hadn't, maybe they'd believed, as so many others had, that I'd done what I was accused of doing because of love or duty, that the prosecutors had gone too far. But just for that afternoon, as Jeff whipped around the curvy roads, I thought that maybe someone had believed what I said.

". . . Gulden, a former Harvard honors student, with the murder of her mother, Katherine. Mrs. Gulden, the wife of the chairman of the English department at Langhorne College, died in February and an autopsy . . ." the radio bleated, and then the signal wavered and a Brahms concerto took its place. We rounded a corner and heard a fragment of Ed Best talking, and then the weather. Tomorrow would be sunny, highs in the seventies. Spring had arrived.

No one had planted flowers in the tubs at the bottom of the porch steps and the azalea by the side of the garage looked as though it had died, although a few green leaves on one stem had made a valiant effort. Jeff turned off the engine. "I thought you might want to go inside," he said. I stared at him, then back at the house. "Pop will be here in fifteen minutes. He called me when he heard. The first thing he said was 'Perhaps now I can see your sister.' Not 'isn't it great.' Not 'whoopdedoo.' Just like that: 'Perhaps now I can see your sister.' I'll never understand him. Never, no matter how hard I try."

Jeff opened the door of the jeep. "I can't, Jeffie. Especially not right now."

"You sure?"

"Perfectly sure." I looked back at the house, my home. "Is it dusty?" I finally said.

"He's got a cleaning lady from the college coming in once a week."

"That's not enough. Has he changed anything?"

"No."

"I can't," I said again.

Jeff climbed out of the jeep. "Okay, wait," he said, and he went toward the kitchen door, and I could see the table in my mind, unpolished, untidy.

"Jeff," I called, and he turned back to me. "I want something."

When he came out of the house he had it under his arm, the glass in the frame glittering as the sunlight caught it. He laid it on my lap, the photograph of my father, my mother on one arm, I on the other, at my college graduation. I unzipped my duffel, wrapped a nightshirt around the picture, and shoved it deep in the bag.

"Isn't there one of you and her alone?" Jeff said.

"No," I said, "I don't think there ever was one."

He drove down the hill, past the shoe store and Phelps's Hardware and the Duanes', and I thought I could see the shadow of Mrs. Duane's pale hair through the window, past the displays of books. The daffodils stood straight on the green, so many of them. If I squinted there was only a yellow blur beneath the flagpole.

"Which way are you going?" I said.

"Train station," Jeff said, and he grinned.

And there on the platform was Jules in her city clothes, her long gauzy black skirt, her cowboy boots, her black leather jacket and black sunglasses, her black backpack and black hair curling wildly around her head. I got out of the car and she ran, her boots making tapping sounds on the platform and the stairs, and grabbed me so hard we both listed to the left.

"I told you to stay in the city," I said, holding her and looking at her, holding her and then looking again. She was thinner than I'd remembered, and her eyes looked different.

"I had eyeliner tattooed on," she said, blinking. "It hurt like a bitch but it's one less thing to do in the morning."

"Oh, Jesus, Jules," I said.

"You were on the AP wire," she said. "They spelled your name wrong. They made you Golden."

"Yeah," I said.

"You are Golden," Jules said, and she climbed into the jeep.

"I just didn't think you should be alone for the ride," she said, once I was in back and she next to Jeff.

"Excuse me, but what am I, the chauffeur?" Jeff said. "Yes, Miss Julie, ma'am, where we going, Miss Julie?"

"Oh, you know what I mean," she said.

Every news station had something about the grand jury, and so we turned on a music station and played it loud. Jules decided we should put the top down, and our hair whipped around our faces, sticking to our lips and teeth, blinding us. We rode for an hour like that, singing along with the radio. When Jules turned around to talk to me I leaned forward, one hand on my duffel so it wouldn't blow away.

"I found a new place, two blocks from mine!" she shouted, the only way she could be heard. "It's prime, honey. A fireplace, two bedrooms, a bathroom with a window." I'd almost forgotten how much a window in the bathroom meant in New York City.

"How much?" I said.

"Only three hundred more than I'm paying now. Let's do it, El. I have to make a decision tomorrow or let it go—you know how they are. You'll find a job and three hundred will be nothing."

"Or I'll sell my story to television."

"So you'll find something. C'mon."

"I don't know, Jules. No guy right now? No hot prospects?"

Jules held back her hair with her long fingers. "There was a guy, now there's not a guy, then there'll be a guy, then no guy, guy gone. You know the routine."

"I do," I said.

"That shithead," Jules said, and we both knew who she meant.

"Yeah, well," I said.

"Yeah, well, nothing. If I run into him I'll take him apart."

"No men for me right now," I said.

"So let's take this place."

"All right," I said, and Jules bounced up and down in her seat like an excited child.

"You're the best, Julie Julie Boboolie," Jeff said.

Jules leaned toward me until her hair touched my arm softly. "If only he was a little older," she said.

"I heard that," Jeff yelled. "That's completely and totally unfair. Younger men are happening. Younger men are a trend."

"Oh, stop," Jules said. "You can't settle down with a trend." Jeff accelerated and we came over a rise in the highway and there, poking into the air like a quiver full of arrows, was the island of Manhattan, the Emerald City, a glorious mirage.

Jules turned around and smiled at me. "Click your heels together three times and say there's no place like home," she said.

"Yeah, and if I do where will I wind up?" I said. And over the ramp and through the tunnel all of us were silent, until on the other side we came into the center of it, came out next to a hotdog cart with a yellow-and-blue umbrella and steam rising from the square hole in its center, to a young black man with a squeegee, the skin tight on his facial bones, who jumped back and yelled, "Hey, motherfucker!" when Jeff turned on the wipers, shifted gears, and took off down Ninth Avenue.

"I'm not sure where I am," I said.

"I know, honey," said Jules. "Welcome to the island of lost souls."

"You two are a pair," Jeff said.

"I'd marry her in a minute if I could," Jules said, turning around to smile at me and pat my knee.

"There's no place like home," I said. "There's no place like home."

"We're not in Kansas anymore," Jules said.

"There's no place like home," I said again as we headed south to the Village.

EPILOGUE

My beeper went off during the second act of a new musical about children in a tuberculosis hospital at the turn of the century. All down the row of velvet seats in the rich darkness of the theater, I saw heads turn and eyes glisten out of the black disapprovingly, as the tinny birdsong issued, muffled, from between my wallet and my checkbook. I reached down into my purse, switched it off, and looked at Richard, smiling ruefully. "Always, always," he whispered, squeezing my upper arm and sending me up the aisle, crouched a bit so as not to disturb the audience, to call the hospital.

It took me a long time to find a job after I moved in with Jules that spring eight years ago. Perhaps I could have found another berth in journalism, even had my old job back at the magazine. But I would have been hired as an oddity, a talking point, book-party gossip.

Besides, I knew too much about the business now from the other side of the notebook. It was not just the stories that had been written about me during the investigation, and afterward, too, nor the fact that Jon sold a first-person account of our relationship to a magazine which put it on the cover along with the omnipresent photograph of me, the inappropriate effect of my Mona Lisa smile.

It was the idea of facing a future skimming the surface of life, winging my way in and out of other people's traumas, crises, confusions, and passages, engaging them enough to get the story but never enough to be indelibly touched by what I had seen or heard. Jules left, too, went into book publishing because she said that hard covers had a dignity that slick glossy paper and flimsy newsprint did not. Every New Year's Eve she offered me a million dollars to write the story of my recent life, and every New Year's Eve I called her a fucking slug, and then we got drunk together. I love Jules. Every New Year's Eve she says if I were not a woman she would marry me tomorrow. She says when they change the laws we should do it anyway.

Afterward some people said—and a few wrote—that it was inevitable that I would go to medical school, but the truth was that I did not think about it until I began visiting AIDS patients at the hospital around the corner from my apartment. I stayed with Jules for six months and then got a place of my own, paid for it with temp work and an evening job as a waitress at a fairly famous bar and grill, where I waited on young Wall Street types with incipient paunches beneath their custom-cut shirts, as well as the occasional up-and-coming movie actor.

I slept with a lot of men during those months, just to feel something. Several of them reminded me of Jonathan, but not one of them reminded me of Chris Mortensen. Perhaps that's why I had no regrets about them. When Jeff told me nearly two years after that Easter weekend that Chris Mortensen, from high school, remember him?, short guy, had been killed in a head-on collision between his pickup and the McNultys' dump truck—the McNultys, naturally, were not even scratched, although they folded their garbage collection business because the younger lost his license for driving while intoxicated, something the elder had done the year before—I searched his face carefully for something hidden there. But he looked guileless. Maybe it was just a bit of Langhorne gossip. Maybe not.

I was lonely, that first year back in New York. Except for Jules, I had only two kinds of friends—those who had abandoned me because of what had happened and those who took me up only because of it. I was also approached by those who wanted me to champion the right to die, assisted suicide, passive euthanasia, to become a poster girl for the cause, as though there had been no denials, no dropped charges, no insistence that I had not done what they believed I should be so proud of doing. One doctor devoted to helping people with multiple sclerosis die by hooking a hose to a car's exhaust pipe came in person to my apartment, hose in hand. I closed one of his fingers in the door.

My decision to become a doctor had nothing to do with any of that. Not long after I moved into my own place, a studio with a stove and small refrigerator hidden behind louvered doors in a closet, the man across the hall, an actor, began to lose flesh from his long bones, in a deadly progression that seemed so natural to me that I scarcely registered it at first. When I went to see him in the hospital in October, bright blotches now disfiguring the face that had once brought him soap-opera roles and coffee commercials, I was importuned by the head nurse to visit some of her other patients. When she asked me twice to spell my name— Gulden? Gulden? Oh, like the mustard—something relaxed inside me.

I did it for myself, the visiting, because I was so lonely. And perhaps for Brian, too. After our mother died he avoided me, and I assumed that it was because he, too, disbelieved my denials. But then one day he came into the city from Philadelphia on the train. I met him on the platform at Penn Station, the air warm and faintly tinged with gray, as though we were lovers in some old movie coming together again after many years, crowds eddying around us as we caught one another's eyes. And we did catch one another's eyes, staring full into each other's faces, and then he smiled, that sweet bright smile, and I held him for so long a time that people would have been justified in thinking we were lovers.

"Oh, El," he repeated over and over again.

At dinner that night at the restaurant where I worked, where they fed us free, he told me that he was gay, that he thought sometimes that his quiet all his life had been a way of holding back the words that frightened him so. All the time I thought he hated me for something I hadn't done, he believed I would be repelled by what he was doing. It was joy, knowing both of us were wrong.

Even today he has still not told our father. But that night, as we sat for hours over coffee, this seemed less important to him than the sure knowledge that our mother would have accepted him.

"She wouldn't have cared," he said.

"No," I said, "she wouldn't."

That's not exactly true, of course. My mother would have cared very much, would have cared that her best beloved baby was assigned a path that might cause him pain and ridicule, that his life might be harder because of it. She would have cared very much about the daughter-in-law she would never have had—quiet, pretty, so dear, she surely would have imagined her—and the grandchildren there would never be. But it was simpler to say that she would not have cared. We made her simpler after she was dead. No, that's not true, either. We'd made her simpler all her life, simpler than her real self. We'd made her what we needed her to be. We'd made her ours, our one true thing.

It's all anyone wants, really, to make life simple. Sometimes people have wondered why I'm not more bitter about what happened to me. And I was bitter for a long time, but at base I understand. Death is so strange, so mysterious, so sad, that we want to blame someone for it. And it was easy to blame me. Besides, when people wonder how I survived being accused of killing my mother, none of them realizes that watching her die was many, many times worse. And knowing I could have killed her was nothing compared to knowing I could not save her. And knowing I'd almost missed knowing her was far more frightening than Ed Best and his little army of shrunken suits.

In all that time in New York, finding my way again, inventing a new one, I never saw my father. In the beginning it did not seem to be deliberate. I no longer celebrated holidays; he rarely came into town. For a year he was a visiting professor in England; for my last two years of med school I worked so hard that I sometimes went for days seeing no one but my classmates and whoever happened to be admitted to the hospital.

I have never gone back to Langhorne. I don't believe I ever will.

Jeff did not attend his own college graduation. He said that he thought ceremonies were stupid, but I wonder whether he wanted to keep my father and me apart. A month after Jeff graduated I received a letter addressed in that familiar sprawling angular hand. I was on my way to work when I picked up the mail and I put it in my backpack to read later; for days it haunted me amid the detritus at the bottom of my bag, the ChapStick, the spare change, the keys. Then one day I went to look at it, to hold it in my hand and consider slitting it open and letting the words tumble out. And it had disappeared.

I searched my tiny apartment, but could find it nowhere. I pulled books from the shelves and flapped them wildly, hanging on to their spines. I looked in the crippled folds of my pullout couch and in the kitchen cabinets. But I never found it.

Perhaps I pulled a subway token from the bottom of my bag as I ran toward a turnstile, and the letter fluttered to the cement floor and from there to the tracks. Maybe I took out my wallet, distracted in the delicatessen, and it dropped down between the ice-cream case and the counter, to be found and discarded during a remodeling years later.

As we psychiatrists like to say, there are no accidents.

I see my brothers often, and perhaps they see my father but do not say. Brian left Penn and runs a framing store in Philadelphia, and seems happier than he ever did, although he is still looking for someone to love. Jeff went to summer school after I was cleared, or exonerated, or whatever you call it when no charges are brought against you for something everyone really believes you did. He went to law school and now he is a prosecutor in Manhattan.

Neither of us misses the irony of that, although I like to think he did it because he wanted to make sure the right people got indicted. It's the same office in lower Manhattan where Jon worked that summer, but although he performed well Jon was not offered a job at the D.A.'s office, nor did he get any of the clerkships for which he applied.

In the newspaper accounts, which I read one summer day on microfilm in the New York Public Library, just before I began med school, when I was between a temporary receptionist's stint and two weeks playing handmaiden to the executive vice president of an ad agency, he had said that his legal training made him understand keenly the moral need for him to come forward when my mother's death was ruled suspicious. But Jeff told me that many of the lawyers in his office had thought it was "low rent," as one put it, to testify against your lover, no matter what she might have done. Besides, they found his ambition fearsome. "Walk over his mother in golf spikes," one said.

Ah, Jon's mother. How his life would have been different had she reconciled herself to boredom in Brooklyn and carted him to PBA picnics and the Aquarium at Coney Island. He is at one of the big firms now, although not the one with the atrium. I presume that no one there much cares that he ratted me out. There walking over your mother in golf spikes is probably a term of art. There he puts in his seventy hours a week.

I put in mine each week now, too. I am as driven as I was before those months I spent at home; I am simply not as sure of myself or of all the things I once believed. When I enrolled in medical school one of the tabloids put my picture on page five, a photo of me sitting in the cafeteria that was obviously taken by one of my fellow students. ANGEL OF DEATH NOW A DOC? the headline read, and although there was a flurry of protest and a visit with the dean, I was allowed to finish. After a while people seemed to forget.

I never forget. My remembering has gotten more vivid as the years go by. I never considered going into oncology. I knew enough, after my rotations, to know that my mother was in every way a typical patient except that she died more quickly than many with her kind of cancer. But she would have died nonetheless. If I had been her doctor I would have treated her just as Dr. Cohn did, with precisely the same results. I would have asked for the autopsy, too, just as Dr. Cohn did, the professional curiosity that so changed all our lives.

"As her daughter, would you have behaved differently?" my therapist asked once, with an unaccustomed gleam in her eye. And the answer is that, knowing then what I know now, I would have. I would have given her more opportunities to talk, to complain, to fantasize, to weep, to speak. But that is what I am in the business of doing now, and it sounds easier in retrospect. I did the best I could at the time. We all did, I think, even my father, with his distance, his terror, his spoonfuls of rice pudding.

Sometimes still I think I see her in crowds, see that shiny crown of burnished hair bobbing along just a few heads away, just a little too far away to reach. The other day, thoughtlessly, I bought an old recording of *South Pacific*. I remembered that we had watched the movie one night when the pain in her back was especially bad, but somehow I had forgotten being a small girl, sitting in front of the stereo while she taught me to sing: "I'm stuck,/like a dope,/with a thing called hope,/and I can't get it out of my heart . . ."

Sometimes things leap out at me now, a funhouse of memory, some forgotten, others supressed. Even at the theater that night, just before my beeper went off, a few bars of music had made me think that I should call her when I got home. Sometimes I even pick up the phone and begin to dial. The sunflower pillow is on my couch. "Do you needlepoint?" the occasional female guest asks. "No," I say.

"George Eliot!" my brothers and I yell, when it's late and we've had too much to drink, and we all laugh. They help me remember, and I help them.

Most of my patients are young women embarked on a quest for perfection, eaten up by it. Early on, one of them, a brilliant girl who had tried to starve herself to death the summer between Exeter and Yale, said to me in the middle of a session, when she was getting a little too close to some personal truth, "My mother says people say you killed your mother."

"Does she?" Her mother was an extraordinarily beautiful woman, the trophy wife of a financier who had herself recently been shed for a younger trophy. She always had swatches of fabric in a big velvety leather bag, and gold pens, and gold-bound books with room layouts on graph paper inside them and her name embossed in gold on the covers. Once it crossed my mind that, had my mother been wealthy and idle and cold, she would have been this woman. But if my mother had been wealthy and idle and cold, she would have been someone else entirely.

"She said you got off on a technicality."

A slight tilt to the head, a nod. That's what I do when I want the patient to go on.

"I can understand why you'd want to. I'd love to get rid of my mother."

I looked at her poor transparent arms, sticks in the sleeves of the T-shirt she wore as a rebuke to the silk blouses in her closet, and thought that the person she was trying to kill was surely not her mother.

"But if you did it," I said, "what next?"

"What?"

"Your mother is disappeared, dead, gone, however you put it. What then?"

"Like how?" she said.

"Just think about it," I said.

When I was in therapy as part of my training I told my therapist that since my mother had died I no longer knew who I was. I felt as though I had lost my connection to the past. The future seemed to me, as hers had been, the blink of an eye.

The irony was that before she was ill I had been so sure of who I was, of what I wanted. I was George Gulden's daughter and I wanted to make him love me. And in many ways I am still very much like him. But I am also the last living member of the Gulden Girls Book and Cook Club, and I will never forget it, nor ever be the same for it. I will never again be able to think that Anna did the right thing when she closed the door and ran after Vronsky; I will always think of little Seryohza shivering in the hallway, waiting for Maman to return, as I sometimes wait for mine, pausing with the telephone receiver in my hand to make a call and then remembering that the woman I need to speak with has been dead for nearly a decade.

My mother left her mark on me at the very end, so that perhaps now I see my father as she did, admiring and covertly pitying at the same time. My father is not a bad man. He is only a weak one. And he only did what so many men do: he divided women into groups, although in his case it was not the body-and-soul dichotomy of the madonna and the whore but the intellectual twins, the woman of the mind and the one of the heart. Elizabeth and Jane Bennet. I had the misfortune to be designated the heartless one, my mother the mindless one. It was a disservice to us both but, on balance, I think she got the better deal.

Jules always says that someday I'm going to write a big blockbuster self-help book, that we'll call it *Women Who Love Men Who Love Themselves*. My last year of medical school I fell in love with an intern named Jamie, a Californian with white-blond hair and hands so skillful that he was a cinch for surgery and infidelity. It took me six months to discover what everyone else knew, that his mood swings were a function of methamphetamines and his favorite position was with a nurse in an empty single.

I like to think he was the last of the string.

Richard is an orthopedic surgeon, the medical equivalent of a carpenter. He has been my friend for a year and my lover for another and now he wants to be my husband and he will be, I suspect, if I can overcome the fact that I feel about him much the way I feel about my brothers. Once when I was fitfully cruising the living room of the chief of surgery's apartment at a party, drinking too much wine and pretending not to notice the powerful chemistry between Jamie and the chief's third wife, the one in the black strapless dress, Richard said to me roughly, "My problem is I'm too nice to you."

"It's my problem," I said.

"You bet your ass it is, sweetheart," he said, folding his brawny arms over his chest and kicking at the carpet.

He is nice. The night we went to the theater he had tickets for a Knicks game. I only knew because I found the tickets in the drawer in his kitchen where he keeps the scissors. And when my beeper went off, a dozen different men, even other doctors, would have frowned or fidgeted. He only squeezed my arm and sent me off. An adolescent psychiatrist does not have the same interruptions as, say, an obstetrician. But there are emergencies nonetheless. I am accustomed to them now.

There was only one pay phone in the lobby of the theater, off behind a column. A man in a double-breasted suit was using it. When he saw me standing behind him, he took a cellular from his pocket. "On the fritz," he said with a mixture of ire and apology. And he began talking numbers, money, dealmakers and breakers with someone on the other end.

I paced a bit on the theater's Oriental-patterned wall-to-wall and looked at my watch. Two minutes and I would tell him I was a psychiatrist with an emergency. Even an investment banker would hang up. People always did, envisioning a man on a rooftop, a girl with a razorblade at her wrist. I paced a little longer, standing in front of the glass doors to Forty-sixth Street. On the other side, smoking a cigarette, stood my father.

He tossed the butt onto the ground and put it out deftly with his toe, then turned slightly toward the lobby and saw me there. He tilted his head—is that where I got it, that gesture I thought was only mine?—and then gave a half-smile, part recognition, part ironic distance and parted the glass doors with his elegant hands.

"As you've doubtless noted with great disapproval, I've substituted cigarettes for liquor," he said, without preamble.

"Great—keep the liver, lose the lungs. A winning equation."

"Age does not wither nor custom stale your sharp tongue."

"Actually, it has. That was the old me talking. I think you should give up smoking but I also think giving up drinking is an excellent idea."

"Your medical opinion."

"Yes."

"I never imagined you would be a doctor," he said, looking at me closely, as though it would have changed my face. Or perhaps he was looking for my opinion of him in my eyes. Instead I wore the studied neutrality of my profession.

"And an alienist," he added.

I threw back my head and laughed, and so did he, and for just a moment I thought nothing has changed, nothing.

"Only you would use that term," I said. "So Victorian."

"And you work with children," he said.

"Adolescents," I said. "Depression, suicide, other manifestations of despair."

"The stuff of fiction," he said.

"No, not really," I said. "On paper you can make them do what you want. In practice you have to convince Anna not to throw herself in front of a train."

We stared at one another. "You're looking well," he finally said.

"And you," I replied.

"You like the play?"

"Not much," I said. "I'm surprised you're here."

"I have a friend who studies set design," he said. "Her teacher did the scenery."

The banker hung up the pay phone. "It's all yours," he said to me. "Emergency," I said to my father as I lifted the receiver.

It was not much of one: a young woman who'd tried to drink herself to death at a small liberal arts college in Ohio and who'd just begun taking antidepressants wanted to double the dose because they weren't working. "I told her it takes a while for them to take effect, but she won't settle down until she's heard it from you," said one of the nurses on the psychiatric floor.

"Tell her I will see her first thing in the morning," I said. "And tell her the antidepressants should begin to work by the end of the week or I will change her dosage or her medication. And remind her that I'd assigned her to read *Wuthering Heights* along with the medication."

He was still there when I got off the phone. I knew he was. I would have felt it if he had left. His eyebrows were raised.

"You assign the Brontës to the mentally ill?"

"It will help her understand compulsion," I said, "and it will take her mind momentarily off her own. And despite what you think, I always liked the Brontës." I smiled. "I have to get back to my seat."

"I would like to say one thing," he said, and the look on his face was stripped, frozen, like the look on his face that day we hit the deer.

"It's not necessary," I said.

"I would like to," he said. "It's important that you believe what I said in my letter. That I never, ever blamed you. I would have done what you did in your position. Perhaps I should have."

"What?" I said.

"I never blamed you for what you did. It was the right thing to do. It took a good deal of courage. Real courage. Valor. I couldn't say that at the time because of the circumstances. Perhaps I said it badly in the letter. I never blamed you. I wish I'd done it myself."

I looked into his face and there was nothing there, no guile, no subterfuge, nothing except the truth of what he was saying.

"Oh, Papa," I said.

"I admire your courage."

From inside I heard the first plangent strains of a violin sketching out the beginning of a love song. Two fools, I thought, looking at him. Two brilliant fools: he thinking it was me, me believing it was him. Like an O. Henry story, except that it had blighted both our lives. Suddenly it seemed incredible that all this time I had thought him either courageous or cunning enough, depending on his motives. It was too dirty, too real life, those crushed pills, that bowl of custard, that crystalline moment of decision. Neither of us could have managed it.

But in the end what was important was not that we had so misunderstood one another, but that we had so misunderstood her, this woman who had made us who we were while we barely noticed it. Sometimes I try to reconstruct it now. Maybe after I heaved her from the bath she began to horde her pills, to ask for them when she did not need them, to keep them in a cache beneath her underwear or in a box with her anniversary pearls, so that some winter morning, when the light was gray, she could gulp them down and sleep easy.

Perhaps it just came to her, that afternoon, when I went out to find my father and he was on his way home to her and she found herself alone. Perhaps she pulled herself to the table by the window where I kept the vial. Perhaps she bit them, chewed them to bits, and waited for dark to fall.

Maybe they were even in the rice pudding after all; maybe her last domestic act in that pretty kitchen was to grind the pills to a powder and mix them in the little container that she knew, eventually, would make her last dessert. Now that I know, now that I'm not so blind, I can imagine her thinking to herself, as surely as I made this little world with my own two hands, with the turpentine the paint the yarn the floor wax the tung oil the flowers the kindness the care the need the fear the love so I will leave it.

"What then?" I'd asked my patient about the fantasy death of the woman who'd made her out of her own body, and now I had to begin asking myself all over again. The only thing sadder than life, Edith Wharton once said, is death. But sometimes it seems she had it backward.

My father looked old and empty, like the skin of a cicada, the illusion of the thing. I suppose in some strange way he honored me with his assumption and I was damned if I would tell him otherwise. Let him think of me as a heroine from some little story. He became part of the crowd that night, the great throng that believed speaking the truth was inconsequential, a cover for what I had really done. It was easier when I believed I was covering for him. Now I would have to reinvent him.

And her too. Sometimes now I say to myself, logically, that I could not have known, that the knowledge that she had asked my help convinced me that she could not help herself, that at the end I had every reason to believe that she was too sapped, too weak, too far gone.

But the truth is I didn't really think she had it in her. And being so wrong about her makes me wonder now how often I am utterly wrong about myself. And how wrong she might have been about her mother, how wrong he might have been about his father, how much of family life is a vast web of misunderstandings, a tinted and touched-up family portrait, an accurate representation of fact that leaves out only the essential truth.

I wondered as I made my way back down the aisle in the theater, and I've wondered since, who I should tell about what I now know. Bob Greenstein wouldn't care; if my job is to search for truth, his is to seek scenarios. I wonder whether knowing what really happened would help Jeff smooth over his differences with our father. But perhaps those differences go back much, much further than any question of pills or responsibility, back to those days when the two of us, my father and I, would move into his den and leave the boys on the porch, leave them to the love of their mother.

Mrs. Forburg? Teresa? When I see them now, we never talk about the past. We talk about Mrs. Forburg's travels around the country, where she teaches retired adults about the Great Books in elder hostels. We talk about Teresa's daughter Gina and how hard it is for her husband the pediatrician to make time to see the little girl when he is spending so many hours each day taking care of other people's children.

If I could tell anyone what I know now, perhaps it would be the woman in the blue suit. Somehow I feel that she deserves to know it, so that the story for her can have a beginning, a middle, and an end.

And someday I will tell my father. Someday soon, I imagine, although there is a great temptation to leave the man I once thought the smartest person on earth in utter ignorance. When we parted he had asked, "May I call you?" like a suitor. And I had handed him my card, as though our meeting was a piece of unfinished business.

It never occurred to me, in the dim light of the theater lobby, to blurt out the truth as I had suddenly discovered it. I have learned my profession well. Before I tell him what really happened, as far as I know it, I need to understand it myself. I need to understand how, learning as much about my mother as I did during those long days we spent together, I had somehow missed her essence. And he, the person who should have known her best in all the world, had missed it, too. Or perhaps she had only duped him, with the deft and docile ways she found to make his life just what he wanted it to be, duped him into thinking that there was less to her than met the eye.

I will find a way to make it parse, as Jules still says. Doing what I do now, I surely should understand that all our lives have some mystery at the core, and many of them go unsolved. If I had not come to that play on that evening, if I had gone to the Knicks game with Richard instead, if my patient's medication had taken effect, if the nurse had not called, if the banker had not been on the phone, if my father had not taken up smoking, if, if, if, if, my own story would have ended with a different sort of father, a different sort of mother, and, of course, a different sort of daughter.

When I went back to my seat Richard took my hand and smiled in the darkness. When the lights came on after the curtain call, he kissed my cheek. As I looked at him I realized that, while I would never be my mother nor have her life, the lesson she had left me was that it was possible to love and care for a man and still have at your core a strength so great that you never even needed to put it on display. I realized that Richard was nothing like my father but very much like my mother. And I thought that I would marry him very, very soon and take my chances with all the rest. Perhaps then I could afford to know my father again, to fall within the now truncated circle of his thrall.

"Everything okay?" Richard asked.

"Is everything ever okay?" I said.

"Is it really true that a psychiatrist can only answer a question with another question?"

"I don't know, what do you think?" I said. I squeezed his big hand, walking out into the night air, and then I added, "The patient is fine. I prescribed Cathy and Heathcliff until her medication kicks in."

We stopped on the sidewalk. The audience eddied around us, dissecting the play, but I did not see my father again.

Richard reached down and checked my pulse. "And how is my patient?" he said.

"Have you ever had the feeling that you had things all figured out and then suddenly you find yourself back to square one?"

"I've never felt that I had things all figured out," he said.

"You are a better person than I am."

"Simpler."

"Better."

"Have it your way," Richard said, and we began to walk. A black man with rheumy eyes asked for a quarter. "No change," I said. Richard dug into his pocket and gave him a dollar. "Get a cup of coffee, guy," he said.

"Life's a bitch," I said.

"Yeah," Richard said, "but consider the alternative."

"Is that George Burns or Émile Zola?" I said.

"I thought it was me, actually. C'mon, I'm starved; let's go eat."

"Food," I said. "That's what I need."